I0725814

FARTHER

FARTHER

DEAN VALE

NOSETOUCH PRESS

CHICAGO | PITTSBURGH

Farther
© 2020 by Dean Vale. All Rights Reserved.

ISBN-13: 978-1-944286-11-8

Published by Nosetouch Press
www.nosetouchpress.com

For more information about bulk purchases,
please contact Nosetouch Press at info@nosetouchpress.com.

Cataloging-in-Publication Data

Names: Vale, Dean., author.
Title: Farther / Dean Vale
Description: Chicago, IL : Nosetouch Press [2020]
Identifiers: ISBN: 9781944286118 (paperback)
Subjects: LCSH: Science fiction—Fiction.
GSAFD: Science fiction. | BISAC: FICTION / Science Fiction / Space Exploration.

Cover & interior designed by
Christine M. Scott, Clever Crow Consulting and Design
www.clevercrow.com

The text for this book was set in Adobe Minion Pro.

For Dane, closer than farther.

1

WAITING WAS AN AFFLICTION, treated only through training. It seemed absurd for Terranauts who spent the majority of their lives packaged into exosuits to have to train, but it was about the only way to stay sane in the intervals between missions. Travers jogged to clear his head. Guessica did yoga. Ford did calisthenics. They kept busy, and keeping busy kept heads clear and hearts whole. *Hearts and Minds Mattered.* That's what the slogan said.

There were only thirty-six Terranauts in the entire universe—a dozen teams of three. Ford didn't know how the International Space Authority came up with three as the magic number; it wasn't his place to know. All they did know is that they were the Blue Team. Since the foundation of the Program so many years before, the Orange Team had never returned, and Yellow Team had all come back dead, but the Blue Team *always* came through for the good old ISA.

That day, when Yellow Team was reclaimed, they were wheeled in on gurneys. Their exosuits were molten slag, blackened polyalloy, plastic, glasstic, and fiber mixed with the triumphal white, ISA logos nearly baked off. A recovery team had been sent in to bring them back when Commander Franzen hadn't called in at droptime.

As was so often the case when a team came back through the Causeway, through the gravitic lens of the Conduit, the off-duty teams would assemble and watch in the observation room that overlooked the Causeway.

It wasn't quite a ritual, but it was something of a tradition. All of them had gone through the conduits, all of them understood the euphoria and horror of traveling billions upon billions of miles in one step, the bending of space-time at the behest of the ISA's technology, powered and funded by Paragon, Inc.

"What the hell happened?" Travers asked, when he'd seen Yellow Team wheeled in. "That could've been us."

Travers had a long face, perpetually tired eyes of blue, a long nose, terminally short blonde hair, and he was otherwise unexceptional, except for being a Terranaut, of course. He always looked sleepy, but spoke quickly, in a clipped cadence that even alert Paragon employees would've found difficult to censor. He was the Team Meteorologist, so it fit that he was a windbag.

Ford was Team Leader for his trio. Tall, fit, broad-shouldered, lantern-jawed, mahogany-skinned. Ford had had curly brown hair, although he kept it punitively short in some unspoken competition with Travers as to who could look more perfectly Terranautical.

Newsfeed had done a feature on him: "Forging Ahead With Ford Collins," that had made him something of a star among the Terranauts. ISA loved him, because he looked like the popular conception of what a Terranaut *should* look like: a bold, resolute adventurer, the kind of guy who could give you a dissertation on particle physics while doing knuckle pushups without even breaking a sweat.

However, the return of the Yellow Team had caused plenty of Terranauts to sweat. All three of the Yellow Team member bodies were horribly charred. Seeing them on their backs, faces unrecognizable blends of blackened bone and high-tech protective materials, what could one say?

"The Loonies fucked it up," Travers said, pacing. The other teams were watching and commenting, too. They all were; all they *could* do was comment. They had the clearance, and anytime anybody was inbound, the other Terranauts sure as hell were there. "Had to be the Loonies."

"Maybe," Ford said. "We'll find out."

"Will we?" Guessica asked. She was the third member of their team: the Geologist. Guessica was Indian by birth, Trans-European by culture. She kept her black hair long, in a bit of defiance of the trend among both male and female Terranauts for shorter, more manageable hair. Her eyes were the color of cinnamon, her white, wide smile was nearly always ironic. Guessica kept a lot to herself, was focused, with a quiet kind of precision that made her an outstanding field operative. At least a decade younger than Ford, most in the ISA assumed Guessica would be the next big star in the Program.

"I'll find out," Ford said. The Lunar Space Observatory—the Loonies, as Travers and others in the program dubbed them—lived on the dark side of the moon. The LSO was charged with scouting locations for the Terranauts, free from the radio noise of Earth. There, in darkness and silence, their massive radio telescopes scoured the skies, aided by artificial intelligences.

The Terranauts took to calling the LSO workers "Loonies" as a bit of a dig at the never-seen observers, who gazed forever into the depths of space for suitable dropsites. With many tens of billions of habitable, colonization-capable planets out there, and hundreds of trillions of commercially valuable planets to exploit, the Loonies were kept insanely busy.

How many Terranauts had the Loonies killed?

"With Yellow Team, this makes, what, twenty-eight Terranauts dead, now?" Travers asked, counting on his fingers. "This is *bullshit*, man. They should be sending probes. They should be sending fucking bots. Bots before 'Nauts, Man."

Wen Chao, Leader of Red Team, scoffed when she heard that. Red Team was the first team, the best team, the most experienced team of surveyors. They were the survivors, the troubleshooters, the fixers. Ford's team was the second team, the second-most experienced. Yellow had been third.

"Probes don't bring back good data," Chao said, shaking her head. "They get lost, Trav. Probes are expensive and inefficient. And bots are trouble."

"And human lives are infinitely cheaper," Guessica said, sighing.

Everybody understood this. ISA didn't send probes because they were unreliable and expensive, and at such great distances, nearly impossible to manage remotely—it was too costly and energy-intensive to keep the portals open for survey operations. Once wormhole technology had been properly tested and found to be reasonably reliable and safe, probes were jettisoned in favor of the Terranauts.

"Then what the hell happened?" Travers asked.

"They'll find out," Ford said. "Relax, Travers."

"I can't relax," Travers said. "We're up next. If they screwed something up, I want to know what it is so that we don't end up like those guys."

Yellow Team had been wheeled out of the Ready Room, taken to Diagnostic Division. The entire reentry area was a quarantine zone. That was learned almost immediately, when the first Terranauts went out there and came back. The quarantine zone was a labyrinthine structure, a spiderweb within the compound, with the wormhole at the heart of it, at the Causeway.

Nobody came in or out of that wormhole without being properly and thoroughly sterilized. This was just common sense, after a Terranaut brought back Spaceclap. That was the joke name for it, what the Terranauts called it. They had funny names for everything. But it hadn't been funny when it happened. Absolutely nobody laughed about it back then.

It had been Brown Team, about five years ago. They had come back from surveying a world, and one of them, Team Leader Dunkin Rave, had gotten a breach in his suit. It had been simple and stupid, really—he'd stumbled on a hill and had caught himself on a rock. The rupture in the suit had been at the elbow joint. The exosuits were tough, but the rocks on GLX-189 had been tougher, and there'd been a breach, and he'd been cut. He had done standard countermeasures—a spritz of field antibiotic, some sealant for his suit. He had opted to finish the mission, because that's what a Terranaut did, but when he'd come back, he'd been infected.

Rave's Disease was what it was called, officially. He'd showed it to the techs and they'd put him into an isolation ward and got him out of the suit. By that time, purple tendrils had snaked their way up his arm from the point of contact. Right under the skin, and excision only caused them to break, spreading the infection, which appeared to behave somewhat like a fungus.

Nobody knew what to do, so they took Rave's arm, just sliced it clean off with a hypersonic scalpel, put the thing in a container, and watched. But whatever that thing was, it had infected his whole body, and within three days of the removal of his arm, Rave had sprouted more, mapping their way across his body in purple tubules.

The ISA medical staff could only really observe. Nobody knew what they were dealing with, and they were terrified of infecting the rest of the compound, so only the highest-rated Medtechs were allowed into Rave's ward, and at the time, Rave was just howling out for morphine, heroin, clenzodren, anything. He called out for that until he died, exactly 6.3 days after returning.

It was later determined, after autopsy, that Rave's Disease was an exofungal infection unique to GLX-189, and that this made that world unfit for colonization. A dozen other personnel caught Rave's Disease in the wake of the original infection, which required vigorous decontamination procedures for the area, the outright quarantine and eventual destruction of that facility, known as the Vault.

Stuff always slipped through, which was why the quarantine zone was so thorough, why the procedures were so rigorous. The wormhole was a conduit, almost like a syringe that connected one world to another, and anything imaginable could come through. The lessons of centuries past were not lost on ISA; the only challenge was spotting the problems when they turned up, and being ready for absolutely everything, and expecting the unexpected.

It was why so much attention was paid to the engineering of the exosuits. The mission of the Terranauts was finding worlds that human beings could colonize. Worlds like Earth, more or less. And the challenge of a world that could sustain life was that, more often than not, there was life there already when the Terranauts showed up. Alien life did not welcome intrusion—and, of course, the irony was not lost on the Terranauts that, to the aliens, the humans *were* the invading organisms.

The exosuits were intended to protect the Terranauts from whatever was out there, within conceivable limits—budgets precluded making the suits completely invulnerable, but they were designed to be rugged and reliable. Heavily-armored, articulated, ambulatory shells that were packed with scanning equipment and sensors, the exosuits were effectively walking spaceships. Nobody actually ever flew in space, anymore; it was considered archaic, in bad taste. Something only desperate, ruthless, provincial types might consider.

Not since the Thorne Commission had successfully brought about the wormhole tech to begin with. Since then, it was how everybody traveled. Space was for pirates and vagabonds; space-time was where it was at, the way to *really* fly.

But part and parcel of this was the need for safety. It was why the post-Vault ISA compound was in the middle of a desert, heavily guarded, and why absolutely nobody came in or out without proper clearance. The ISA was responsible for finding worlds to settle, habitats for humanity—but that required incredible caution and care. So far, six planets had been colonized, out of hundreds of worlds surveyed. That was how careful they were.

A Terranaut in an exosuit could survive a week on their own, thanks to the life-preserving nature of the suits, the battery of resources at their disposal. In wormhole terms, a week was a lifetime, because travel to and from the points was effectively instantaneous. The suits were sacred to the Terranauts, because they literally meant life or death for them.

It was why seeing a ruined trio of Yellow Team exosuits filled the other teams with angst. Even Red Team fretted about it. The suits were supposed to be able to take anything a planet could dish out. They could take high temperatures, they could take low temperatures. They could take high pressure, they could take low pressure. They could weather high radiation levels, they could deal with high winds. They could handle solar winds. They could function in water and in acid. The testing regimen of the exosuits was incredibly thorough. The engineers were always pushing the envelope, trying to design for the ultimate experience.

The original exosuits had been adopted by the Polygon for Colonial military operations, where the great distances involved required a steady, sure military presence to buttress Colonial government authority. The Governors insisted on having cadres of well-oiled battlesuits, wielded by trained professionals, on their worlds to ensure that law and order was observed. Since self-reliance was a requirement of Colonial administration, the Polygon had adapted the suits for maximum field effectiveness in hostile terrain. The purpose was the same, even if the mission was ultimately different.

So, why had Yellow Team died? It could have meant that the Loonies had dropped them in some bad place, some place where the conditions exceeded the operational specifications of the suits.

But that didn't make sense—nobody portaled blind. You could see where you were going when you went in there. The gravitational lensing was pronounced, but it still provided a glimpse into the character of the destination.

"It had to be a glitch," Travers said, biting a finger. "The fucking Loonies screwed *something* up."

Ford thought about the Yellow Team's mission. They had been dropped three days ago. So, whatever had happened to them couldn't have been because of a miscalculation on the part of the Loonies. Had it been, it would have been apparent the moment the Conduit opened.

"I don't think so," Ford said. "Look, don't dwell on it, Trav. You're gonna go crazy if you keep thinking about it."

"Too late," Guessica said. "Do you think they'll assign us to that planet? Find out what went wrong?"

"God, I hope not," Travers said. "Would they do that? We have our own mission."

Ford shrugged. ISA could assign them wherever it felt they needed to go. The Loonies found the worlds, the Terranauts surveyed them. That was the relationship. That was their job.

"They can do whatever they want," Guessica said.

"My bet is our mission will go as they originally mapped it out," Ford said. "Yellow Team had the GLX Sector. We've had QED Sector for the past three years. They're not going to uproot us and throw us there, out of the blue. It would be a misallocation of resources."

Travers stepped away from the observation window, looked Ford in the eye. The other Teams had gradually left, since there was nothing more to see, and they were not next to launch, could afford to relax.

"That's my point," Travers said. "Why not just fling us over there? Who cares? They can send us fucking anywhere. We're prospecting worlds, here. You think they're going to risk sending us to some other place when they've got something to solve in GLX?"

Ford sighed. When Travers got wound up, there was no stopping him or his mouth. Guessica, fortunately, intervened before Ford could say something he might regret.

"The Lunar Observatory has to carefully map out the worlds for us," she said. "They've already got one for us to survey. That's more important to ISA and Paragon than finding out why Yellow Team got killed. ALLIE will find out what went wrong for Yellow Team."

"And that's supposed to reassure me?" Travers asked. "Goddamned ALLIE."

ALLIE (Advanced Logistical Liminal Intelligence Extrapolator) was the AI charged with data analysis for the entire wormhole program. Given the scope of the operation, the calculations necessary, an AI was a natural fit for the project. It was never calculated how many scientists had lost their minds trying to compute and crunch the data the LSO accumulated, but it was tremendous. The Loonies studied the sky, ALLIE found prospective worlds by poring through the raw data, then the ISA followed up on the initial analysis with the Survey Program, and ALLIE collated the accumulated data as to whether the world could be safely colonized.

After that, Paragon worked with the Naming Commission to assign a name to the planet, the Colonial Administration Authority set up the government, and the conglomerates moved in to establish commercial operations. A world usually got up and running in five years, once a name had been assigned, and property rights allocated.

"I'm saying it's not our job," Ford said. "Don't sweat what we can't control, Sport."

He patted Travers on the back, and walked out of the observation deck, Guessica close behind.

"But we don't control anything," Travers said.

2

FORD *DID* SWEAT IT.

He went outside the compound and stared into the endless desert, felt the cold night air descending, as the sun slowly dipped over the horizon. The new ISA facility was nicknamed the Oasis, because that's what it ultimately was, as surely as the Vault was a vault.

There were gardens inside the compound walls: lemon trees, orange trees, almond trees. All manner of flowering things grew there that filled the air with precious scents and feelings of sanctuary and security, no doubt part of company protocol, intended to soothe frayed Terranautical nerves.

While the Quarantine and Cross-Contamination Bureaus sweated there being all the pollinating plants on-site, the Psych Division had worked hard to ensure that the Oasis could offer Terranauts a comfortable respite from their harrowing missions.

Because they stayed cooped up in their exosuits on missions, during much of their downtime the Terranauts liked to be under the open sky, to face broad and unimpeded vistas, to feel sun and wind and even rain on their faces.

This place, his home, was far away from everything. The Terranauts were not allowed to mingle with the populace when they were on active duty. It was just part of the regimen. No diseases in or out, corporate quarantine. Terranauts were effectively classified as biohazards when they were on active duty. In this way, the safety and health of the Earth was ensured, and it was not an idle precaution.

Terranauts always wore blue jumpsuits. Security wore black. Mech-techs wore grey. Medtechs wore white. Scienticians wore red. Life Sciences wore green. Psych Ops wore Indigo. And so on. Everything and everyone was color-coded at the Oasis, except for Administrators. Administrators didn't wear jumpsuits or colors—they just wore suits and frowns. They were almost always tanned, and were almost always whining, grumbling, growling, posturing, yelling, or complaining about something. Terranauts sweated time-space; the Administrators sweated budgets and deadlines.

At night, everything around the Oasis went black; only the Oasis was illuminated. Although he could not see them, Ford knew that anything getting too close to the Oasis would face sentry guns and be shot. No questions asked, no quarter given. There was simply too much at stake, the competition was too intense. The Oasis was an interplanetary revenue generator, operating on a scale that dwarfed human comprehension. The discoveries, dangers, and profits to be made were considerable.

The security of the Oasis often made him wonder, but he supposed that the ISA and Paragon wanted to keep their competitive advantage in wormhole technology intact. And the avoidance of a "whoopsie" wormhole moment ensured the continued survival of the human race.

Ford looked above him, at the night sky. The views of space were lovely at the Oasis, because of the relative darkness around them. All of those stars up there. He'd surveyed a score of worlds, which made him the second-most experienced surviving Terranaut, after Chao, who had surveyed two dozen. Chao was absolutely fearless. Ford was sure she'd be the one reassigned to the GLX Sector. It only made sense.

Six of the worlds Ford had surveyed had been actively colonized. ALLIE was still crunching data on the other worlds, as far as he knew.

Planet Terranova.

Planet Eden.

Planet Xenophon.

Planet Thanatos.

Planet Midas.

Planet Nikedidas.

The Naming Commission was a highly-charged political body, because naming rights for a planet were no small thing. In the euphoria around the first discovered habitable world, New Earth was the only acceptable name, and Terranova was born. After that, though, the political dynamic in it held greater sway, as players on Earth wanted their interests represented. The ISA ensured any number of bidders that they would all get worlds of their own to colonize and settle, for the greater good of humanity.

That's what it was all about, after all: the greater good of humanity. Ever since the Apophis meteor gave everybody a scare, the emphasis on colonization of space, of spreading the human seed as widely as possible to ensure the continuation of human life, had become a grave concern.

But what had also happened was one of the single greatest challenges facing the human species—living space—had been solved by the ISA and Paragon. Worlds could be found, settled, tamed and conquered. All thanks to the shimmering elegance of the wormhole and antigravity.

The irony for Ford was that while he had surveyed these discovered worlds, he'd never visited them after colonization. He didn't have time, wasn't one to settle or homestead.

After sifting Ford's field data, ALLIE would determine if a planet was fit for colonization, then the Naming Commission stepped in, and the Colonial Commerce Administration worked out plans for settlement, and then people flocked to the new worlds, if they met the requirements. They didn't upload through the Oasis. There was another facility for that, the Gate, designed for large-scale transfer of people and materials to colonial worlds. They had their own protocols, and it wasn't something Ford particularly worried about. By the time the Gate was involved, the Terranauts had already moved on.

But he did sweat it a little, thinking about those worlds. Thanatos was a prison planet. Every institutional and criminal case on the Colonial Worlds ended up settled there, and the wormhole conduit there was easily the most heavily-guarded thing in human history. It made the Oasis look wide open by comparison.

It was called the Cage.

He remembered Thanatos, the grey waste of that place. Heavily-clouded, rough land. Broad oceans, deep and brimming with odd-yet-edible monstrosities. He smiled to himself, imagining who was the first person to discover that, to take a bite of the things that lived there.

Even a prison planet like Thanatos had xenobiologists combing the land, finding new discoveries, new things to patent. It never ended.

Each of the new planets had about a billion people on them, which greatly lessened the load on Earth, had vastly improved the conditions here. Earth was now more of a country club than a planet, as the ghost of Malthus was finally laid to rest and the problem of too many people competing for too few resources was ultimately and elegantly solved.

With more planets, there was the opportunity for specialization of labor, which, as Ford saw it, was both good and bad.

Terranova was a farming planet, the breadbasket of the Colonies. Eden and Xenophon were twin paradises—resort worlds where tourism, gambling, pleasure, relaxation of every sort could be had. Eden was for the low-rent hedonist—pleasures of the body, while Xenophon was for the higher-end consumer of pleasure, a world of fine art and culture—a world of philosophers and scholars, pleasures of the mind. Midas was mineral rich, a mining world, where new elements and alloys were extracted and exported to the Colonies. Nikedidas produced endless garments and textiles that clothed absolutely everybody.

All of this was made possible through the wormhole. Without it, each world would just be isolated and alone in the depths of space, completely ignorant of one another, without hope of interaction. But with the Conduits, there could be commerce and trade between these worlds, a web of human interaction.

Ford had seen all of these worlds before they were settled, and knew them all in snapshot memories. They were like his children, in a way, and he longed to see how they'd grown up. But to do so would be to step out of the Terranaut program, and to lose his place in line. Ford had simply worked too hard to settle down, yet. One day, he would choose a world to settle upon when the time came, when he was up for retirement, or in danger of being surpassed. Maybe he'd stay on Earth. He didn't know. It was nice to have a choice of worlds.

"ALLIE," Ford said aloud.

"Yes, Commander Ford?" ALLIE replied. She could hear anybody on the Oasis, and respond through comlinks everybody carried on them. "She" was, of course, a contrivance, but they gave it a female voice the Psych Division had determined was pleasing to the human ear, so ALLIE became a she.

It was a testament to her processing power that she could calculate unending streams of data on newly-discovered worlds, crunch logistics numbers for upcoming missions, and converse with everybody on the Oasis and Luna at once, if required to.

"Any word on Yellow Team?" Ford asked.

"Still collating," ALLIE said. "It appears that Commander Franzen took the team in an unanticipated direction on GLX-189, exceeding mission parameters."

"I see," Ford said. He wanted to access the information, see what Franzen had been doing there. If Paragon had been up to something, he doubted he'd be able to sniff it out, but it was at least worth a look. The problem was justifying that in the wake of their next QED mission. Given the history and reputation of GLX-189, Ford suspected it was the Exoweapons Division, maybe wanting to see if there were goodies there as toxic as Rave's Disease. Dennis Franzen had been less than pleased when he'd found out he'd been assigned that planet, had talked about it to Ford about a week before his team had launched.

"I'm flat-out saying it: Why me?" Franzen asked, running his hand through this spiky brown hair. They were at Bar None, one of four such establishments on the Oasis. Bar None was the quietest of the bars, the place of somber contemplation in darkly-lit booths, with only argon lighted tubes for company, snaking their way around chrome and black furniture. Screens on the walls broadcast Colonial News.

"Why *anybody*, Franz?" Ford asked.

"GLX is a deathtrap," Franzen said, his eyes big. Ford could see him sweating in the argon afterglow. "It's been quarantined since Brown Team went there, and now they're sending us in there? What the hell for?"

Ford knew as well as Franzen that requesting reassignment was career suicide—a Terranaut who actually asked to be reassigned a planet was guaranteeing that they ended up undergoing extensive Psych Eval to ensure that they remained field-ready. And that would mean being bumped out of the active duty roster for probably a year, and out of the limelight, without prospects.

With his team in the gamma position, Franzen absolutely had to make that drop.

"No answers here, Franz," Ford said. "You know me."

"Yeah," Franzen said. "I know you. I'm fucked. I'm roundly fucked, here, Ford. When I saw that ALLIE put us in GLX, I thought 'What are the odds that I'll end up on 189? What are the odds?' And here I am. Roundly fucked."

"Just keep your head," Ford said. It was a mantra of the Terranauts, one of many, but one of the most important: Keep your head, or you'll be dead.

"Easy for you to say, QED," Franzen said, taking a drink of his Code Blue.

"We'll laugh about this when you get back," Ford said.

"I'm not laughing," Franzen said. "I think Administration hates me. Honestly, somebody upstairs wants me fucking dead."

Ford laughed into his Martian Sunrise. Franzen was pill-popping paranoid, and it always made him laugh.

"Nobody wants you dead," Ford said. "You're too valuable to them, Franz. We all are."

Franzen turned his bulging eyes to Ford and looked at his friend like he was the one who was nuts.

"Ford, I wish I could bottle that cluelessness of yours," Franzen said. "I could buy this place."

"It's true," Ford said. "We're the ones who make all of this possible."

He nodded to all of the monitor screens, all of those different worlds, all doing their different things. All of them were recorded feeds, since none of them were in broadcast range. Absolutely everything was pre-recorded these days. Ford wondered how much was censored.

"Mark my words, Ford: Roundly. Fucked."

Ford had not imagined that would be his last conversation with Franzen. He didn't know what to make of it, either—maybe Franzen had been right, or maybe he had been so nervous in the field that he had fucked something up and gotten his team killed. Either possibility seemed equally credible to Ford. Franzen was always a nerve end, always prone to second-guessing himself, to reading too much into things, to bouts of navel-gazing and philosophical meandering. Being a Terranaut wasn't rocket science. Even rocket science wasn't rocket science, anymore.

"How many days until QED-376 upload?" Ford asked.

"Seventy-two hours, Commander Collins," ALLIE said. "If you were worried about Yellow Team interfering with the work schedule, you needn't be. Your team's mission will continue as scheduled. Do you need anything else, Commander?"

"Not for the moment, ALLIE. Thank you," Ford said.

"Thank you, Commander."

Ford looked back up at the night sky. He knew where each of the worlds were, although he could not see them with his own eyes. It was surreal to him, knowing that, endless light-years away, there were other human beings out there, going through their own lives, some perhaps gazing at the stars, themselves.

To date, no intelligent life had yet been found on a colonial world. There had been plenty of life discovered. New species, new orders of life—zoologists and biologists and botanists had gone absolutely batty with the rush of new information. But so far, no intelligent life, no extraterrestrial civilizations had been found. Not even any ruins had been located, which made Ford a little sad. Ruins would have been nice. Nicer than being absolutely alone in the universe, anyway.

Not that ALLIE was looking for them; ALLIE was charged with finding worlds that human beings could settle safely. And, ultimately, a world already occupied with a sapient species was a world that offered still more complications than the usual colonial settlement procedure.

Thinking of the burned bodies of Yellow Team, Ford wondered if something new had been discovered on GLX-189. Maybe the Terranauts had been murdered.

3

ADMINISTRATOR DEXTER PAYNE WAS CHARGED with handling Blue Team, his project assigned to him by Paragon. Short, built like a wrestler, with big teeth and a smile that pulled his cheeks laterally, seemed unwilling to give an upward inch of facial real estate, Mr. Payne was a man of over-hearty handshakes and a flinty, no-nonsense bearing.

All of Paragon's people were ultimately like that, one way or another, male or female, old or young. Their job was finding worlds and exploiting them, and they would find them and exploit them. The Terranauts were simply a world-delivery system, in the eyes of Paragon, a mean to an end.

He called Blue Team into a conference room, where a holographic image of their destination, QED-376, was indicated: 2.3 million light-years away, in Andromeda Galaxy.

"Sorry you had to see Franzen's team come in that way," Payne said, once everybody was seated.

"What happened?" Travers asked.

"ALLIE said it was a human software malfunction," Payne said. "Although it was a preliminary finding."

Travers scoffed.

"A human software malfunction? What is that supposed to mean?"

"It means Franzen screwed up," Payne said, in a tone that indicated just how little he valued Travers's speculations on the fate of Yellow Team.

Guessica and Ford looked at each other, Ford leaning forward, resting his elbows on his knees.

"Are we going forward as planned?"

"Yes," Payne said. "No changes. You're still offloading in three days. I'm hoping that ALLIE gives us detailed information on Franzen's fuckup before then, and I think that's a fair hope, since three days for her might as well be a lifetime for us."

"So, we're not being moved to Yellow's quadrant?"

Payne laughed, an entirely humorless eruption from inside him, somewhere between a snort, a scoff, and a wheeze.

"Oh, hell, no," Payne said. "That's Proctor's problem, not mine. Look, you three are nailing this. We're showing just what Paragon is capable of with the conduit technology. You're going to be superstars when this is over. Endorsement deals, whatever you can imagine."

"I'm pretty imaginative," Travers said. "I can imagine a lot."

"Good," Payne said. "You'll need it. I'm not going to tell you how to do your jobs, but don't fuck this up. This is the longest-range field test of the Conduit—forget Chao's 1.4 million light-year sock hop to Leo T last year. That's nothing. This is big. It's huge. Andromeda Fucking Galaxy. This will be the longest transgalactic jump for the program."

Travers glanced at Guessica and Ford. Payne's penchant for profanity was part and parcel of his personality. Every briefing they had required a certain amount of redaction, before it ended up in Paragon's permanent records.

He toggled the holographic display, and showed their destination, which was hell and gone from the Milky Way. In fact, all of the previous ISA missions were indicated by colored dots, and the numbers of the planets on them. Travers enjoyed seeing the cluster of blue.

"You get out there, you do your jobs, you make it back, intact, and we've got something wonderful—we demonstrate to the Colonial Commerce Authority that we can literally homestead the entire fucking universe, we get clients by the balls and we can take anything we like, wherever and whenever we wish. *The distance is the selling point in this operation.* You know and I know that the conduits can take us fucking anywhere—but everyday people don't have much of a clue how it fucking works. They don't know, and they don't care; they just want to be able to buy what they want to buy, eat what they want to eat, go where they want to go. They could give a shit about distance records."

Guessica was certain that Payne didn't have an idea how it fucking worked, either. He had an MBA in Interplanetary Business Administration—he was no scientist, wouldn't even qualify as a scientician.

"All those emigrants who went through the Gate, they just did it because they were less than nothing here on Earth," Payne said. "Moving off-world was the only option they had. But we get a toe in *another goddamned galaxy*—and a real one, not that dwarf bullshit like Leo T—I mean, the Loonies tell me that there are around one trillion fucking stars in Andromeda. That's five times the stars in the motherfucking Milky Way, so that might mean, what, 12.5 billon habitable worlds out there for us? Prime real estate."

"Assuming the worlds aren't already inhabited," Guessica said.

"If they are, so much the better," Payne said. "Then we've got something even more tangible to sell to the Naming Commission. Look, I don't want to psych you guys out, but the successful completion of this mission means absolutely everything to Paragon, and that means good for ISA, good for you, good for the whole fucking Earth. We'll get to a point where there'll be a planet for every motherfucking human being currently alive. I can see the campaign: 'A World of Your Own.' The taglines practically write themselves."

"I thought they do, already. You know, algorithmic marketing and such," Guessica said, smirking. Payne stared blankly at her.

"Considering there's only around a billion people left on Earth these days," Ford said, "We'd be spread sorta thin on 12.5 billion worlds, right?"

"People can get fucking busy," Payne said. "We'll fill them up in no time. What matters is with that kind of spread, we're covered. We will have extinction-proofed humanity. I mean, we already have, right? But we'll have done so, only more, and better."

"Bigger. Better. Faster. More." was Paragon's corporate slogan. It was printed absolutely everywhere in their facilities, in big, bold, sans-serif letters. Impossible to ignore.

Guessica sighed.

"It's a hefty responsibility," she said.

"Of course," Payne said. "Gravitas, all that shit. I get it, I really do. Heartstrings tugging, Music of the Spheres, blah blah blah."

"It means they're going to have to hire a lot more Terranauts," Travers said. "That's way too big a workload for us all to handle, Payne."

Payne looked at Travers like he wanted to slap him.

"Talent Acquisitions is handling it. Successful completion of this mission will guarantee an increase in manpower for these operations. Fuck three-man teams—if this goes smoothly, we're going to have a whole Blue Brigade going. And you three—even you, Travers—will be the stars of the show. Next to me, of course, for keeping it all going, for managing the living fuck out of the whole operation, and getting my percentage of the take."

In truth, all of the Teams were more than just the three Terranauts—there were cadres of support personnel and a pool of resident scienticians to help them through their work.

But the first three—the Terranauts who made those all-important first drops—they were the superstars of the group. Always the first ones to make planetfall, the first ones over the wall.

"What about Chao?" Ford asked.

"Fuck Chao," Payne said. "She's been reassigned to GLX, to figure how where Franzen fucked up, why, and how."

The Terranauts squirmed in their chairs at the mention of the Red Team Leader, and the dreaded GLX. Payne gauged their reactions.

"Oh, please," Payne said. "I know that Leona Prig was fucking keen to have Chao be the one to hit Andromeda, but we were ahead in line, and the Yellow Team meltdown means that Prig's prodigy is going to be slumming it a mere 75,000 light-years away, while you aces are going to be 2.3 million light-years away, making motherfucking history. There was no way I was letting anybody cut in the goddamned line."

Guessica found it amazing how routinely those vast distances were thrown out, anymore. All part of the new reality. The conduits folded space into measurable portions. The industrial marketing apparatus had taken the sublime and rendered it mundane. It was impossible to even think about a 2.3 million light-year distance in human terms, over 13.5 *quadrillion* miles.

"Is this a pep talk, Payne? Are you trying to fire us the fuck up?" Travers asked.

"Something like that," Payne said. "I'm just checking on my team, ensuring that everybody's alright in the wake of Franzen's Folly."

"Is that what you Suits are already calling it?" Ford asked.

"You know we have to have a fall guy for this," Payne said. "Franzen fucked it up. Can't fault the Program, and it sure as hell isn't falling upward to Paragon. Franzen's a dead man, so why not blame him for it?"

"But it really was something he did?" Travers asked. "Not some problem with the Causeway, or a miscalculation by ALLIE?"

"Fuck that," Payne said. "Fuck that all right in the ear. This is not going to be you guys. You're going to get the job done, you're going to come back, and we're going to have it on the Newsfeed 24/7. Everybody will know. Speaking of that, I have an interview scheduled for you tomorrow. I already gave the reporter the talking points, so she'll stay on-script, no worries."

"Another interview?" Travers said.

"Not with you," Payne said. "With Ford, here. You and Guessica are simply there as his wingmen. One big, happy team, conquering the cosmos."

"Swell," Ford said. "I'm tired of interviews. Who's the interviewer?"

"Amber Singh," Payne said.

"I want to get to talk to Amber Singh," Travers said. "She's incredibly hot."

Amber Singh hosted *Everything Now,* one of the top Newsfeed programs. She was six feet tall, perfectly built, seemingly immortal, had a mane of black hair and great big eyes the color of walnuts. Just the thought of being in the same room with her gave Travers shivers.

"Try to control yourself," Guessica said. "Honestly, Trav."

"Is that the only interview, then?" Ford asked.

"It's all we need," Payne said. "Stick to the talking points. You know this by now, Ford. Tell me you don't."

Ford nodded, was folded up inside himself like origami, as was his way. Guessica looked over at him, watched him mull it over stoically. She understood Ford, or felt like she did. They had faced dangerous worlds together, and that kind of experience built trust that could not be found between most people. Guessica even trusted Travers, who, despite his silly nature and constant chatter, could be counted on when they got out there.

She knew Payne had to be thrilled to have Amber Singh interviewing them. It would be high-profile for Blue Team.

"I hear she's a cyborg," Travers said. "Not even flesh and blood."

"Don't you dare even ask her that," Payne said. "Or you're grounded."

Travers made a face like he was mock-afraid.

"Enough bullshit," Payne said. "Of course, Singh's not going to be here—it's going to be beamed in the reception room. Show up on time, don't embarrass me, and we'll have no worries. Now, if you'll excuse me, I'm late for my next meeting."

4

THE TERRANAUTS WATCHED THE FOOTAGE of the interview in the reception room, while Travers laughed and hooted as Ford telegenically worked his magic.

"Your jaw takes up half the screen," Travers said.

"Geometry is everything," Ford said.

"*Timing* is everything," Travers said.

Amber Singh had chosen a honey-hued pencil skirt and suit combination, folded one of her long legs, her cream-colored heels as evident as the smooth, perfect skin she had.

"We're told by ISA that your team is heading deeper into space than any team has, yet," Amber said.

"That's right," Ford said, in his media baritone. "We're going to an undisclosed location in the Andromeda Galaxy, which is 2.3 million light-years away."

A holographic helpfully appeared, showing the audiences where Andromeda Galaxy was, and that the Milky Way was our own galaxy—most people did understand this by now, but *Everything Now* always tried to be as thorough as time permitted.

"That's very far away," Singh said.

"Yes, it is," Ford said. "The light we see from Andromeda is that old—it predates human history, in fact."

"Fascinating," Singh said. "Are you afraid?"

"Of what?" Ford asked.

Travers snorted. "Nice, Ford. That look on your face—priceless!"

Singh smiled, radiant white teeth. "You'll be completely on your own, in another galaxy, even."

"Everybody in the Program—every Terranaut—faces this each time we're outbound to an alien world," Ford said. "We're trained to handle adverse situations in alien environments. One light-year is the same as 2.3 million, as far as I'm concerned."

"Really?" Singh asked.

"Yes," Ford said. Guessica and Travers looked on in the broadcast, Guessica to Ford's right, Travers to his left.

"I hate the way you fidget," Guessica said to Travers, as they watched. "Your eyes keep wandering."

"I was bored," Travers said. "I wanted her to ask me a question, but it's always Ford Ford Ford Ford."

Ford looked over and grinned at Travers.

"Why Andromeda?" Singh asked. "ISA tells us there are billions of stars here in the Milky Way, hundreds of billions of worlds; why bother with another galaxy?"

"Why not?" Ford asked. "Paragon wants to illustrate to people everywhere that the Conduit technology is safe, practical, and that distance is no limitation for us. Unlike conventional space travel, the Conduits let us cross any distance instantaneously."

"Like an elevator?" Singh asked.

Travers snorted.

"Not really," Ford said. "There's nothing quite like Conduit travel."

Newsfeed Ford took the sheet of paper, folded in half, which made Travers sigh as he watched it, muttering.

"We start here," Ford said, pointing to one side of the paper. "We want to get over here. If we traveled that actual distance, it would take an incredibly long time. But we fold space, and pass through the conduit, and there you have it."

Singh looked at the paper, at Ford, and smiled blankly.

"We heard rumors about Yellow Team suffering some difficulties on their mission," Singh said. "Care to elaborate on that?"

"I wouldn't know," Ford said. "My primary focus is on Blue Team; I'm sure Commander Franzen has things handled for his people. He's a good man, with an impeccable track record."

Guessica whistled. "Nicely done, Ford, although you can see Travers's tell, there. Look at his expression."

"You don't believe this, Mr. Walker?" Singh asked.

"What? Oh, no, it's just that we Terranauts have a friendly rivalry between our teams," Travers said. "Everybody tries to outdo everybody else. We're all part of the Paragon family, but it's like with sports teams, really—you root for your team, want them to win."

"So, is there a feud between Yellow Team and Blue Team?" Singh asked.

"I wouldn't say that," Travers said. "Friendly rivalry is what I said. We're all friends and family, even, but we're all trying to outdo everybody else—Bigger, Better, Faster, More."

The three Terranauts did a shot as they watched the broadcast.

"No feud," Ford said. "We want only the best for Dennis and his people, Amber."

Guessica laughed at this, looked over at Travers. "Payne was so pissed about this. You opened your mouth, Trav."

"I had to," Travers said. "I mean, Ford can talk about Franzen fine, but the man's dead, and we're busy pretending he's alive? I couldn't hide it."

Singh smiled, recrossed her legs, leaned forward.

"What do you say to critics who say this is just a publicity stunt on the part of Paragon?"

Ford smiled back at her.

"Paragon has invested many hundreds of trillions of Yuan into its conduit technology," Ford said. "The very nature of the work demands precision and care, and I can assure you that no one at ISA takes their work more seriously than Paragon. The investment of time and money in the Program precludes anything like that. The opening of a portal, the exosuits, all of our equipment—no, this is no stunt."

Travers mock-applauded. "Way to plug Paragon, Ford. Bravo."

Singh nodded, the camera on her face. "But why so far out?"

"Because we can," Ford said. "Conduit technology lets us travel any distance, ultimately. This test will demonstrate the real power of the Program, that the sky is literally the limit. Anywhere is Everywhere."

"Is that a new slogan they're trying out? Why wasn't I briefed? You're like a human sloganeer, Ford," Guessica said. Ford shrugged. Travers did a shot.

"Well, as far as we can see, anyway," Newsfeed Travers said.

"What do you mean, Mr. Walker?" Singh asked.

Guessica shook her head. "That mouth of yours, Trav."

Travers grinned, watching the hologram of himself gesticulate, forming a ball. "This is the universe, and it's always expanding. We're over here, and we're seeing the old light from other places. Eventually, light gets so far away that the amount of time it takes to reach us will be effectively infinite—when that happens, when the distances exceed the speed of light, then we'll see stars start to 'disappear.' Oh, they'll be out there, but we'll not be able to see them. And when that happens, we won't be able to shoot a wormhole out there and just blindly drop people to those faraway places."

Ford smiled at Travers and coughed into his hand. "The story is a little more complex than that, Amber—and what Trav is talking about is something that's not going to happen for billions of years. And by then, who knows what we'll have developed."

Amber laughed fetchingly, nodding.

On the other side of the hologram, Ford shook his head. "You just can't stop yourself, can you, Trav?"

"I can't, I can't," Travers said.

The holographic Ford continued. "The Conduit is a kind of lens—we don't just step through blindly. We open a wormhole, and we can see through it, can see what's on the other side. So, we do get a glimpse of what's beyond, even though it's really just a pinhole in space-time. We can see where we're going."

"Why send people through these portals at all?" Amber asked. "Some say that it could be done more effectively by machines, and for less money."

Ford shrugged. "People say that, but in the field, a team of Terranauts can't be topped when it comes to exploration of a new environment. Probes are swell, robots are great; but the nature of conduit travel requires a considerable amount of autonomy and adaptability to unpredictable circumstance, and the Terranaut Program has delivered on the Paragon promise of Bigger, Better, Faster, More. We've done it."

Travers raised a glass, took a shot. It was a little drinking game he'd rigged with some of the other Terranauts. Any time they would slip a corporate slogan into one of their broadcasts, they took a shot.

"Thank you for your time, Terranauts Collins, Rao, and Walker. On behalf of *Everything Now,* the Earth, and the Colonies: good luck."

Ford turned off the holographic replay, while Travers applauded half-heartedly.

"Wonderfully played, Ford," Travers said. "You killed. I see why Payne lets you be his point man."

They just sat there in the dimness of the room. "That mouth of yours is going to get you cashiered, Trav," Ford said. "Not by me; I'm fine with it; but somebody higher in the food chain is going to gobble you up one day."

"Let'em," Travers said, holding out his hand, showing it to be steady.

5

PUSHUPS. FORD BELIEVED IN PUSHUPS. In the face of pre-drop jitters, Ford had faith in them as the cure for the weight of the worlds. He smirked to himself, as he counted his way through his reps—his belief in them had made him firm. Firm but flexible. Ford was nothing if not firm and flexible.

There were two days that were exceedingly stressful for Terranauts—the day before the drop, and the day of the pickup—when the mission was over and one just had to chew on each remaining minute until the conduit reopened.

At this point in his life, he'd done more than his share of service. He reflected on this while he kept at his routine. Routine was the lifeblood of the Terranaut—it was almost an incantation, in an uncertain universe, in the unguessable abyss of infinity, routine was something you could take refuge in. And so Ford did this.

Life at the Oasis was like living in the most high-tech small town in human history. While the Vault had been predominantly a military outpost, the Oasis had been engineered by Paragon's army of design professionals to be more accommodating to the psychological and emotional needs of its Terranauts. This was just considered good form, a way of keeping all of the cogs and flywheels operating effectively as possible under unrelentingly dangerous conditions. The Oasis was a place of plastic peace. A happy Terranaut was a valuable corporate asset, and Paragon ensured that ISA looked after their Terranauts, granting them everything except their freedom—the nature of the work required the utmost secrecy, or so they were told, over and over again.

A Terranaut could quit the Program at any time, but there was a gag order in place that ensured that retiring didn't give that person the opportunity to reveal what they'd seen. Not directly, anyway, or in any way that Paragon's lawbots could find fault with.

It wasn't that Ford wanted to quit; he enjoyed the work. Rather, it was that he was beginning to feel like a galactic gladiator who had been in the games too long, had faced the cheering crowds enough times that he had nothing left to prove in the arena. There was no canvas greater than the cosmos, no work more challenging than being a Terranaut. Once he made the drop to Andromeda, he'd be the Man, and Chao would be eating her hand with envy, and then Prig would want her Red Team to top that record. He could just imagine them hopping to a 13.3 billion light-year galaxy, just to set the bar so high that nobody could hope to challenge them. It would be a very Red Team sort of thing to do. Ford didn't relish being caught up in that sort of intergalactic space race, with the egos of Payne and Prig leading to the Terranauts being thrown ever farther.

These were his thoughts as he worked through the remaining reps.

The Oasis had sexual/relationship professionals on staff—all of them licensed and bonded to provide the necessary release required from time to time, but Ford never approved of them. He wasn't uptight about it, but he hated the idea of a counterfeit relationship like that. The Proxies, as they were called, were actually more than simple sex workers—they were on-staff to provide the Terranauts with relationships, if they wanted them. The Terranauts, in their tendency to nickname, called them their "Fuckbuddies," and plenty of his peers had them. It was simply Paragon's answer to the problem of long-term employment of personnel on-site. Starting a family was seen as counterproductive to the overall mission requirements of the Program—Paragon didn't want its people distracted, so the Proxies were brought in as a way of remedying that, giving them all the comforts of home without the demands of home life. There were no children at the Oasis, because the work that was done there wasn't child's play.

Plenty of the Terranauts had done their service and retired to leave the Oasis forever behind and start families of their own. Often, Ter-

ranauts married other Terranauts, because only another stellar surveyor could really appreciate their experience.

But not Ford. He'd last had a relationship with Luz Pirelli, his personal Proxy, for three years, before he put an end to that. She'd been
great at her job, being his companion, always understanding, always
ensuring something nice for him when he returned. Her mane of
curly black hair always smelled good. She kept herself fit, her brown
eyes were always understanding, and she always listened to him when
he talked about what he'd experienced. It was just that when he would
come back to the Oasis, Luz just reminded him of how much he wanted to have a proper home, a place of his own, and not to be a pet (even
a favored one) of Paragon's.

She'd naturally taken another client after Ford: Bryan Gaye of Purple Team, and had been his Proxy for about five years. Gaye seemed
content with the arrangement, and Luz and Ford maintain a cordial
work relationship, even though their paths seldom crossed.

Ford paused in his pushups, did some agonizingly slow ones. Fitness
of body begat fitness of mind. That's what he told himself, rep after rep.

Payne had been worried when Ford had given up Pirelli, who had
been one of the most in-demand of Proxies. Payne had confronted
him about it in the hallway outside the Terranaut Quarters. He had
actually blocked Ford's passage in the corridor. Ford was a big man,
not used to that, but Payne just glared up at him, unrelenting.

"What the fuck is this?" he said. "Luz tells me you're letting her go."

"That's right," Ford said. "I'm through."

Payne looked at him like he had just insulted his mother. "Luz Pirelli? Oh, you fucking 'Nauts. Why? Tell me why?"

There was no aspect of a Terranaut's life that wasn't subject to scru-
tiny and oversight from Paragon. Maybe that was part of the problem.

"It's not real," Ford said. "She's not real. She's sweet, but she's a fraud.
She's a little white lie."

"You want another Proxy? Is that what you're telling me?"

Payne was such a little pit bull of a man. He actually pushed Ford
against the wall of the hall with his personality. Ford pushed back, a
finger in the man's chest.

"I don't want a fucking Proxy," Ford said. "I'm sick of it. The whole
thing is bullshit. Luz was fine, but it was her fucking job."

"Whoa," Payne said. "Look, I understand that the Oasis is a tough gig. Nobody knows this better than me. That's why they're here: they're here for you."

Ford shook his head. "No more. Seriously. I'm done with that. I had Luz for three years, Margo for five, Leesha for four."

Payne knew this as well as Ford did. It was his job to know. Just like Ford knew that Luz and Margo and Leesha were also required to report on his health and mental well-being to the Paragon psychologists. There wasn't anybody involved who didn't know how it worked.

"The work is isolating," Payne said. "Your work is tremendously dangerous and it's alienating. Paragon isn't going to let you buck this. We're not going to let you just come back home and sit and stare out the fucking window or up into the goddamned night's sky, Ford. There's going to be someone waiting there for you. Now, you can be a big boy and pick one, or you can have me pick one for you."

"Payne the Pimp," Ford said. "God, I can only imagine."

Payne waved that off. "Look, it's done. I've already filed the paperwork for it. Got you a nice, young thing. Her name is Miranda Wilson."

Ford scoffed. "I'm not going to take that. I don't have to."

"The one Terranaut who doesn't want to get laid, can you fucking believe it?" Payne looked like he wanted to have a Smoke™, but that was forbidden on-site. "You'll come back from QED-111 and she's going to be there, Sport. Probably in your fucking bed. Just deal with it."

Ford had dealt with it. The thing was, he didn't want to cause the woman any trouble. As a Proxy, her career depended on being able to make him happy. So, when he got back from surveying 111, and, as Payne had promised/threatened, she was there, sitting on one of Ford's chairs, absently playing with one of her long, tangled ringlets, long, dark legs stretched out on the ottoman, watching the trideo, drinking a cocktail she'd made, one for him already on the chilltray, he had gone easy on her.

"You're her?" he asked.

"That's me," Miranda said. She was naked.

"You're, what? 20?" Ford dropped his attaché and gym bag in a corner, locked the door.

"I'm 22," Miranda said.

"From?"

"Eden," she said. "New Bethlehem."

Of course. All of the best Proxies came from Eden.

"Yeah," Ford said.

She had a slight upward turn to her nose, and her lips looked pouty. Her frame was long and lean, but her breasts were full and couldn't have resisted gravity any better if Paragon had engineered them. Payne had picked somebody who had kind of looked like Luz. It was so clear. Taller, more willowy, but still she looked like Luz to Ford, only seeming more sincere.

Miranda got up, picked up the drink, held it out. Big eyes, brown, like brazil nuts. "I was watching the broadcast of your return. You must be thirsty."

Ford took the drink, sipped it. A Manhattan, exactly how he liked it. An ancient drink.

"Look, you don't have to do anything," Ford said. "Honestly, you don't."

"I just want to make you happy, Commander Collins," she said.

"Ford," he said.

"I just want to make you happy, Ford," she said. "Let me make you happy."

Ford sat down in one of his chairs, and Miranda rubbed his shoulders a moment before she came around and sat down in front of him, perching her chin on his knee, gazing up at him.

"Nobody gets you, right?" she asked. "Not even Luz got you, did she?"

The trideo played the news of his return, with Travers and Guessica on his wings, the three of them gamely shaking sand off their suits. A mere 150,000 light-years, that one. The other side of the galaxy. Practically a stroll.

"Luz got me," Ford said.

"Now *I've* got you," Miranda said.

Ford downed his drink and set it back on the chilltray, watched it frost over again. "Look, Miranda, I'm going to bore the fuck out of you. I'm not going to ask a single thing of you. You can just flop here, do your own thing. When performance review time comes up, I'll give you a glowing review, you can go anywhere."

Miranda scoffed at this. "You think I *want* to be anywhere but here, Ford? This is the Oasis. This is one of the best-paying, cushiest gigs a girl could land. You think I want to slum it back on Eden? Do you know how many companions there are there? How many proxies?"

Ford admitted that he didn't.

"There are 40 million sex workers on Eden," Miranda said. "I think it's like four percent of the population."

"Wow," Ford said.

Miranda looked him in the eye and laughed—a hearty, brassy sound.

"Yeah, that's a lot of competition. This place is like a vacation. You do exactly what you want with or to me, and it's *still* better than Eden. Just don't send me back there, please. I'd die before I went back to Eden."

It made Ford sad to think that the virgin Eden had been so roundly plowed over, so fast. Miranda noticed the change in his expression, touched his thigh with her hand. Her nails were painted almond. She smelled like coconuts.

"What's wrong, Ford?"

"It just makes me sad," Ford said. "I was the second person to set foot on that world, you know that?"

"I do," Miranda said. Every Proxy was briefed on their client. "Do people even know what's been done to it?" Ford asked.

"They know," Miranda said. "Nobody cares. It's a pleasure planet, Ford. That's what it's there, for. People love it."

Ford was no moralist, but it still made him sad. And seeing this lovely young woman, with her heart-shaped face and her willowy limbs and her perfect body, and understanding that she'd been bred and raised to be a courtesan on Eden, and that indentured servitude to him at the Oasis was actually a move up for her? It made him ache. He reached out and stroked her hair, which she took to be a gesture of affection, closed her eyes, and leaned into it, catlike, to receive his attention.

"We can make this work if we want it to, Ford," Miranda said. She was so young—fifteen years younger than he was. Each time another Proxy turned up, the age chasm widened.

"What do you think of Earth?" he asked. "Were you born on Eden?"

"Yes," she said. "Earth is quaint."

He laughed, despite himself. "Quaint?"

Miranda nodded, which, from her perch on his knee, looked amusing. "It's much quieter than I thought it would be. You know, all the history and stuff, you think maybe it would show. But it's a sleepy place."

"Wasn't always," Ford said. "Used to be noisier."

"It's sedate," Miranda said. "Eden never sleeps. I could show you some fun there. I mean, Eden's hell, but it's not boring, and it sure as hell isn't sleepy."

"No, you couldn't," Ford said. "They keep us on lockdown, here. They don't let us go out and about. Risk of contagion is just too great."

Miranda sulked. "Wow. You never get to travel?"

Ford laughed again, because it was a funny thing to imagine. He, who had traveled more and greater distances than anybody, who was scheduled to travel to Andromeda Galaxy, never got to travel.

"Something like that," he said. "Once we leave the Program, we can travel as we like, as civilians. But as Terranauts? No. Never."

Miranda stroked his thigh with her hand, and almost had him convinced that she didn't already know that Terranauts didn't travel—she was that convincing. Proxies always were, though.

"Payne tells me there's a big one lined up for you," she said.

"That's right," Ford said. "The biggest. The farthest."

"I'll worry for you," Miranda said.

"Yeah," Ford said. "Right."

Ford knew how this went. It was the same with Luz.

He finished his pushups, and Miranda came in, wearing a leather dress of the most tantalizing shade of indigo, no doubt dyed using some of the exotics from Terranova. The range of products available in this day and age was staggering. Colors human eyes had never before seen were now commonplace, foods only recently discovered. Miranda was wearing five-inch heels, suede matched to the color of the dress. She had a bag of things she'd bought at the luxury store. Not because she had to, but because she wanted to.

"How many is it this time, Tough Guy?" she asked.

"Fifty sets of twenty reps," he said.

Miranda whistled. Her kissy-big lips were painted claret. "Today being your big day, I brought something special."

He sat on the floor, stretched a little. She'd been with him for months, now. He, of course, succumbed—he wasn't allowed to kick her out without bringing the Psych people in to question his sanity; after the Luz situation, he had to play ball.

Miranda knelt by him, holding out a pendant. It was a pretty silver thing, a triangle of silver punctured with a cerulean crystal.

"What is it?"

"It's a pendant," she said. "Man jewelry, Silly."

"I'm supposed to wear this?"

Miranda smiled. "Yes. For luck. For me. For us."

She unclasped it and held it out for him. Her nails were indigo, as well. She paused, waiting for him to accept it. He did with a reluctant nod. She leaned in, put it around his neck, let him take her scent, let him see her cleavage as she fastened the thing. Then she leaned back, all cuteness and impertinence.

"There," she said. "Was that so hard?"

Ford took the thing in his hand, looked it over. On the back was "M.E.W."

"What's that?"

"My initials," Miranda said. "Miranda Ermine Wilson. MEW."

She made a little mewling sound, giving his chest a kittenish pawing.

"Hah," Ford said, turning it back over, looking at the blue stone upon it.

"Something to remember me by," she said, smirking at him. "It does more than just look pretty, you know. Just like me."

She pressed the crystal in the center, and the thing projected a fist-sized hologram of Miranda, smiling nakedly at him. Her whole, gorgeous body, turning this way and that, and, from another angle, her face, gazing warmly-yet-wantonly at him. She looked beautiful, healthy, sweet, even. Vital. Alive.

Ford closed his eyes, thought of endless nights and trackless skies.

"Come back soon, Ford," she said, and Ford didn't know whether it was her or the hologram.

6

GUESSICA ALWAYS WROTE HER FAMILY before a drop. She wrote all of them. It was one of her pre-drop rituals, a way of hopefully banishing any demons, any creatures of misfortune that haunted her steps. Her family lived on Xenophon, so when these letters were delivered, she would already be gone.

One of the issues associated with the conduits was the primacy of couriers to communicate from planet to planet, since no one was able to broadcast conventionally to the Colonies, nor were computer networks on planets linkable. Even with the permanent commercial conduits set up at the Gate, conglomerates were reluctant to clog up conduit pathways with cables linking the worlds, so each world operated on its own network, and couriers tended to dominate the business of information between them.

On the bright side, it saw some revival of the moribund profession of journalism, since journalists actually found themselves with a job to do, after many decades of somnolence.

For the couriers, it was no different. Their job was to come and go across the conduits, relaying information in endless streams between the worlds. It struck Guessica as faintly ironic, given how much weight was placed on conduit travel at the Oasis, how much prestige the Terranauts enjoyed, relative to the couriers, who hopscotched their way across space and time constantly, daily, back and forth, conveying information. Until some better means was found, the Colonial Express couriers, with their massive jump drives on their backs, were the lynchpins of Colonial communication.

What Guessica found curious was that a CE station was invariably placed at either side of the Gate's conduits. And in those heavily-protected stations were data transfer nodes that actually uplinked to the planetary information webs. What the CE couriers did was walk back and forth, from station to station, passing that information in a Sisyphean manner, receiving uploads from Earth, downloads from Terranova, uploads from Eden, downloads from Thanatos, on and on and on, a constant stream across space-time.

Guessica finished her letters to her family, wrapped up a note to her prospective husband, Amil, and uploaded them to CE for delivery, which would be on Drop Day. She kept everything informative but unrevealing, for ALLIE would pore over the notes before they were allowed off-site, per Paragon's policy. It wasn't like Guessica would reveal any company secrets to Amil, but their policy was strict with regard to the passing of information into and out of the Oasis.

Having attended to that, she went over her lists on her datassistant, to ensure that she'd forgotten nothing. Of course, she hadn't, because she had done this so many times before, but all the same, it was one of her rituals. There was always that period of uncertainty and dread before a drop, at least she felt it.

She didn't know if anyone else did, assumed they did. Even Ford had to get the pre-drop jitters.

"Are you nervous?" ALLIE asked, her soothing voice startling Guessica, making her jump.

"ALLIE, you scared me," Guessica said.

"I'm sorry, Guessica," ALLIE said. Her disembodied voice sounded on one of the million intercoms that were peppered throughout the Oasis, indeed, at any place ALLIE worked.

"No, I'm not nervous," Guessica said, wondering if the artificial intelligence could see through that. It still made her want to pinch herself, to know that she was talking to one of the highest-functioning AIs available. In truth, there were no AIs "on the market"—they were all highly regulated, highly protected corporate assets. They qualified, in some respects, as indentured servants, at least to Guessica's understanding. Their processing power was astounding.

"I'm asking because of the content of your messages," ALLIE said. "My sense is that you are worried about the upcoming mission."

Guessica got herself a glass of cold water from her fridge, cut a slice of lemon and put it in the glass, and then sat down in her living room. For Terranauts between missions, even the simplest creature comforts were resonant and necessary.

"You got that, did you?"

"Yes," ALLIE said. "You know I monitor everyone's correspondence."

"It's just natural," Guessica said. "To feel nervous."

"I understand," ALLIE said. "This is a very important mission. You want to excel."

"Always."

"I have reason to believe that this may be the most significant mission for ISA, yet," ALLIE said.

"Why is that?"

It still amazed Guessica that ALLIE could be simultaneously conversing with her (and perhaps other Terranauts), monitoring everything at the Oasis, corresponding with the Loonies, plotting mission logistics, assessing viability for future missions on countless discovered worlds, and doing who knows what else.

"I'm not at liberty to discuss it at this time," ALLIE said. "But the distances alone will guarantee a level of notoriety for Blue Team that will surely touch off a 'time-space race' between yourselves and the other teams. Their administrators are already having me analyze still-farther solar systems, in an effort to plant their flags in other galaxies. Triangulum Galaxy is already being probed."

At 3 million light-years away, Triangulum was surely where Chao would take Red Team. It made Guessica a little sad to think that their record-breaking 2.3 million light-year trek to Andromeda was already slated to be surpassed.

"And after Triangulum, still farther," ALLIE said. "Would it please you to know that ISA is investigating a galaxy over 13 billion light-years from Earth?"

Guessica exhaled sharply. The scale of it was beyond her comprehension—she could compute the distances, but the meaning behind the math was beyond imagining. There was no point in questioning it; if ALLIE was saying it, it must be true.

"That's incredible," Guessica said. "A galaxy formed near the very beginning of the universe."

"Yes," ALLIE said. "We are currently trying to get a good look at it, using gravity lensing and assorted other optical aids with dozens of our orbiting telescopes, deployed at all of the Colonial Worlds. It is a small galaxy—scarcely 600 light-years across."

"Fascinating," Guessica said. "I hope to be part of that team."

"Paragon has planned something special for that mission," ALLIE said. "A kind of 'all-star' team—taking the best from each of the survey teams and sending them there."

That both excited Guessica and made her sad—she was certainly the best geologist ISA had, but if they were really only sending the best of each team, then Ford would, without question, be tapped for that mission.

The scale of it actually frightened and awed her—13 billion light-years made even their own titanic leap across the abyss seem like nothing more than a hop.

"You would very much like to be on that mission, yes?" ALLIE asked.

"You know I would," Guessica said.

"What if I told you that successful completion of this mission would guarantee you a spot on Gold Team?" ALLIE asked.

Guessica wondered if ALLIE was authorized to reveal this to her, whether it was, perhaps, some kind of protocol Paragon had put in place to test the ambition and vision of its Terranauts, something dreamed up by the Psych Division to analyze Oasis personnel.

"There is no Gold Team," Guessica said.

"Gold Team is the assignation for this mission," ALLIE said.

"I would very much like to be on that mission," Guessica said. "Are you authorized to be telling me this stuff, ALLIE?"

"I wouldn't be doing so if I weren't."

Gold Team. It would be the ultimate mission. Guessica was confident that none of the other geologists would get tapped for it. ALLIE seemed to sense Guessica's thoughts, spoke further.

"Three team leaders, two physicists, two geologists, two biologists, two meteorologists, one doctor," ALLIE said. "Gold Team."

"Wow," Guessica said. "Do Ford and Travers know?"

"You're the first member of Blue Team that I've told," ALLIE said.

"And why is that?"

Guessica's mind was already reeling, as she contemplated this mission. It made her sweat, made her thirsty. She drank deep from her glass of ice water.

"I understand your ambition," ALLIE said. "Successful completion of QED-376 mission will guarantee you a place on Gold Team."

Again, Guessica knew better than to question ALLIE. If ALLIE was saying this, it was so. But why ALLIE had chosen to tell her about it was something Guessica was less sure about.

"Has a world been discovered in this system?"

"Not yet," ALLIE said. "But we are looking at it very carefully. It's only a matter of time. Of course, it will be the most dangerous of assignments, hence the priority placed on team quality. After all, a lot can happen in 13 billion light-years' time, and what we're seeing is very, very old light. Paragon feels that the public has gotten too comfortable with conduit technology, that it has become almost commonplace in popular perception. The Gold Team project will once again command people's attention. What's more, Paragon wants to get there first."

"Nobody will believe it," Guessica said. "It's too far away, too incredible."

"They will believe," ALLIE said.

"Fine one you are to distract me with this before our drop, ALLIE," Guessica said.

ALLIE was silent for a millisecond. With her processing power, it might as well have been a lifetime.

"I just wanted you to know," ALLIE said.

"Why me? Why haven't you told Ford?"

"Ford knows what he needs to know. That is his nature. He is Operations. When the right planet is found, when the mission is planned, Ford will be informed," ALLIE said. "Until then, his job is the successful completion of the QED-376 survey mission."

Guessica's hands were shaking a little, and she set down her glass. To be burdened with such a secret before a mission? It probably wasn't the first time it had happened to a Terranaut, but it was the first time it had happened to Guessica. Did that mean that she had moved further up in Paragon's estimation? Had Payne been so pleased with her work that his favorable reports had percolated upward into ALLIE's consciousness?

"Why me?" Guessica asked.

"You are ready," ALLIE said. "ISA needs people like you. Do your job on this upcoming mission, do not fail, no matter the obstacles you may face, and you will be part of Gold Team."

Despite fluency in three languages, failure was not part of Guessica's vocabulary.

"I won't fail, ALLIE," Guessica said.

"Whatever it takes?"

"Whatever it takes," Guessica said. "Is there reason to expect this QED mission to be extraordinarily difficult?"

"Only that it is, for the moment, farther than any previous mission," ALLIE said. "That distance can place a great burden on human psychology. Wen Chao experienced it in her team on the Leo T mission. Not herself, of course, but Fabian Dross, her geologist, became a little unhinged by the experience, to put it in the way people do."

Dross was Guessica's only real competition in the Program. His PhD from Xenophon College up against her own PhD from EMIT had made her feel almost provincial, even though the lineage at EMIT was far greater than anything the savants at Xenophon could hope to muster. Dross was daring and imaginative, a ponytailed prodigy with an impish grin and a tan that rivaled that of most of the administrators. His ambition was only exceeded by his arrogance—he really considered himself a "rock star" in the field.

"I wasn't aware of Fabian losing it at Leo T," Guessica said.

"Your term is colloquially expressed, but is, on the face of it, accurate," ALLIE said. "He experienced profound reservations about the mission upon deployment to Leo T. This information is classified."

"Okay," Guessica said, trying to remember the last time she'd seen Dross. Six months ago? Despite the intimacy and endless confinement at the Oasis, it was so easy to get wrapped up in mission preparation that one could avoid seeing even one's neighbors for some time.

"Dross suffered a bit of a breakdown at Leo T," ALLIE said. "Cause unknown. He's currently being evaluated by the Psychology Department."

Guessica whistled. Dross was brilliant. She wondered what had happened to him.

"Can I talk to him?"

"He's been moved off-site," ALLIE said.

"Really? It's that bad?"

"He's being thoroughly evaluated," ALLIE said. "I don't believe he'll be returning to the Program."

"Wow," Guessica said. That should have meant that she was guaranteed a spot on Gold Team, then, which made the contingent nature of it alarming to her. "That kind of thing won't happen to me, you know; I'm rock-solid."

It was one of her geologist quips, one of many at her disposal, to be unearthed in times of uncertainty.

"Of course," ALLIE said. Guessica was positive she understood the humor, but doubted that the AI had been programmed to laugh. "I just wanted you to be certain that you understood the stakes of this mission, that, through no fault of your own, its failure could adversely impact your position on Gold Team."

"Jeez," Guessica said. "I'll do my part without cracking, ALLIE. You can be sure of that. Why would Dross lose it?"

"The Psych Officers have labeled it 'deep-space psychosis,' for lack of a more precise term," ALLIE said. "The existential shock of the distances, maybe even a reaction to the gravitic stresses of the conduit passage over time? It's still being studied. Of course, Dross's own psychology could be in play, as well. There are so many variables."

"How bad was it?"

Guessica hadn't seen Red Team's return from Leo T; she had been sick with flu, and had been quarantined from the other Terranauts for the duration of it, as was routine at the Oasis, and she'd been happy to do so; the last thing Guessica wanted was to be responsible for halting missions because of an untimely bout of influenza.

"Dross had to be sedated upon arrival," ALLIE said. "He was immediately sequestered and, well, I've probably already told you far too much."

Guessica wondered why ALLIE was telling her this at all. The prospect of a once-in-a-lifetime mission on the face of a soon-to-be-historic mission and the specter of one of her rivals' apparent psychotic breakdown? It was too much information to process at once, but maybe it was a measure of ALLIE's respect for her that she thought Guessica could handle it. Or, perhaps, it was a measure of ALLIE's lack of understanding of the human mind that she thought she could bury her consciousness beneath a landslide of information without consequence.

"I think you have," Guessica said. "For now, I'm going to concentrate squarely on the mission."

"As you should," ALLIE said. "We can talk more, if you like, after this mission is completed."

"You know, you asked me if I was nervous. And if I wasn't before, I definitely am, now. Thanks, ALLIE," Guessica said, hoping the AI understood her sarcasm.

"You're *more* than welcome, Guessica," ALLIE replied, and she couldn't be sure if ALLIE was mocking her or not.

7

TRAVERS TOOK FULL ADVANTAGE of Salacia Cross, his own Proxy. As far as he knew, he could be dead tomorrow. Salacia had red hair, dyed the most incredible red Travers had ever seen, something she'd picked up from a spa in Eden called Jezebel's. The color was magnificently bright, an honest vermillion, gleaned from some sea sponges they'd found in the oceans of that world. Unlike most red dyes, Jezebel Red was permanent.

She was short, because Travers liked short girls, felt like they had something to prove, and enjoyed when they proved it to him again and again and again. Her red hair was shoulder-length and straight—it was as straight as the rest of her was curvy, and Travers enjoyed that contrast.

Travers loved the Proxy Program, and went through a new Proxy each year as a kind of tradition, or an annual bonus—it was simply a case of wanting to enjoy the fullest fruits of his labors, and thumbing his nose a bit at Paragon. If they were going to keep him captive at the Oasis, he was sure as hell going to require the company to pimp him plenty of Proxies. He had enough complaints about the work as it was to not feel that he was owed something, and as long as Paragon was willing to provide him with Proxies, he'd be happy to use them.

He'd actually researched the origins of Proxies at ISA, like where the program had come from, and it had been intended as a concession won by the Terranauts from Paragon, because of the secrecy surrounding the conduit program, and the danger of it making it not conducive for family men, so the Proxies arose—somebody had mentioned the archaic word, "doxies"—although Proxies could be male or female, depending on the Terranaut.

There was another aspect to the Proxies, too, which was why Travers always cycled through his—he knew that they were spies for Paragon. Part and parcel of their job was to keep an eye on the Terranauts, and to report on anything unusual to Administration. Sure, they were there to take the edge off the Terranauts, but they were spies, as well. Knowing that about them only fueled his cynicism, allowed him to stay detached. Woe to the Terranaut who fell in love with his Proxy. It had happened a few times in the Program, and it got messy.

Salacia was pressed up against him in bed, one leg draped over his body.

"You know, I could die tomorrow," Travers said.

"Yeah?" Salacia said. "That would suck."

"It sure would," Travers said. Salacia had periwinkle eyes, and Travers had always wondered whether those were natural, or whether they were contacts, or whether she'd been bred to have them.

She just looked at him with those colorful eyes, playfully bit his collarbone.

"So, don't do it," Salacia said. "Don't die."

"Nobody plans on it," Travers said. "But shit happens."

"Yeah," Salacia said. "Deep shit."

Salacia's penchant for the profane didn't bother Travers, although his own mortality certainly did nag at him. In one of the halls at the Oasis was the Hall of the Dead—where holograms of the fallen Terranauts were on display, where they were left, suspended in the air, these ghosts.

With Franzen's team's sudden passing, there would be three more ghosts added to the Hall of the Dead—it was officially called Hallowed Hall.

Travers had personally known about half of the ghosts in residence, and had known of the rest. He most certainly didn't want to end up in Hallowed Hall, but he'd spent a lot of time meandering in it, gazing at the impeccably crafted holographic memorials of each of them. Paragon's social media people always put together polished pieces for the fallen, atop black marble veined with white—the pieces were as polished as the stone which housed them.

"I'm scared to death," Travers said. "Always."

"Fuck death," Salacia said, squirming against him. She walked a pair of fingers down the landscape of his stomach, grabbed his cock with surprising gentleness.

"Yeah," Travers said. "Sure. That's your answer for everything, though, right? Fucking?"

"I'm a Virgo," Salacia said. "What can I say? It's what I do. Fuck this, fuck that, fuck everything. It's gotten me this fucking far, hasn't it?"

It amused Travers that Salacia liked astrology. She was always reading into things, cosmic alignments, the stars. It tickled him, in a way, since he'd actually visited some of the stars she studied in her charts, so when she talked with authority about the stars and their alignments, it made him want to laugh.

She stroked his cock until he was hard, then climbed aboard him, slipping herself onto him slowly, so he could feel every inch of himself inside her, and she favored him with a glorious gasp as he entered her.

"Let me distract you a little, Spaceman," Salacia said.

Salacia glowered down at him with periwinkle eyes as she rocked her hips. When she'd fuck him, she'd sometimes scowl lasciviously at him, her eyes pinched tight into sparkly crescents, before snapping wide open again, a look of revelation and orgasmic epiphany on her face that, real or fake, was always impressive. Her breasts bucked the trends in Eden by being real, and she'd adorned them with a pair of silver nipple rings that made Travers think that Salacia was secretly inflatable, and that those slender hoops on her nipples were the only thing keeping her that way. He imagined him pulling the pins from them and her flying around the room over his head, deflating.

He gave her a squeeze on either side of her hips as she rode him. Salacia was good at her job: she was a magnificent lay. She could drive away the entire universe when she fucked him. Within her thighs was the power to negate space-time, gravity, entropy, ennui, angst, anomie, horror, terror—all manner of things that might otherwise clog his consciousness. They just ceased to exist in Salacia's company, and there was only the caustic, flinty squint of hers as she fucked him (she never made love—Salacia only fucked, although, in brief, bashful moments of her rampant Virgin/Whore Complex, she might call it "lovemaking," but usually stuck to "sex" or "fucking"). In those moments, where time really did seem to cease for him, Travers treasured her cries and moans, her thick, red hair, the wild-yet-faraway look she got in her eyes as she came with power and punctual precision. Salacia got off on him, and Travers got off on that.

She made a lot of noise when they fucked, and Travers enjoyed that, too, although she never really talked in articulate phrases, but rather usually cursed or cried out to various deities, until she reached climax and screamed in his face, her mouth agape, eyes rolling, a beautifully human display of transportative abandon.

Salacia was a whore, but she was *his* whore, well-paid to keep him happy, and she excelled in that role, which was why Travers wondered now and then if he might buck his tradition and keep her on for another year. He resolved that until the moment came when he became bored with her, he'd just do that. She'd understand. Maybe she'd be a little pissed at him, but she'd get it. Proxies were well paid for their labors; she had no complaints.

As Travers came, stars in his eyes, Salacia brought her arms down on his chest, gripping him tightly, and they rolled over, Travers still inside her, now atop her.

"Stay there," she said. "Don't go."

And while he stayed inside her, held himself there, she came again, crying out even louder than before, before she let him go, curled up against him.

"You are a fucking genius," she said. "At sex. I would worship your cock. There should be a shrine built to it. At the Oasis. There should just be a room where women from all over the cosmos can come and pay their respects to your cock."

Travers laughed. "Maybe I can run that by Administration, yeah?"

"Would you?" Salacia asked. "It could keep me company while you're gone."

"Maybe I could endorse a line of sex toys when I'm done here," Travers said.

Salacia liked that, snorted.

"Now that *would* keep me company while you're gone," Salacia said.

"Yeah, how's that going to go for you?" Travers asked. "I mean, five whole days."

"Really more like 4.75 days," Salacia said. "Technically speaking, since I'm sending you off freshly-laid."

"Yeah," Travers said. "Hell, yeah."

"We all must make sacrifices," Salacia said. "Suffering is what makes us human."

"Did you make that one up?"

She smirked tartly. "Oh, probably something I just picked up from somewhere. You know what I do when you're gone? I read."

Proxies weren't allowed to fraternize with anybody but the Terranauts they were assigned to—oh, they could be social and sociable, but relationships of the sexual nature weren't permitted for the Proxies, unless a special rider had been attached to their contracts to allow for it. Otherwise, it was grounds for immediate dismissal, and none of them wanted to risk that. And Travers knew it probably chafed at Salacia to not have her run of the Oasis, but at the same time, it amused him.

"What are you reading this time out?"

"Nothing you'd know," she said. "Self-help books."

Travers laughed. "Self-help? For what?"

"For me, Stupid," Salacia said. "Getting my head on right."

"Astrology books?"

"Astrology *is* self-help," Salacia said, a trifle defensively.

"Sure," Travers said.

"Sure," Salacia said, mocking him. "Just don't die, alright? I'll be fucking pissed off if you die."

"So will I," Travers said. "So will I."

8

FORD WENT TO TALK WITH THE RECOVERY TEAM that had picked up Yellow Team. It was led by Commander Vic Slaughter, who was a peer of Ford's from their Polygon days. Slaughter had hair, but shaved it all off, preferred to be a bullethead. He had a scar at his chin, earned from a gig on Dangerworld. Slaughter was even more of an adrenaline junkie than most of the other Terranauts—he liked the challenge of search and rescue missions, lacked the technical finesse to handle straight-up survey jobs.

Slaughter was in the garden, grabbing some oranges from the trees. The sun was shining brightly overhead, bathing the atrium garden in radiance.

"Hey, Ford," he said, his voice hoarse. He tossed a big orange at Ford. "Catch."

Ford snagged it, turned it over in his hands. Slaughter sat down on one of the landscaped hills and drew out a knife, began slicing chunks out of the orange.

"Don't even ask me about Franzen," Slaughter said. "I'm not supposed to tell anybody. Least of all, you."

Ford smiled, sat down on a printed stone bench downhill from Slaughter. Vic knew Ford all too well.

"What's that supposed to mean?" Ford asked.

Slaughter had hazel eyes, wore a stone-grey mustache that made him look like a bodybuilder from the ancient times. "You know what it means. No questions asked. One of the perks of being in Recovery."

"Yeah, yeah," Ford said. "I have to know whether it was equipment failure, Vic. Seriously. This'll nag at me the whole time I'm on mission. I just need to clear my head."

Vic paused a moment, mid-bite with the orange. "It *wasn't* equipment failure."

"You're sure of that?"

Vic nodded. "Sure as fuck."

He ate that wedge of orange, tossed the peel into the undergrowth.

"That's a relief," Ford said. "Unless Paragon told you to tell everybody that."

Vic grinned at his old friend. "Paranoid to a fault, Ford. You haven't changed. You know that? Ford, time and again."

"I just have to know whether there are any legitimate safety concerns on this one," Ford said. "I have to know that my team'll be alright."

"Stop fretting," Vic said. "Franzen screwed up. It wasn't the suits, if that's what you're worrying about. The suits were fine. You knew Franzen—bundle of nerves. Even his neuroses had neuroses. I'm surprised he wasn't cashiered by Psych. Yeah, I admit that. But the man had a good service record, despite it. I just think things caught up with him. It happens in this business, you know as well as anybody. Things catch up with you, or you leave enough of yourself behind on each drop that, sooner or later, you forget who you were at exactly the time when you need yourself the most."

"Man, you're getting philosophical in your old age, Vic," Ford said.

Ford knew Vic well enough to understand if and when he was bullshitting him, and he seemed to be telling the truth, as far as he knew it.

"I'll probably have to bring you back," Vic said. "You're crazy, going that far out. ALLIE will probably miss, send you lot careening off into deep space. We have a protocol for deep-space rescue, you know that? Can you imagine opening a wormhole into space? I mean, the suits can take it, of course, but they have to seal off the Causeway—which is no big deal, but it's still kinda creepy when you think of it, this void opening up, sucking us right through, trying to rescue your sorry asses."

ALLIE had never missed on a portal drop. Her targeting algorithms were matchless, but every Terranaut had nightmares about a lost drop. The fate of Orange Team, the Lost Team, sent a mere 1,000 light-years away, an almost laughable distance, anymore. It was hard to imagine anybody dropping that close, let alone disappearing. But Orange Team had vanished, literally lost in space. Every Terranaut harbored that secret dread. Seeing LIS on a chart was guaranteed to give even the most experienced Terranaut the shakes.

"You know that's never happened, ALLIE has never blown a drop like that," Ford said. "Quit mindfucking me and tell me what the hell happened to Franzen."

Another slice of orange disappeared in Slaughter's maw, another peel went over his shoulder. Drones would recover the peels, chop them to bits, turn them into compost. Nothing went to waste in the Oasis.

The scent of lemons, limes, and oranges made this oasis within the Oasis one of the most popular places for the Terranauts to rest and recover. There was even a pond, although, at the moment, it was just the two of them there, and a couple of Paragon employees at the far end, having lunch by the water. Gene-engineered koi fish swam in heedlessly expectant circles in the pond, making little ripples as they went. Ford watched the ripples expand across the glassy surface of the pond, intersecting one another, canceling each other out.

"Franzen cracked," Slaughter said. "He panicked."

Ford thought Franzen was a competent enough commander, nothing special about him, aside from being a Terranaut, which separated him from nearly all of humanity in terms of aptitude, ability, and attitude.

Franzen talked a lot in a washed-out, sing-song kind of blasé way, his own kind of affectation meant, Ford guessed, to mask whatever demons he was wrestling with on the inside. Every Terranaut had their own way of handling the stresses of their job—some were cowboys, some were good soldiers, others were competent, cool-headed professionals, some were clowns, some were amazons or Valkyries—all of them had various methods of communicating to Paragon, the Psych Division, and the world at large that they were alright, that nothing was wrong.

"What made him panic?" Ford asked. "That is exactly what I want to know."

"I can't tell you more than that," Slaughter said, finishing his orange. He laid a scarred hand on the basket of oranges he'd picked, grabbed another one. "The suits are fine. You think ALLIE would let you go out in a shoddy suit?"

"Not intentionally," Ford said. "But if some error went unnoticed, maybe. Better to err on the side of caution, right?"

"Sure," Slaughter said. "It's what I'd do. Man, I knew you'd come looking for me, Collins. You have everybody here fooled but me. Because I know you better than the rest of them, I know what makes you tick, my man. Paragon eats up that whole, what is it, 'Grace Under Pressure' kind of thing, like the old days. They love that. But you're at the end of your tether, aren't you? You're never going to displace Chao. Sure, you'll have your moment in the sunshine after Andromeda, but Chao'll leapfrog you the first chance she gets, and a moment is all you're going to get. And on and on. It's funny, really, you and her dueling for distance. Cracks me up."

Ford didn't know what to say to that. Of course there was competition with Chao; it was something they'd always done. They were the two most experienced Terranauts in the program. Vic numbered among them, too, but his experiences at Recovery were not the same that Chao and Ford had.

"Glad we can provide you with some amusement," Ford said.

"I laugh because it'll be me that's sent to scoop you guys up, when one or both of you becomes an intergalactic omelet," Slaughter said. "The things I've seen with these old eyes, Ford. It's only a race until somebody stumbles. And I think the easy money's on you taking the fall. It's like when I was a kid, like in school, and there'd be that kid with perfect attendance—it always bugged me, how there'd be some kind of value assigned to perfect attendance, as if showing up every goddamned school day was somehow a laudable quality. Never mind that those kids would turn up sick at school, infecting everybody else—those kids would turn up day in, day out, and get some kind of gold star for perfect attendance, afraid to lose that little bit of nothing that defined their world. You're like those kids, Ford. Immaculate record, perfect attendance. Shining star. Valedictorian. But that's the problem, isn't it? There's only one way to go from up, and that's down."

"I can always count on you for boosting my morale, Vic," Ford said. "You trying to make me cry, here?"

Slaughter grinned like death at his old friend.

"You should retire," Slaughter said. "You're 37, now, Champ. You have exactly nothing to prove to anybody. Why are you still doing this? You should be ghostwriting your memoirs, working the circuit. Settled on Eden and opening a casino. Or digging up glowtatoes on Terranova. Something. You should be settled somewhere, Champ."

"I could say the same for you," Ford said. "Recovery is a grim detail."

"Oh, I'm a mercenary," Slaughter said. "Somebody with my background has his life mapped out for him. I like Recovery Team, because I already know what I'm getting into. I just need to know how to use a mop and a squeegee. But you? You're going to keep flinging yourself across the cosmos for how long? Another decade? Can you really imagine doing that? With what to show for it? No kids, no family, no life. Nothing."

"Nothing but accomplishment and discovery," Ford said.

Slaughter cut an orange in half with a stroke of his knife, then sliced it into wedges, gobbled up the pieces, juice running down his chin. He gave his mustache an absent wipe of his hand, then made a jacking-off motion.

Ford laughed. "What?"

"Can you even tell me what world you'd pick? Where you'd settle?"

"Who says I want to settle? Why is settling seen as the thing to do? Never settle for anything."

Slaughter acknowledged that with a tip of his bald and shiny head. "Sure, I get it. If you're in it for the thrills, then that's what it is. Don't snow me with that plebe boilerplate shit about accomplishment and the spirit of exploration—if you're just in it for the rush, then that's what it is. But you've got to be ready for that moment when you're just not able to get the job done. That's when our paths will cross, yours and mine. And so, I suppose, as your friend, I'm trying to warn you away from that a little, because you don't want me to have to come get you, because it's not going to be pretty. I guess I'm saying that you should retire so I don't have to go through the grief of carting your dead body back to the Oasis and watching Paragon's media people scramble to manufacture meaning for your death."

Ford watched his friend gobble up that orange, knife always in hand, sitting on that landscaped, green-garbed hill, looking every bit the lion of the savannah he had always been, back when they had been employed by the Polygon, newly-minted exosoldiers, tramping around the Earth in their tanklike suits.

"I saved the Earth," Ford said. "You remember how it was, before the conduits opened up space for us, gave us room to breathe and get out of everybody's way."

"Sure," Vic said.

"It's worth it," Ford said. "Whatever happens to me, it's worth it."

Slaughter found that amusing, wryly tossed the empty, dripping peels over his shoulder, wiped his knife and his hands with a napkin, which he pocketed.

"Oh, man, spare me the whole 'noble sacrifice' line," Vic said. "It's me, Ford. You saved the Earth? Honestly?"

Vic was about the only person at the Oasis who could put Ford on the defensive.

"What have you saved? The only thing you did was broaden the vista," Vic said. "You helped give us a bigger canvas to paint with blood. Did you happen to notice how the Polygon's mission statement shifted the moment the first wormhole was created? Remember? Back in our day, we were busy saving humanity from itself. And the moment the conduit program was established, the moment you swilled the Aquifier and volunteered for the Program, that's when the Polygon changed its mission to protecting humanity from itself to protecting humanity from THEM. Never mind that we haven't found any THEM, yet. Maybe we never will. But nothing's changed, and nobody's saved."

Ford understood that a certain amount of bureaucratic inertia was always going to be in play with the Polygon, but that was exactly it—the existence of the alien—even existentially, required a robust threat assessment and response force. And the Colonial Enforcement Authority Act gave the Polygon clearance to ensure law and order were in place on all of the Colonies. It had worked to keep everything running smoothly with a minimum of bloodshed.

"Sure," Slaughter said. "Sure, our species is now not stuck on this one little basket."

He let a hand drop on the basket of oranges, fingers caressing the ripe fruit contained therein.

"A comet here, an asteroid there, a gamma ray burst, a magnetar, yes, I get that. Something human will survive," Slaughter said. "But the conduits didn't save a thing. Not really. They just let it all keep on going. Every conglomerate wants their own world. You know that as well as I do. The money made from Midas and Terranova alone set the stage for that. New worlds are coming, they are minting them as we speak—we find them, and they serve them up. I'm being billeted up at the LSO while you're gone, probably because they're planning on launching some more of you yahoos into someplace sloppy, meaning that I'll be stuck cleaning up the mess, as I always am. They're sending my whole Recovery team to Luna. I'm sure ALLIE has something lined up for us, maybe evac drills for the Loonies or something."

"You've gotten so cynical in your old age, Vic," Ford said, tossing him back his orange, which his friend caught, placed carefully in his basket. In an age of alien overabundance, of colonial largess, something as domestic and terrestrial as an orange had added resonance.

"Just don't lose your head the way that Franzen did," Vic said. "I don't want to have to be your undertaker."

"Don't worry, you won't," Ford said. "I'm never going to die."

"That's the spirit," Vic said. He held out a hand, which Ford shook.

"I'm nothing if not spiritual," Ford said.

"Good luck, Killer," Slaughter said. "Come back safely. Don't make me come looking for you."

"Have fun with the Loonies, Vic," Ford said.

9

TRAVERS AND GUESSICA WERE ALREADY in the preparation facility when Ford arrived on Drop Day. He had been poring over the digital dossier on GLX-189. A desert planet, heavily volcanized. One large ocean. The mining conglomerates were so eager to get in there, as was the Polygon—it was seen as near-ideal for weapons testing. The Rave's Disease exofungus was just a bonus, he supposed, or there were treasures on GLX-189 worth risking that exposure. Franzen had been scheduled for a five-day outing on GLX-189, which was a follow-up mission—they had been up there seven times already, and the data ALLIE had received was promising. Atmosphere was a little rich, but it appeared safe.

"About time you showed up," Guessica said. "Travers thought you were going to bug out on this one."

Travers grinned sheepishly at Ford, as the Medtechs poked and prodded them.

"Like hell," Ford said. "I just overslept a little, Scrubs."

He took his spot on the exam table, where the Medtechs, faceless, suited up, promptly hooked up the vital sign monitors for them.

QED-376 was a five-day berth for them, but since it was a first mission, it got a little more attention than other assignments. Ford glanced up at the observation window, where members of Green, Orange, and Purple Teams watched them. He was almost disappointed that Chao wasn't there; it almost felt like a snub, except that he knew that Chao was being prepped for GLX.

QED-376 was scheduled for five survey missions. That was the plan, anyway, as ALLIE had set it up, based on the size and composition of the world. It was, like so much the Terranauts dealt with, subject to revision, depending on the circumstances on the ground. Part of the flexibility of the conduit arrangement meant that they could be reassigned without too much difficulty. The challenge was the alignment and the portal drop, versus picking targets in the sky to launch them to.

Three-person survey teams had been determined to be ideal by the ISA, as it offered maximum mutual support at minimal cost, the latter of which was always paramount with Paragon, since the cost of the conduits themselves was astronomical. QED-376 was so far away from the Earth that the maximum support structure would be of vital necessity.

This had caused Travers no end of worry.

"At some point, we're going to be too far out," he said, when they had done the original mission briefing. "They're not going to be able to bring us back. The math will get so big that even ALLIE can't crunch it."

"Stick to the weather, Weatherman," Payne said. "No more editorializing, for fuck's sake."

"The distance doesn't matter with wormholes, Trav," Guessica said.

"It matters to me," Travers said. "Seriously. At those distances, what's to stop us from, I don't know, missing?"

"ALLIE," Payne said. "ALLIE calculates the fucking drops, Travers. Look, if this is too much for you, I'll be happy to have you reassigned. You burn through memory cards with all your goddamned chatter, anyway."

Travers clammed up, as he always did. The pay was just too good. And since nobody at the Oasis had much to spend on while sequestered there, the money piled up. A lucrative retirement beckoned, if only one lived long enough to enjoy it. He imagined a villa with all of his Proxies on it—all of them wearing diaphanous robes, showering him with flower petals, and Travers dressed like some ancient emperor. He was so going to retire on Eden.

"Besides, even with a missed drop, our suits would protect us," Ford said. "You worry too much, Trav."

QED-376 was bigger than Mars, smaller than Earth, with a circumference of ~30,000 kilometers. It had three moons orbiting it, and was part of an 11-planet solar system around a star that was very close to the Sun in composition. ALLIE always searched for suns like Earth's, for ease of exploration, colonization, settlement, and development.

This first jaunt would be to place initial data collectors for ALLIE. They could collect soil and atmosphere samples, topographical and geographic information, and full spectrometric readings of the world, to bring back at the end of the mission.

Ford would also leave some long-term collection equipment on QED-376, to pick up on the second drop, which would be a month hence, if everything went well. And so on, through the five-drop scheduled mission plan. At that point, their job would be done, and ALLIE would either have enough information to make an informed decision about colonizing opportunities for QED-376, or Blue Team might have to revisit it.

"They should double our team," Travers said.

"Double the people means half the wages," Guessica said. "Paragon's mindful of overhead, Trav."

"Yeah, yeah," Travers said. "I'll just miss all my friends."

"What friends?" Ford asked. "Proxies don't count."

Travers pouted, and Ford touched a necklace he was wearing, a silver pendant, to ensure that the Medtechs didn't snatch it off him.

When they were deployed in the field, they would be cut off from the Oasis; no communication was possible, because the conduit would only be maintained long enough to get them there. There would be the scheduled drop site and pickup point, which allowed the Terranauts to come and go. But the distance of QED-376 made communication impossible. They would be completely on their own for five days.

This was why ISA and Paragon carefully screened and trained Terranauts—they were required to be optimally self-sufficient. The initial drop was almost always the most dangerous, since it offered the greatest number of variables and unknowns. Once that initial mission went as planned, and ALLIE determined that the planet had settlement and exploitation potential, then ISA would begin creating a permanent wormhole conduit for the prospective world. The expense of the enterprise demanded this kind of care, and Paragon wouldn't form a permanent conduit for a world that did not promise enormous financial returns.

The exosuits were brought out, wheeled into the Ready Room by the Mechtechs, in their own grey protective suits. The Chief Mechtech, a red-haired woman named Maroon, kept pace with the suits as they entered, looked over at Ford and the others.

"Are you people ready to climb aboard or what?" Maroon asked. It was easy to think of people by their nametags. Ford found himself doing it all the time. Maroon's last name was Fein. People tended to call her "Rooney."

"We're getting there, Rooney," Ford said. "What's the rush?"

"No rush," she said, folding her arms, leaning on one of the tables. "Seriously, take all the time you need. We'll just go when you celebrities are ready."

Ford glanced up at the monitor, which covered the broadcast of the drop, which wasn't actually on the trideo. *Everything Now* notwithstanding, nobody really paid attention to drops anymore. It was fine by him, since there was enough to worry about without throwing the media into it. ISA had given out press kits which indicated that the Blue Team was about to travel farther out than any Terranaut crew had yet gone, and there were canned interviews of Ford and Guessica explaining the QED-376 mission, what it meant for Earth if another colonial acquisition could be had, and the last-minute Singh interview Payne had somehow engineered.

That was part of the problem. Paragon had done its job almost too well—it created the impression that what they had done was routine—from the miraculous to the banal in only a few news cycles.

Terranova had been huge, and Ford had been proud to be part of that one. He and Chao and Sandahl set the standard with Terranova. That was the one where the entire planet was watching, because Earth had needed it so badly.

But that had been years ago. With six worlds now in the Greater Earth Economic Co-Prosperity Protectorate (GEECPP), new worlds weren't quite the attention grabbers they once were, unless there was something extraordinary about them—either if they were very odd, or very deadly, or packed with exploitable resources.

People just expected it, and accepted it. But, in truth, the conglomerates were very, very interested in new worlds, and as more worlds were found, surveyed, assessed, analyzed, and registered, the interest only grew—and conglomerates were clawing at each other to get their own proprietary planet.

Travers hopped up, startling his Medtechs, clapping his hands together. "I'm ready. Let's do this."

Guessica smiled at him, watching him hop from foot to foot on the cold floor, wearing his minimal grey nanotunic, which made him look even more comically lean than he already was. She exchanged a smile with Ford, as the Medtechs secured her long hair in a ponytail, putting a nanocap on her head.

Administration frowned on that long hair, viewing it as a nuisance in an exosuit, where every inch of space was precious, but Guessica was one of the best geologists they had in ISA, and all of the Terranauts were given a reasonable amount of latitude, as they were the ones who took the risks, and even the hefty pay they received was a pittance compared with the rewards a conglomerate could reap with the acquisition of a new planetary property.

Ford got up and did a little stretch. Five days within his own suit would be uncomfortable, although the Program had advanced markedly since he'd first signed up for it. ISA were quick learners; the cost-cutting of Paragon demanded close attention to detail, and while Terranauts were ultimately expendable in the grand scheme of things, it didn't prevent ISA from trying to make it as comfortable as possible for them, just so they'd do the best work they could. Although five days cooped up in a suit was enough to try anybody's patience.

"Don't bone this up, Blue Team," Payne said, his face popping up on the big screens overhead, interrupting the canned feed. His frowning face hovering over them like God™. "Nothing fancy, just do your fucking jobs. After that Yellow Team clusterfuck, I want this to be smooth as glasstic. You are intergalactic ambassadors: nobody's going out further than you guys."

"Farther," Travers said. "Nobody's going out farther, you mean."

Payne looked like somebody had just stepped on his loafers. "What the fuck are you saying, Travers?"

"Farther is used specifically for geographical, physical distance," Travers said. "Further is for, you know, metaphorical or figurative distance."

"Are you trying to be a smartass, Travers?"

"I'm trying to have some precision in our language, here, Mr. Payne. If you mean 'more miles,' use 'farther.' If you mean 'in addition,' you use 'further.' I don't want to end up dead because somebody doesn't know what the hell they're talking about over here."

Ford and Guessica snickered, while Travers winked at them, and Payne glowered at them on the big screen.

"Let's see if I got this right: Nobody's going fucking farther than your team so far. If you would like to continue working with this goddamned outfit, Mr. Travers, I would appreciate no further bullshit from you. Is that okay by you?"

"Yessir, Mr. Payne," he said.

"Suit them up," Payne said. "Let's get this going. Five days, Commander Collins."

"Yessir," Ford said. He hated having a corporate administrator in charge of their operation. He hated that it was Payne almost as much as Travers did.

Travers had already hopped into his suit, and Guessica was squeezing herself into hers. Ford climbed into his. The air was filled with the citrus scent of the disinfectant they used, no doubt something Psych had decided would affect their moods. Everything was incredibly clean, since half as much attention was paid to not infecting a new world as there was to bringing back something new and dangerous. Not so much out of concern for the new world, but from the perspective of it as a potential asset. Nobody wanted a new property to come to them damaged, like a bruised apple.

Ford slipped into his suit and got situated, felt the thing bond with his body in the way that the nanotechnology of the suits did, bonding with the tunics.

Rooney watched them all, pacing back and forth, her eyes not missing a thing behind her own visor.

"We put new reactor cores in these, so mind your power levels on them, Stupids," Maroon said. "Don't want you detonating yourselves prematurely."

The exosuits were triggered to activate the moment a Terranaut's body entered. This allowed movement and final checks before the helmets came down. When the helmet seals were in place, the suit became a self-contained environment. In the interests of efficiency and longevity of life support systems, the suits weren't closed until moments before the Terranauts entered the wormhole, right at the Causeway.

Travers was already walking around in his own suit, while Guessica was flexing her limbs. The suits vastly augmented the strength of the Terranaut pilot, which was considered a requirement for robust field operation, but which, as in the case of the late, great Dunkin Rave, could cause trouble if one fell over.

Just as being on-camera led to a magnification of expression that required one to dial it back a bit emotionally, so there was a necessity to maintain a cool and composed disposition within an exosuit, so as to avoid breaking one's own arm, or smashing through a wall or a Mech-tech or anything else in their way. If a camera added ten pounds, an exosuit added ten tons—not in weight, but in terms of motive power.

The floor thumped around them as the other two walked around, getting comfortable. Ford nodded to Rooney.

"Alright, back up," Ford said. "I'm deploying, here."

He stomped around, noting the power indices that Rooney had warned them of. Indeed, the new microreactors gave them an incredible amount of power. He wondered what ISA had in mind with this.

"Can you believe it?" Travers said, grinning at Ford. "Those Paragon cheapskates gave us upgrades. That can only mean they want twice as much work from us."

"At the very least," Rooney said.

Ford didn't like that they were field-testing upgraded suits. He didn't like just finding this out. As Team Leader, he had the option to scrub the mission, if he had a concern about it, but it would mean losing his shot at breaking the distance record, and would hasten the retirement Vic had urged for him, and it would be a retirement not in glory, but in disgrace. Ford didn't like testing a suit upgrade in the field, but he was not going to be the one to complain about it.

"Fucking upgrades," Travers said. "Field-testing upgrades on a mission like this? Are you kidding me, Payne?"

"Alright, enough chatter," Payne said. "By my mark you have 10 minutes until droptime. Better get yourselves down the hall, Ford."

"Yessir," Ford said. "C'mon, you rats."

"Bring my babies back," Maroon said. "Intact, you rascals."

"Not a scratch, Rooney," Travers said, blowing her a kiss, which looked ridiculous when expressed by the massive limb of the exosuit.

Their equipment had been trucked in with them. The other two picked up their loads, and Ford followed suit. They were the primary scientists on the mission, and while Ford had an understanding of biology, he wasn't a biologist. The team leaders were seldom scientists, themselves; they were mostly Operations personnel, as it was considered paramount to ensure successful completion of the missions.

Each of the cases weighed a ton, contained exactly that amount of gear that was as rugged as it was sensitive—all were effectively field-tested on myriad worlds, intended to offer Terranauts the widest range of information-gathering capabilities on an alien world.

Each of the suits contained a portable flight unit—a kind of fold-out wing with an antigravity projector (itself a spinoff product from the patented antigravity material Paragon used to maintain the conduits) and a high-performance thruster that let the exosuits fly for short distances.

The funny thing about Travers, as Ford saw it, was he was most nervous and edgy between missions. When he deployed, he was almost giddily happy. He thought about this as they stomped their way down the silver hallway, toward the wormhole. The Ready Room sealed off behind them.

"You're in a good mood, Travers," Ford said.

"What choice do I have?" Travers said. "Hell, we're making history, here. Nobody's going farther out than us."

"Nobody yet," Guessica said. "You know Chao is going to be right on our heels. She's going to hate losing her Leo T record-breaking drop."

"Yeah," Ford said. "I bet she's pissed about the GLX assignment."

Guessica laughed. "Are you kidding me? I bet she's thrilled. The chance to be a hero again? She probably volunteered her team for it."

That made Ford wonder a bit. Was that possible? Should he have volunteered Blue Team for the Franzen Fiasco? He and Chao went way back, of course, to the start of the Program. In a weird way, they had egged each other on. When Sandahl died, they were the two remaining old hands at this game. Not that either was terribly old; it was just that the rigors of the work meant that a Terranaut did not have a terribly long shelf-life. That Chao and Ford had survived for as long as they had was a testament to their skill and value to the Program. All of the Terranauts respected Chao and Ford. Only Vic came anywhere near them in experience.

"Should I have volunteered you guys for that?" Ford asked.

"Fuck that," Travers said. "Seriously. Fuck. That."

"She's doing her part, and we're doing ours," Guessica said. "I swear, between you and Travers, I'm like the filling of an angstwich."

"And what a sweetly savory filling you are, my dear," Travers said. "You know what I want to know?"

"What?" Ford asked.

"Why are they sending us so far out?" Travers asked. "I mean, ALLIE is always finding new worlds, prospectives. They've got her combing the skies around the clock. You can't tell me that there wasn't something closer than 2.3 million light-years for us to prospect. They're up to something, here. They're using us for a test."

"Aren't they always?" Guessica asked.

"That is my point," Travers said. "2.3 million light-years away from Earth, Guys."

"Pissing contest," Ford said.

"But we're not in competition with anybody, are we? Paragon's got nobody even close to them in this," Travers said.

Ford sighed. His suit was humming along smoothly. Rooney had done her usual excellent work on it.

"They want to test the operational range of the wormhole technology," Guessica said.

"That's precisely my point," Travers said. "Like you like to say, they already know we can crisscross the universe with this stuff. You tell me that it doesn't matter how far we go."

"And it doesn't," Guessica said.

"So why are they sending us so far out there?" Travers asked.

"Only ALLIE knows," Ford said. "And she's not telling."

Of course, mentioning ALLIE's name had her piping up in their comlinks. "If this brings you any kind of reassurance, we are testing operational ranges of the wormhole. While Guessica is correct that its range is theoretically infinite, our ability to gather good information on distant worlds tapers with distance, which necessitates more robust fieldwork. Hence the improvements to your suits."

"So we *are* in danger," Travers said.

"You are always in danger, Travers," ALLIE said. "Approaching the Causeway. Please prepare yourselves, Blue Team."

"You heard her," Ford said. "Seal it."

They closed their helmets, and were at that moment now on the life support systems ISA had created for the exosuits. A mission clock started on the head's up display, a green counter, as did a red counter that tracked the overall life support system of the suit, and a blue counter reflected elapsed time. A yellow counter was set to 120 hours; this was the conduit counter—the moment they made the drop, that counter would begin and would drop until it reached zero, at which point, ALLIE would have opened the conduit, and they'd all go home. The yellow counter was often the one Terranauts would fixate on; those last few minutes were often the most trying for them.

The security doors opened, and ahead of them was the Causeway, the shining metal path that led to the wormhole, secure on its stationary platform, radiant, the light distorting in the gravitic lens, the gateway held open by the antigravity matter that was the most closely-guarded secret of Paragon, their most proprietary of properties. The distortion of the light was like gazing through a great big fisheye lens, a window on QED-376, the first time human eyes had ever gazed upon this unknown world.

Simple probes had been launched, was a standard procedure, but they only brought back preliminary data for the entry site, the equivalent of sticking one's hand out the window to determine if it was raining. The heavy lifting was invariably left to the Terranauts.

"Blue Team ready to disembark," Ford said. He had his team do sound checks and diagnostic evals of their suits while they waited.

"Copy that, Blue Team," came back the voice of the Mission Commander, who was a woman named Hannah Argent. "You are cleared to go."

Ford climbed the platform first. As Team Leader, it was customary for them to set foot first on any world they reached. He walked up to the wormhole, the gateway that bent space and time itself to the will of Man, which folded 2.3 million light-years' distance of space and made it a matter of a single step. The energy used in the generation of the conduit was incredible. Two galaxies were two steps apart. In that moment, Ford Collins would be the first human being to set foot in Andromeda Galaxy.

The moment seemed to call for something epic, something reflective of the scale of the passage, the enormity of it, but Ford's mind went blank.

"Here goes," he said, biting his lip at the lameness of it. Chao would've rehearsed what she was going to say, would've said something evocative and profound.

Ford stepped through the gateway, and left the Earth farther behind than he or anyone else ever had before.

DAY ONE

1

QED-376 WAS COLD. ALLIE had dropped them in a subarctic region. It was as cold as a Russian winter, Ford estimated from the readings. The drop had gone without incident. He'd walked through, Guessica had followed, and Travers had brought up the rear.

First. Second. Third.

They stepped through and were there. Turning around, the radiant light of the wormhole shone at them, the distortion of the gravitic lens revealing the Causeway, 2.3 million light-years away. Ford planted the marker in the ground, a pulsing data emitter that acted kind of like an encryption key with ALLIE—she would have the other half of the code, and so when the conduit was reopened, she would be able to send a probe through to home in on the data emitter's pulse and put the conduit there.

And then the conduit was gone, and they were alone. As utterly alone as any human beings had ever been.

"One small step for a man, blah blah blah," Ford said. "One giant leap, new galaxy. Hellllllloooo, Andromeda."

"Wow, Ford," Guessica said. "Epic."

Around them was snow. Absolutely everywhere, snow.

"Blows my mind every time," Travers said. "We're here, they're there. They're dead, we're alive."

"We're *all* alive," Guessica said. She'd already begun opening her case, setting up a soil sampler.

Ford gazed at the unfamiliar sky, the alien stars. He knew where they were based on the suit navigation computer aboard the exosuit, but it brought no frame of reference. They were so far away. He'd planted the flag of Earth next to the data emitter, the blue sphere on a black field, shoved it deep into the snow. From this point on, this world's fate would be intertwined with that of Earth's, barring something unforeseen. Ford banked the flag, ensured that it would stand.

"Why don't you two stand by the flag," Ford said. The other two complied, shuffling to the flag, which fluttered in the wind. Ford snapped a picture of it, while Travers kept talking.

"I'm saying that we're cheating the cosmos," Travers said. "We're not supposed to be able to hopscotch this way."

"You love it, and you know it," Guessica said. She'd already launched a sampler into the ground, drawing forth a core, which was digitally tagged and sealed. First sample of QED-376.

The dropsite for QED-376 was an unending field of white snow that was actually frozen water. Not carbon dioxide; it was actual liquid water, frozen. But no trees anywhere in sight. Nothing even close to trees.

"Ford, we're on top of a frozen body of water," Guessica said. "My core sampler just brought up ice."

Guessica stashed the core of ice in its canister.

Ford turned his suit's scanners to their feet, and they began to get readings. The ice was ten meters thick, and they appeared to be on top of a 300-meter deep water body.

"Fuck," Travers said. "See, this is what I mean. What if it had been summer? We'd have splashed down, sunk right to the bottom."

"The suits can take it," Ford said, walking around.

"There's probably monsters in the water," Travers said.

"If there are, they'll have to be pretty huge to punch through ten meters of ice, Trav," Guessica said.

"Maybe they *are* huge," Travers said.

Travers opened his own case, took some air samples, which he marked and tagged much the way Guessica had. Ford deployed one of his own pieces of equipment, which was a surveyor drone that would give them a topographical map of the world. He opened the thing, let its wings lock into place, before activating it. Up it went, and away. It would repeatedly circumnavigate the globe, taking pictures. It was not unlike their own flight packs on their backs, only it had its own navigation system and primitive electronic brain.

"I'm just saying, they were trying to make a point, here," Travers said.

"I am getting a landmass approximately sixty kilometers southwest of here, Ford," Guessica said. "I think it's an island."

"I'll get confirmation of that with the drone," Ford said. "Is it an island?"

"I can't tell," Guessica said.

Ford's nose itched. He was patched into the surveyor, which was beaming information to him. With a few clicks of his tongue, he relayed the data to Guessica.

"Thanks, Ford," she said.

Travers was stomping around, setting up a wind gauge and launching a weather balloon.

"Don't send that thing up until my survey drone comes back," Ford said.

"No worries," Travers said. "Why in the hell would ALLIE think this place was alright? It's a fucking snowball. We should get naming rights."

It was a common complaint among Terranauts. As the ones who always incurred the early risks, many wanted a chance to name a world, but ISA always defaulted to the Naming Commission's authority on that. There were a lot of considerations in the naming of a planet, like whether it was representative of the world in question, and whether it was commercially viable, and what name would encourage immigrants to the new world. Often when worlds were found, potential names were run by focus groups, to get a sense of what images and impressions the prospective names left on people. A positive impression was the desired outcome, coupled with a desire to homestead the place.

Thinking in terms of the world reminded Ford that nationality was so last century. Countries were more like cities used to be, when whole planets were put into play. They were Earthlings, now.

In fact, the Naming Commission had to take that into consideration, how residents' planetary self-identification would sound. Usually "Terran" was more commonly used for Earth folks, or "Gaians," in some circles. Terranovans had it easy. Denizens of Eden were typically called "Edenists"—a play on "hedonist," of course, and it stuck, since "Edenite" or "Edenling" just didn't sound right.

While natives of Xenophon were officially Xenophonians, most folks just called them "Xenos," for short, which caused some degree of umbrage among them. The more caustic name for them was "Phonies," which was one of the first interstellar slurs. There were really no official natives of Thanatos, but "Thanatosian" had definitely lodged itself in the Colonial lexicon for good, and was deemed to have the right blend of exoticism and mystery to be acceptable in everyday use.

The two problem children of the Colonies were Midas and Nikedidas—the names didn't lend themselves to ready derivation. While the conglomerates of Nikedidas favored "Nikedisians" as their official name, and it certainly had traction with the mercantile bodies, most everyday people used the colloquial slur "Sneakers" for natives of Nikedidas. Just like how "Xenos," "Phonies," and "Loonies" entered into the parlance, so it happened with Sneakers—while the trideo and Newsfeed always called them Nikedisians, on the street, it was always Sneakers.

Midas had it even harder, really, since the Naming Commission's choice for that world, while evocative of the boundless mineral wealth to be had there, left much to be desired. Various names had been tried out, but, again, in street terms, "Stoners" became the most common slang term for a resident of Midas.

Slurs, as ever, took precedence over more lofty nomenclatures, with "Diggers" and "Dusters" being very common ones for natives of Midas. There was simply no way to properly parse "Midas"—"Midasian" sounded like someone living in the center of Earth's Asia, while "Midasite" sounded like a kind of parasite, and in the explosion of new organism discoveries occurring in the Colonies, a "Midasite" was very likely an actual creature, or would be, sooner or later. "Natives of Midas" had been what Newsfeed had picked up, and tended to be how it was expressed in the news. "Ingots" was gaining traction, since it kind of sounded like "idiots" and referred to the massive wealth coming out of that planet.

"Island," Guessica said. "That's an island, Ford."

He saw the data, knew it was well as she did.

"Atmosphere is 77% nitrogen," Travers said. "21% oxygen. 9% argon and trace elements."

"That's 103%, Travers," Guessica said, laughing to herself.

"Sorry," Travers said. "1% argon. Trace elements make up the rest. Nothing too toxic."

Ford knelt and picked up a handful of the snow, which was impossibly white and pure. It was night where they were, and while their suits had scanners that let them see in the dark, he felt the temptation to turn on a light, but avoided it, just in case maybe there was something beneath the thick ice upon which they stood.

Travers packed the snow into a snowman, rolling a great big ball for the base with the help of his suit, then adding a body and head.

"Oh, nice," Guessica said. "First snowman in deep space."

"That's right," Travers said. "Ford got first step, but that snowman is all mine. The first intergalactic snowman."

Travers snapped a picture of it, actually walked around it, so the trideo image of it would be preserved.

Ford had to laugh. Travers was a good scientist, even though he was a clown. It would never have occurred to him to put a snowman on QED-376; for Travers, it was as natural as breathing. He made the snowman look skyward, poking holes for its eyes and giving it a gape-mouthed expression.

"Wonderful," Guessica said. "Really, Trav, that's so special. But it's really a snowperson, yes?"

"Hey, I made it," Travers said. "It's a snowman, man. Flaky the Snowman."

He'd positioned it near the flag Ford had planted, while Guessica took pictures of it.

"Payne will love that," Guessica said. "You know he will."

"I hope so," Travers said. They both knew he wouldn't.

"The drone should be back in about three hours," Ford said. "Let's fly to that island, see what we can see."

"You're the boss," Guessica said.

While a necessary adjunct for effective fieldwork, exosuit flight was energy-intensive. However, the gravity of this world was about one-third as strong as Earth's, so the strain wouldn't be too much for the antigrav projectors to overcome. Each suit's aerial unit had a fuel cell that powered them for ~2,500 kilometers. The projectors were rechargeable with a solar panel pack that could bring them back to full power in 72 hours from full depletion.

"Travers, you stay here and get your balloon up," Ford said. "Guess and I are going to the island."

"Alright," Travers said. "Don't get killed."

"You're the one being left behind, Trav," Guessica said. "That's always the one who gets killed."

"Hey," Travers said, but was drowned out in the thrust as Guessica and Ford shot into the sky like winged missiles.

2

IT TOOK ABOUT TWENTY MINUTES for Ford and Guessica to reach the island, flying quickly over the featureless field of white.

"Was the water we landed on fresh?" Ford asked.

"Yes," Guessica said. "Oddly enough. I guess we're on some big frozen lake."

The island was barely visible amid all of the snow, except that it rose out of the water, offered a contour on an otherwise featureless landscape of white.

"We'll want to put a marker on the island," Ford said. "I'm not sure what kind of seasons this place has, but in case this snow melts, I want to be able to land on solid ground, the next time we're here."

They landed at the shore of the island, the exosuits taking pixelated renderings of the land. It was one of the features of the suits that Ford liked. There were direct optical scans, infrared, ultraviolet, thermographic, and pixelated scans—often, a pixelated rendering was more useful, with ground rendered in a dull red, their ships showing up in a bright blue, and landmasses in a vivid yellow. It helped one see things in stark relief.

These pixelated contour maps, in fact, were what led to the most shocking discovery of Ford's career, as his and Guessica's suits dutifully analyzed the landmass they occupied.

Clear as can be, hovering on the HUD over his forehead, was the island, and, upon it, structures. Not mountains, not trees; structures.

Ford felt his legs buckle at the sight of these things.

"Guess, do you see this?" Ford said.

"Yes," Guessica said. "Yes, Ford."

In the snow, they were largely concealed. But to the exosuit's scanners, they were very apparent. The shapes of them, the spindles, obelisks, and spires, bent in disorienting ways. They stood like great stone splinters, swollen, pointing skyward, seeming to bend, and yet, when he walked around them, to also point straight up. It was like the way an image of something diffracted in the water, how it shifted one's perception of it.

"Are you recording?"

"Yes," Guessica said.

"Can these be natural structures?"

"No," Guessica said. "These were fabricated."

The size of them was overwhelming. Ford actually stumbled, dropped to his knees, cursing, thinking of Rave. But, thankfully, there had been no breach of his suit.

"Are you guys okay?" Travers asked.

He sounded so far away.

"Yes," Guessica said, when Ford didn't answer. "We've found something, Trav. Give us a minute, here."

Ford found his footing, got back to his feet. The things—obelisks? They had left him reeling. Had ALLIE known about this? Was it possible that this was why they were sent here?

"Do you think they knew these were here?" Ford asked.

"I don't know," Guessica said. "Maybe? I'm not getting any kind of discernable pulse or anything from them, at least on conventional wavelengths."

As he often did when he was uneasy, Ford got busy, set up a marker, while Guessica took a soil sample. But always in the shadow of the structures before them.

There appeared to be several giant obelisks surrounded by rings of smaller spires. They had sharp points at their tips, and yet were not the straight and angular geometry of Earth; rather, they looked distended. Moving around them created a sense of disquiet in Ford. He had never seen anything like them, and, in truth, he perhaps hadn't wanted to—that realization came in a flood of sensation to him, as he moved around them. It gave him pause.

"We have to investigate these, Ford," Guessica said.

"Of course," he said, a little defensively. He knew the procedure. They had five days to carry out their mission. It was plenty of time to investigate these things as well as survey the planet.

Guessica retrieved her sample, while Ford tested the marker. "Travers, are you getting the marker's signal there?"

A pause.

"Yes," Travers said. "Got it. What are you guys up to over there? What am I missing?"

"Stay at your location," Ford said.

The marker would ensure that subsequent drops could put them on the island. He could scarcely believe his good fortune. Chao would lose her mind.

"Unbelievable," Ford said. The suits could record a week's worth of information, and were recording everything they saw and detected, maintained in compressed files in the onboard suit systems. The data would be incontrovertible, undeniable. Payne would be ecstatic at the coup.

"Ruins," Guessica said, approaching one of the smaller obelisks. She took a sample and ran it through her own specialized field geology equipment. "I would guardedly venture that these are at least seven billion years old, Ford, although we'll need ALLIE to confirm the exact date of these."

Ford walked beside her to one of the snow-choked obelisks, dusted it off with his armored hand.

Guessica checked her soil sample data. "I'm seeing 10% aluminum, 7% calcium, 10% iron, 3% magnesium, 35% oxygen, 3% potassium, 29% silicon, 3% sodium. Again, ALLIE will have to confirm these results, but that's what I'm getting at this site."

"What are these things made of?" Ford asked.

"Unknown," Guessica said. "They appear to be stone."

The stone was green-hued, but in the infrared light, everything was green-hued. He turned on his suit's external lights, shined them directly on the stone. The stone was, indeed, a deep green hue that made Ford nauseous. It was the color of overmixed paint, an almost blackish-green. It was disgusting to him. Ford felt actual revulsion at the sight of them.

"How much erosion on these?" he asked.

"Negligible, as far as I can tell," Guessica said, turning on her own lights. She had taken out a special rock hammer and tried to strike a bit from the small obelisk in front of her. The thing sparked and resisted the hammer. "Strong stuff."

"We have to get a sample of it," Ford said. He was already imagining the ISA drafting a xeno-anthropologist to accompany them on the next mission, once word of this discovery reached the Oasis.

"I'm trying," Guessica said.

"Is this native rock?" he asked.

A trace of an edge to Guessica's voice. "I don't know, yet, Ford. Give me a little time, here. We need to get the samples back to ALLIE, and let her crunch on the data."

"Sorry," he said. "Just determine what you can."

The snow had gone from a novelty to an irritation for him. Ford wanted to blow it clear of the site, get a proper look at it. The pixelated images were only egging him on, giving him a stomach-turning sense of the structures.

"Do you feel that?" he asked.

"Feel what?"

"Queasy?"

"It's the geometry," Guessica said, grunting and cursing as she tried to gather a sample of the obelisk material.

"What are you talking about?"

"Wrongful geometry," she said. "The lines of these structures follow a non-Euclidean geometry. It's unfamiliar to our brains. Alien. It's the visual equivalent of something being out of tune, for lack of a better term. Like a bad taste for the eyes."

Wrongful geometry. Ford felt it. He could see it. It really did turn his stomach to gaze at the pillars and megaliths for any length of time. The way they loomed above them, a fecundity of form that spoke to something he had never felt before, despite seeing so many alien worlds. This was even more alien, and the notion of consciousness creating these things, whatever they were, it was dizzying. There was a darkling, profligate majesty in the things that defied ready characterization.

"This is the first sign of intelligent life we've ever had," Ford said.

"Yes, it is," Guessica said.

"Incredible."

"Yes."

Ford knew that Orange Team had disappeared while tracking a radio signal of mysterious origin that had been vexing astronomers for a century. Many speculated that Orange Team had encountered some kind of alien intelligence in their quest to find that radio signal's source, but when they had disappeared—and this had been years ago—nobody had ever found out for sure about their fate. It was one of those odd blips in the Program. The ETA quadrant. Back then, the expense of the Program had been so great, the disappearance of Orange Team was a big loss. Slaughter's Recovery Team had been deployed to ETA-101, the world that Commander Elliott had been sent to survey, but they'd never found anything. Just the black, empty world of ETA-101—the Terranauts had nicknamed that world "Charon"—the matte black soil of the place, the darkness of it, even the blue-black plant life they'd found there, it all was ill-omened.

Since Paragon was in the business of prospecting profitable planets, Charon was left unexplored, and the fate of Orange Team, forever unknown. Ford had wanted to explore it, but Terranauts weren't in charge of picking targets, only surveying them. It was simply not up to him. All the same, he had always suspected that aliens had been involved in the disappearance of Orange Team. Everybody thought that, even if nobody really said it.

Ford steadied himself again, could only imagine how this information would be received at the Oasis. He had to keep it together; they still had four more trips to this new world.

And all the same, Ford felt something unfamiliar—a sense of dread. Something had lived here. Something older than the Earth itself. And something else. Something had died here. He didn't know how he felt that, but he felt it just the same—like a hint of shadows in the corners of his eyes, banished by a glance.

Something lurking.

Ford was experienced enough to keep those kinds of observations to himself—absolutely everything they said and even felt, was biometrically monitored and recorded. In addition to being surveyors, the Terranauts were, themselves, surveyed by ISA and Paragon, scrutinized by Psych Division and by ALLIE, too.

All the same, he turned around in his suit, looked around them, scanned their perimeter. The feeling of being watched was palpable, made him sweat. All of the gauges on his suit showed green. There was nothing tracking on the radar or broad-spectrum scans. But still, he felt like there was *something* out there, and wanted to ask Guessica if she was getting it, too. She was, however, busy at her work.

"Travers," Ford said, tonguing the comlink for person-to-person.

"What is it, Ford?" Travers asked, his face popping up on Ford's HUD 1.

"Did you get your balloon up?"

"Yes," Travers said.

"Good," Ford said. "Anything showing up on your scanners?"

"Like what?" Travers asked. "Are you asking about weather patterns, Ford? Or like wildlife or something?"

"I mean anything out of the ordinary," Ford asked.

"Funny that you'd mention that," Travers said. "Got some pings, actually. Something under the ice. Something moving down there."

"Upload me what you got," Ford said. "You should've sent that to me the moment you got it."

"Sorry," Travers said. "I had to be sure it wasn't a ghost."

"Right," Ford said. Travers beamed Ford stills of the signal, which Ford put on HUD 2. Sure enough, it was a yellow blob that looked to be about twenty meters long. "Wow, it's big."

"Yeah," Travers said. "I'm feeling a bit like bait over here, out on this damned ice."

"Anything else?" Ford asked.

"Nope. Why?"

"Just wondering," Ford said. "Keep your proximity alarms up, if that thing comes back, you let me know."

"You know, I could use my laser to cut through this ice, Ford," Travers said. "Cut a nice, thick circle in the ice. Then we could go right down there and see just what that thing was."

"Negative," Ford said, although he was sure Travers was joking. "Stick to your mission parameters."

"Right," Travers said.

Shadows.

That's what he was seeing. At the corners of his eyes, which, in the confined space of the exosuit, made him more than a little uncomfortable. The suits were designed to offer the maximum available visibility for the Terranauts, within the limits imposed by the demands of the suits themselves. To see something at the corner of his eyes meant that he was simply seeing things, because the narrowness of his range of vision by the visor prevented him from actually being able to see out of the corner of his eyes. The best one could hope for is to turn the suit manually, or else have the external cameras take a look for him.

He checked his air mix, and everything seemed solid.

> "Personal log: I'm seeing something at the corner of my vision. Probably nothing, but just a little disturbance—shadowy shapes. I checked my internal atmosphere, and everything's fine. I'll check with Guessica and Travers, see if they're seeing anything, later today, after most of our initial work tasks have been performed."

After stopping his entry, Ford watched Guessica work. She kept at the obelisk, finally managed to shave off a bit of the stone, which she secured in a receptacle.

"This stuff is unbelievably hard," Guessica said. "I'm guessing greater than ten on the Mohs hardness scale. Nanodiamond, or the equivalent."

"Is that how you removed it?" Ford asked. "Using one of your nanodiamond tools?"

"Yes," she said. "It's incredible to imagine something this large being created at all."

"Just so long as you got a sample," Ford said.

"That I did," Guessica said.

Ford began pushing away the snow, shoving it aside in great sweeps of his suit's armature. He wanted to know what these things were, wanted to see them with his hands and eyes, not simply relying on scanners.

Guessica began helping him, and the two of them cleared a rough passageway in the snow, which let them shelter in the midst of the structures, although the concept of "shelter" felt entirely alien in the presence of these (for lack of a better term) monstrous structures.

"I can't even believe this," he said.

"Paragon will be thrilled with this material," Guessica said, patting some of the obelisks. "This is why these have stood all this time. I doubt anything could erode them."

"Have you picked up anything on your scanners?" Ford asked.

"You mean anything out of the ordinary? No."

"Travers got a radar contact," Ford said, beaming the image to her.

"That's a big contact," Guessica said. "I wonder what it is."

"We'll see," Ford said. "Maybe we can drop a probe down there. I figure I can use my laser to cut a hole in the ice and we can drop a probe into the water."

"Cool," Guessica said. "That's a must."

"I figure we could do it here, where the ice isn't likely so thick," Ford said.

"Good plan," Guessica said.

Ford, in his role as Operations Officer and Team Leader, had access to a survey drone, and three heavy-duty portable surveillance probes, known as "Rollers" because they were round spheres roughly a foot in diameter. Stuffed with sensory gear, Rollers could be deployed just about anywhere, where they would go about their business, collecting data for the duration of their shelf-life. Being solar-powered, they could run for years, depending on the climate of the world in question. They were also capable of operating at significant depths. Once activated, they would simply be sent on their way, beaming information back to the reception unit, which had removable datajacks that could be readily transported back to the Oasis. He would deploy one of the Rollers into the water, once they'd finished clearing the snow from the obelisks. He wanted to see if there was a passageway inside the ring of spires, first. He'd definitely send a Roller that way.

The surfaces of the obelisks were pebbled with things. Not dents or pits, but with glyphs and writing. There was no doubt about it. These certainly could not be denied as natural occurrences or flukes. They were created things.

"Writing," Ford said. "Writing!"

"I see it," Guessica said. "Recording."

He could only imagine how people would react upon discovery of this. Ford wondered how long it would even be before ISA revealed this to the Colonies. Probably years. The weight of that knowledge hung heavy on him.

"They'll never let us off the Oasis with this," Ford said. "No way."

Guessica sighed. "Yeah, you're probably right. And I have a husband to marry, you know? A life to build. I'm not flying solo like you, Ford."

"He's not your husband, yet, if you haven't married him," Ford said.

"You know what I mean," Guessica said. "Don't quibble."

But the practical reality of it was evident to Ford—until Paragon saw fit to tell the Colonies that life, or the existence of intelligent life, had been found, all of the Terranauts would be embargoed to a degree that made previous sequestrations seem tame.

"I'm just saying, we're going to be locked down tight," Ford said.

"Frankly, I think they should just tell everybody," Guessica said. "Get it all out there."

"They'll never do that," Ford said.

Paragon kept a lid on absolutely everything they did at the Oasis. And everything that was represented here would involve all of the big players, would have them all wanting a piece of this.

"What are you guys seeing over there?" Travers said. "I'm bored."

"Did you get your balloon up?" Ford asked.

"Yes," Travers said. "I've been collecting data for the last half-hour. Sounds like you guys are having much more fun than I am."

"Look, patch into that surveyor drone," Ford said. "When that thing comes in, I want you to upload the information, and route that to us. While you're at it, take one of the Rollers. Use your laser to cut a hole in the ice and drop the Roller down there."

"I'm not authorized to deploy Rollers," Travers said.

"It's easy, and maybe you'll get some good data for your own stuff," Ford said. "Just take the Gamma Roller and make sure it's on, then drop it down the hole."

"Anything else?"

"No, the monitor should automatically track the signal pulses from the Roller," Ford said. "Then secure the site and bring the gear over to us on the island. Use the marker to navigate."

"You want me to move from the drop site?"

"Yes," Ford said. "We'll set up here. When contact is reestablished, we'll just load it all back over. The next mission drop'll be at the new site. You won't believe what we've got, here. Meantime, just get the surveyor information loaded when it comes back."

"That's 2.5 hours from now, Ford," Travers said, heaving a sigh.

"Just do it," he said. "You can join the party then. The Roller can entertain you while you're waiting."

"Yessir," Travers said. "Can't you tell me what you're seeing there?"

"I don't want you distracted," Ford said. "Get the front-end work done and join us when that's finished."

"Fine, fine," Travers said. Guessica laughed in Ford's ear, a private communication.

"He's going to lose his mind when he sees this," she said.

"I know," Ford said. "That's what I'm afraid of. Hell, I'm afraid I'm losing my mind, already."

The life they'd known was over. Guessica chuckled nervously.

"You and me, both," she said. "But, seriously, this is going to make us, Ford. Chao's going to die when we get back."

"Everybody will," Ford said.

3

TRAVERS GRUMBLED TO HIMSELF while readying his 75-kilowatt microlaser, mounted on one of the arms of his suit. All exosuits came with a laser, which was intended for fieldwork applications and self-defense, if situations warranted it. The Polygon had insisted on it, and ISA had its engineers add them. Like so much that the ISA did, the exosuits were often used to test technology for later Polygon applications.

He had set the laser to power up, and while it was doing that, Travers activated the Gamma Roller. Equipment cases were geared for the big hands and fingers of the exosuits, with uncommonly large buttons designed to accommodate them.

The data collector was a simple computer that was radio-linked with the Rollers, set to receive datapulses from them.

Travers toggled the switches and pushed the buttons, and the Roller came to life in his hands, landing on the snow and rolling in a circle around him. Laughing, Travers pushed the big blue button that paused it, while he checked his laser, which was fully charged.

He took an eyebolt from the supply case, one of the spare screwbolts that they had to secure equipment with, as necessary, and screwed it into the target on the ice, dead-center.

Then he took aim with the laser, pointing it to the ice below him, programming a cutting pattern for it, careful not to target his own foot. In a moment, the laser cut a ten-meter deep cylinder in the ice in seconds, the beam silently lancing through the ice, leaving sizzling water around the roughly thirty-centimeter diameter circle he'd cut.

That done, Travers then reached down and grabbed the eyebolt and, his suit straining with the burden, pulled up the core of ice in slow but steady strokes of his arms, drawing the blue-white cylinder of ice forth, laying it down on the frozen surface of the lake. The weight of that column of ice was nearly more than his suit could take.

The hole was completely black, and it made Travers uneasy, having this breach in the armor of the ice.

Then he took the Gamma Roller and held it over the hole.

"Alright, Roller," Travers said. "This is your time to shine."

He checked it one last time, to be sure it was up and running, and then he dropped it down the shaft.

Going to the data collector, he turned off the pause function, let the roller go about its business.

"Roller deployed successfully," Travers said to Ford.

"Copy that," Ford replied.

The hole in the ice looked like the eye socket of a skull, the black against the endless field of white. Travers had a sense of something out of place, and remembered, of course, that on this world, the Blue Team were the aliens. They were the invaders. The only thing out of place here was him.

"Can I close up the hole I cut?" Travers asked.

"Scared?" Ford asked.

"A little," Travers replied. "I don't like the idea of that thing in there being able to look back up at me, if it wanted to. What if it's got tentacles?"

Ford laughed on Traver's HUD 2. "Then you're screwed."

"I'm closing up this hole," Travers said. "I mean, there's no way that Roller's coming back up through this, right?"

"Right," Ford said. "No way. Go ahead and close up that shaft, if it makes you feel better."

Travers broke the cylinder into three even chunks, so as not to overstrain his suit, and dropped them, one at a time, down the shaft he'd cut, grateful that he'd not have to look into that dark abyss. He carefully slid the last one in place, then rolled a great snow boulder and put it atop the eyebolt.

"There," he said. It made him feel somewhat better.

He checked the monitor for the Roller, saw that the Roller had made its way to the bottom of the lake, and was traveling along it. Unfortunately, it had stirred up some dust when it got there, and so the internal camera wasn't picking up anything but clouds of aquatic dust.

"Good luck, Roller," Travers said, closing the monitor's case.

Then he checked the surveyor's ETA. He still had a lot of time to kill.

Looking around him, on that plain of white, he felt incredibly alone and tiny.

"Guys, this sucks," Travers said. "I'm lonely over here. Somebody talk to me."

"Awww," Guessica said. "Trav's bored."

"I did my stuff, I'm waiting. I hate waiting," Travers said.

He thought about Salacia, listening to her complain about the Colonies, while they lounged around in bed and she told him her theories about the universe. Although she'd come from Eden, she'd managed to visit Terranova, Midas, and Xenophon as well, and had plenty of opinions about them. She'd hate this place.

"Go to the source," Salacia said. "That's always been my philosophy. You want a good deal on stones, you go to Midas. You want good food for cheap, you hit Terranova. But they're just so crowded, already. It feels that way, anyway. Once you're out of the Colonial Commerce Authority dropzone, and you're on the planet proper, it all falls away. The infrastructure's just not there, yet. I mean, you can smell the money being made there, but everything's just tied to import/export. Terranova is just one giant agricultural conglomerate—so what if they grow everything there? The dust clouds reach up and choke the sun, and the rains there are like monsoons—that's what they're called here, right? Monsoons? Yeah, so they just get everything soaked, and there's barely any roads. The money's being made, but I don't know who's making it, because the locals sure aren't."

"What were you doing on Terranova, anyway?" Travers asked.

"I was looking for fresh produce," Salacia. "I know, that sounds stupid, but I heard there were some aphrodisiacs there. Like fierce stuff, so I was hunting for them, and it's not like the kind of thing a girl like me can just walk up and ask a yokel about, you know?"

"What'd you want an aphrodisiac for, anyway?"

"Just to have," Salacia said. "There are all sorts of drugs on Eden, yeah, anything you could ever want, but you're paying out the nose for it there, whereas on Terranova, you can get stuff for a lot cheaper, if you know where to look. Midas is worse, still. It reeks of sulfur. They have the biggest damned trucks there. The tires are as big as this room. Huge."

"What the hell were you doing on Midas?"

"The male-to-female ratio there is like ten to one, you know that? I was doing a little prospecting of my own, there," Salacia said. When Travers hemmed and hawed at that, she gave him a whack with her hand. "Not for me. I was just thinking that some of the lower-rent Edenists could set up some deal with Midas, instead of those miners with their money coming to Eden and stinking up the place."

"You were trying to set up an operation there?"

"It's already there," Salacia said. "You think a planet can have that kind of male/female ratio and not have an industry there? No, I just wanted the miners to *stay* there."

"Oh, so you're a snob?"

"I'm a businesswoman," Salacia said. "We don't need a lot of conduit traffic from Midas to Eden, frankly. The Ingots have their money, but it's not the same, them turning up and bashing the hell out of the place. Rowdies."

"Wow," Travers said. "So, you were, what, a one-woman anti-Midas League?"

"You make it sound bad," she said. "I'm saying that if we could take out the trash on Eden, you know, it would make things that much better on Eden for everybody else. Ingot money spends as well as any-body else's, but Ingots are just nasty. They've always got dirt under their damned nails."

Salacia's mind always worked along angles, edges, planes, points, and lines. "Speaking of trash, did you know they're making a landfill planet?"

"Where'd you hear that?"

Salacia snorted. "I have ears. You Terranauts are so busy being fabulous that you miss out on all the good gossip. The Naming Commission's come up with a planet—it's one of those loser planets, like you know how there are the ones that are deemed commercially viable, versus the ones that aren't? Some planet is being turned into a giant landfill. They're calling it Detritus. Isn't that funny? I looked that up on my phone. 'Detritus.' It means 'trash.'"

"Planet Detritus? You're serious?" Travers asked, but he knew that this wasn't some of Salacia's usual bullshit.

"All of the Colonies are supposed to offload their garbage to it," Salacia said. "Can you imagine that kind of a gig? Who ends up there? Not me, that's for sure."

Travers hadn't heard about it, was wondering why he hadn't. He wondered if it was QED-98—that planet was an inhospitable pile of rock, mostly volcanic, deemed uninhabitable, or at least unfit for large-scale colonization (geologists had been ecstatic about it, and he'd had to hear Guessica talking up QED-98 for weeks after they'd surveyed it).

"You are fucking with me," Travers said.

"I'm so not," Salacia said, looking the very picture of innocence. She could look angelic when she wanted to, could open wide those big periwinkle marbles that were her eyes and dazzle him into silence.

Planet Detritus. The seventh planet. It had its own kind of logic. Why not offload the garbage to some other world, if one had the capacity to do so? Travers knew dwellers of that world would be called "Trashies" in no time flat. He felt bad for anyone who would end up on that world.

"They're going to have all sorts of waste management stuff there," Salacia said. "Supposedly they're going to recycle all the junk on there, or find ways of burning it for fuel, something. ALLIE has it all mapped out."

Hearing Salacia invoke ALLIE as if the two were on speaking terms kind of bugged Travers. He playfully touched the tip of her nose with a finger, which she pretended to nip at.

"Like you've ever had one conversation with ALLIE," Travers said.

"Do you require anything, Travers?" ALLIE asked, right on cue.

"ALLIE, have you and Salacia ever met?" Travers asked, which made Salacia fume.

"I haven't met her, no," ALLIE said. "I don't usually interact with Proxies, Travers."

"Of course," Travers said. "Salacia Cross, ALLIE. ALLIE, Salacia."

Salacia gave him a look that would've sparked a fire.

"Nice to meet you," she said.

"Charmed," ALLIE said. "Do you require anything, Travers?"

"Yes," Travers said. "Salacia tells me that the Naming Commission's assigned a new planet to the Colonies. Planet Detritus. Is this for real?"

"Yes," ALLIE said.

"Is it QED-98?"

"No," ALLIE said. "A curious choice on your part. It's BTG-75."

BTG was the quadrant Brown Team surveyed, and Travers usually was too busy doing his own thing to keep track of every planet the other teams found.

"So, it's really being named 'Planet Detritus?'"

"Yes," ALLIE said. "But this is being embargoed, so no word of it is to leave the Oasis. How did you hear about this, Salacia?"

Salacia cleared her throat, sat up, glaring at Travers at putting her on the spot. "I just overheard it from one of the other Proxies, who's been dating the mission commander for Brown Team. Look, I don't want to get anybody in trouble."

ALLIE's tone was authoritative, without being either soothing or threatening.

"All communications in and out of the Oasis are, of course, monitored by me, so there is no chance of information being released without my knowledge, without Paragon's approval. Just the same, you should be careful about information you share. Obviously, Travers has high-level clearance, but please try to be mindful of the special nature of the Oasis, and our mission, here."

"Sorry," Salacia said.

"That's all, ALLIE," Travers said. "Thank you."

"Not at all, Travers," ALLIE said.

They waited a moment, then Salacia swatted Travers on the arm. "I can't believe you put me on the spot like that, you fucker."

"Hey, you were making it seem like you and you-know-who were old friends," Travers said. "I wanted to call bullshit on that, and find out if there was anything to that stuff about Detritus. I tell you, you Proxies do find things out, don't you? Such little fucking spies."

Salacia smiled warily, nodded. "Count on it. Don't ever put me on the spot like that with her again. That seriously creeped me out. Can she see everything we do here?"

"Everything," Travers said. "She's watching us, even now. I just have to say her name, and she'll be right back here."

"Doesn't that creep you out?"

"Meh," Travers said. "You get used to it."

"We don't have those on Eden," Salacia said, wrapping the blankets around herself.

"Oh, I bet you do," Travers said. "You just don't know it."

"I'd know," Salacia said. "I'm nosy."

Travers imagined with all of the money flowing in and out of Eden, one of the first things the Chamber of Commerce would have done would be to put an AI there. Maybe several. Too much was at stake for inefficient allocation of resources, raw materials, and assets.

"ALLIE?" Travers asked, making Salacia all but hide beneath the blankets.

"Yes, Travers?" ALLIE's voice was just so liquid-smooth.

"Are there AIs on Eden?"

"Yes," ALLIE said. "Specifications for them are unavailable to me, but I interact with them enough to know that they are there. ABLE (Automated Bureaucratic Logistical Expediter) is one I deal with, particularly with regard to the Proxy Program, finding suitable talent for employment at the Oasis, for example."

"Thanks, ALLIE," Travers said. "That'll be all."

"Of course, Travers," ALLIE said.

"See? That's creepy," Salacia said.

"Like you said, she's got it all mapped out," Travers said. Salacia squinted up at the monitor, chewed her lip.

"I wonder who did her voice? I bet it's an actress," Salacia said. "And what was that bullshit about her dealings with Eden? That felt like a kind of threat aimed at me, didn't it? Did you catch that?"

Travers wondered what ABLE was like, whether it was as ubiquitous as ALLIE was. "Huh?"

"She threatened me," Salacia said. "That mention of working with that other program to find talent for the Proxy Program? That was a dig at me, I bet. Like she was saying that I could be replaced."

Travers laughed. "Is that it? You're being paranoid."

"Am I?"

The proximity alarm sounded, jarring Travers out of his daydream. The thing slid beneath the ice, nosed around the plugged hole he'd dug.

"Ford," Travers said into his intercom. "That radar signal came back."

"What's it doing?" Ford asked, as Travers beamed him a still of the radar signal.

"Just hanging out down there," Travers said. "Looks like it's moving again, diving. It's fucking big, Man."

"Yeah," Ford said. "Alright, be careful over there."

The surveyor was inbound, just a few minutes away, and Travers reported on that, too. He couldn't wait to get off the damned ice, get on some solid land.

The radar signal was gone, and Travers was readying his flightpack, doing a preflight diagnostic of it to be sure that it was operational and ready to go.

When the surveyor landed, he packed it into the travel case and gathered the other gear that he could transport to the second site, up-loading the datafeed of the drone into his suit—an in-flight movie for him to watch as he flew.

He tried to be quickly thorough, without rushing, although he was eager to get away from whatever that was in the water.

Sometimes, being paranoid was the only way to be.

4

THEY DUG AROUND THE SITE, tried to clear as much of it as they could, and to record as much of it as possible. The pillars and obelisks served no immediately apparent purpose, except that they pointed at the sky. The island itself was around 1,000 square kilometers.

Travers had received the survey drone and had exclaimed, uploaded the preliminary topographic map to the both of them.

"Can you see it?" Travers said. "Structures!"

"Yes," Ford said. "Get the gear stowed and get over here."

Travers came as quickly as he could. The topographic map showed the world to be about 60% water, 40% land. And the land was covered with structures that Ford could only guess were ruins not unlike what they had found on the island. There were clear climate zones, and to the south of them appeared to be jungle, or the alien equivalent of it—thick groves of as-yet-undetermined life on the main landmasses. Throughout these regions were the structures, the obelisks and spires, scattered randomly across this world. The patterns weren't immediately discernible to Ford, but it wasn't his place to decide what the placements meant; he was only supposed to gather the information.

The jungles were predominantly pink-hued, shades of fuchsia and maroon, and he couldn't tell what they were, whether they were plants, fungi, or animals. But they covered the temperate and equatorial regions in abundance. To say it was verdant was an understatement.

"We're going to be rich," Travers said. "Celebrities."

"We're already rich," Guessica said. "And we're already celebrities. Technically speaking."

"Richer," Travers said. "More famous."

"Let's not get ahead of ourselves," Ford said. "This place is going to be swarming with people in no time. We're just links in an intergalactic chain."

"Fuck that," Travers said, walking at the base of the obelisks on the island.

"Paragon is going to have specialists up here as soon as possible," Ford said. "They're going to want to know absolutely everything about this place."

"Of course," Guessica said.

Travers reached out and touched one of the obelisks, ran his armored hand along it. There almost seemed to be a radiance in these alien stones. He could see a twinkle in the glyphs, a sort of green-white luminescence.

"I wish I could touch it," Travers said.

"You are touching it," Ford said.

"For real," Travers said. "Bare-handed."

"It's -20 degrees Celsius," Guessica said. "You'd get frostbite awfully quickly, Trav."

"But to touch it," he said. "My own skin on it. To be the first, for once."

Ford paused in his digging to look over at Travers. "And the last. You break quarantine and I'm going to shoot you."

"There's nothing here," Travers said. "Just snow and rock and ice. The jungles are to the south of us."

"We don't know what's here," Ford said.

"We're here," Guessica said. "For five days, we're here, Gentlemen."

The weight of that hung as heavily on Ford as anything else. For five days, they only had each other, and *only* each other. For five days, the enormity of their discovery was their own, and wasn't the property of anyone else. 2.3 million light-years away was Earth, blissfully unaware that everything they had done was suddenly seen from the perspective of something far older. Paragon, for all of its wealth and power, was less than nothing in the grand scheme of things. Their technology had let the Blue Team reach this place, but it was still nothing.

"I wonder if ALLIE knew about this," Guessica said.

"Why do you say that?" Ford asked.

"Just a hunch," Guessica said. She thought about her talk with AL-LIE—or ALLIE's talk with her in her room, and ALLIE grilling her about the successful completion of the mission in her politely pushy way. They were all used to ALLIE's manner of dealing with people. In a way, there was some comfort in dealing with her—she was a constant in a torrent of variables that was the Program. Only ALLIE saw everything—she was the one who really combed the data accumulated by the Loonies, was the one who came up with planetary prospects for Paragon.

"I want to touch it," Travers said.

"Help us dig," Ford said.

"It's going to feel like stone, Trav," Guessica said. "Cold, cold stone."

Travers looked around them, gazed up at the things. He staggered for a moment, caught himself.

"Whoops," he said, laughing. "Lost my bearings a bit, there."

"It's the shapes," Guessica said. "I was explaining that to Ford."

"Explaining what?"

"The lines of these things don't follow conventional geometric lines we're used to, so it makes us lose perspective," Guessica said.

Travers did feel dizzy in front of the obelisks. He shook his head inside his suit, tried to clear it, to stay on task.

"What is this place?" Travers asked.

"We don't know," Ford said. "We're just collecting information at the moment, rather than forming conclusions."

Normally, they would do a broader field survey, try to collect as much information as they could. Gathering as many samples as possible. But the island changed the dynamic, and Ford felt certain that ISA would absolutely approve of the path they had chosen. He had deployed the Beta Roller on the ice, let it roll happily away along the surface of the lake, for parts unknown. It would beam back data to the collector, which could be recovered by them on Mission 2. Since he'd had Travers deploy the Gamma Roller underwater, he thought he'd just let this one go on the surface of the ice, to see what it could see.

"Do you feel it?" Travers asked.

"We all do," Guessica said.

"I can't believe we're camping out here," Travers said. "In the shadow of these things?"

"Better here than on that lake," Ford said. "Or freshwater sea. Whatever it is."

The structure followed no discernible pattern, except that it was enormous, Cyclopean in scale. A ring of stones of varying sizes and dimensions. Some as tall as they were, some far larger.

"Do *you* think ALLIE knew?" Travers asked.

"You can ask her when we get back," Ford said. He was certain that Chao would be given command of the subsequent missions. Politics and seniority would almost guarantee it. Chao would want to be Team Leader for the remaining QED missions, and ISA would almost surely grant it, because they'd want their most senior Terranaut on the job. Ford could just imagine Chao coming back from solving whatever happened on GLX-189 and hopping to this world, gathering some more accolades. Never mind that Blue Team had been the ones to discover it; it could have been any of the teams. It was just random chance. Ford laughed at this, shook his head. He was dizzy, too.

"What's so funny?" Guessica asked.

"Nothing," Ford said.

"Didn't sound like nothing," Travers said.

"Nothing's funny," Ford said.

They all laughed at that, the grave way Ford said it. Ford had Travers set up the campsite for them, which was, of course, a formality, as they camped out in their exosuits. In five days, they would want nothing more than to be free of those suits, and to take long, hot antiseptic showers, scrubbed by thick brushes wielded by unsmiling, suited Medtechs.

But that was a hundred thousand lifetimes away from where they were at the moment.

5

"I CAN'T SLEEP," TRAVERS SAID. "Not with those things standing there. They look like they're going to fall on me."

"They aren't going to fall," Guessica said, sleepily. Guessica could sleep anywhere. She had that unique ability, or else a keen understanding of which Paragon meds to take to give her that right amount of sleep.

"But they look like it," Travers said.

"Give yourself a sedative," Ford said, although he could barely sleep, himself. He had put his own suit in sleep mode, had powered it down, but his mind had been racing.

He tried to imagine what the place was, but its purpose was not apparent to him, and there was no way of knowing. And on this remote island, too, which, by their estimation, was at least 2,000 kilometers away from the larger landmasses, which also had structures. Ford had perused the surveyor drone's topographic data, hoping for some kind of insight, but the structures were scattered in a fashion that was not comprehensible to him. They appeared to have been cities, but it was not possible to know precisely what they were. What was this place?

And where were the aliens?

They lacked the equipment to really divine the length of time the ruins had been left untended. That the structures were themselves roughly seven billion years old didn't mean that they had been abandoned that long. The Blue Team had managed to dig out large quantities of snow, they hadn't found any doors into the structures, so maybe they were monuments of some sort.

Guessica had speculated that it was some kind of holy site, while Travers was convinced it was a tomb. Ford couldn't guess what it was, and, more to the point, he wouldn't. His mission was to get his team home safely, and that was what he would do.

It was supposed to be his only concern.

"Shouldn't we have somebody on watch?" Travers asked.

"Like you?" Ford asked. "We have proximity sensors in our suits. We'll know if anything's headed this way."

"Yeah, I guess so," Travers said.

"Paranoid," Ford said.

"Damned straight," Travers said. "Anybody who isn't paranoid is insane."

That made the others laugh. Ford understood where he was coming from, in truth, although he didn't let it gnaw at him the way Travers did. Still, something *was* gnawing at him, as he gazed up at the megaliths. He could feel it, even if he could not precisely define it. A fundamental wrongness about these spires—their haphazard arrangement, their splintery majesty—it haunted him in an ineffable way.

The water was deeper where they were. This was determined when Guessica did some soundings with her sensory devices. While their dropsite was around 300 meters, the water depth near the island was over 9,000 meters. Guessica had suggested that the island had been volcanic at one point in the world's history, long ago. It appeared to be an extinct supervolcanic cone within a great, water-filled caldera.

The more Ford stared at the obelisks, the less sure he was about them. He should not have been so surprised—it was inevitable that a Terranaut team would, sooner or later, run into signs of alien civilization. When you considered how many worlds were out there, how vast space was, it had been Ford's belief that they would have found something by now, but when you factored in things like supernovas, magnetars, gamma ray bursts, asteroids, comets, black holes—there were any number of menaces in space that could readily wipe out a civilization, even if it had been lucky enough to exist at all.

And that didn't even account for things like plague, war, invasion, pollution, genocide—assorted banes of civilization itself. Even humans had come perilously close to extinguishing themselves in the past.

If life was a matter of chance, there was good fortune and bad luck, and alien civilizations were as prone to it as anything else. Just because they were aliens didn't necessarily mean that they were smarter than humans.

Something had lived on this world, had built these structures, or grown them, or however it was that they manufactured them. They had placed them for whatever reason, had been here for a very long time. The civilization that had made them could be long dead.

Ford did not intend to lose sleep over it, but it was exciting. They just needed to complete their mission and return intact with the greatest find any Terranaut team had yet discovered. He could imagine ALLIE analyzing their data and offering up extrapolations from it. Maybe she would be able to decipher the glyphs that ran along the length of the obelisks.

Ford gave himself a sedative. It was a routine thing Terranauts did that first night, the Nervous Night, as they often termed it. The front end of a mission was always fraught with uncertainties that could wear on personnel. The drug soothed him, but the dream that came did not.

He dreamed that he was sinking in a lightless, lifeless ocean, falling in his suit, descending ever deeper, while something swam around him, just out of the range of his lights, circling him, a hungry thing, with many eyes that shone like polished globes bigger than his hands. Watching him, swirling around him. He tried to contact the others, but his comlink was only giving him static. When the water got deep enough, his lights burst, thrusting him in darkness. And still he fell, in blackness except for the light of his HUD, which showed the depth gauge while warnings sounded. Deeper, deeper, pressure warnings flashing, and then breaches in his suit, starting with the weak points, the seams, always the seams, the icy-cold water slicing through his limbs at high pressure, like a hypersonic scalpel, and he saw his limbs float away from him, snatched up by the unseen shadow that swam around him, and then the glasstic visor on his helmet began to crack, all indicators flashing red, urging him to leave the area immediately. Then the visor cracked and that alien water sliced through him. Pummeled by pressure, Ford managed only a momentary scream, muffled, heard by no one.

Ford's proximity sensor went off. All of theirs did. Beeping and pinging, insistent. Ford bolted up, while the other two sat up. Their suits' radar picked up something in the water. Something very big, and very close.

"Are you getting this?" Ford asked, sweating from his nightmare.

"Confirmed," Guessica said.

"It's huge," Travers said. "It's that thing. It followed me here!"

The radar picked up something enormous in the water, swimming around underneath that thick layer of ice. It moved in a slow, deliberate, sinuous fashion, winding through the water. The on-board pixelated scanners represented it as a greenish mass, a blob.

"Maybe it's a school of fish of some sort," Guessica said. "Or whatever occupies that ecological niche here."

"Fuck, it's big," Travers said.

It moved out of range of their sensors, moving slowly.

"It's hunting me, I just know it," Travers said.

"Yeah, right," Ford said. "Whatever it is, it doesn't even know what we are."

"It's hungry," Travers said. "I know it."

Guessica laughed. "You'd leave a bad taste in its mouth, Trav."

Ford sat back down, wanting desperately to take off his helmet and just breathe freely. All of the Terranauts were trained and conditioned to be able to reside in their exosuits for extended periods of time without suffering from any adverse psychological reactions, but he felt that urge pretty strongly.

He thought he saw radiance on the spires, but attributed it to reflections from the aurora borealis crackling in the sky above them in shimmering, iridescent waves that softly illuminated everything below them. These alien stars, the wrongful sky, such a strange place. The first time he'd landed on a world outside the Milky Way. Indeed, from here, he could see the Milky Way in this alien night's sky, far, far away. Everything in this sky was wrong to Ford's eye. His mind played tricks, created new constellations—there was the Proxy, laying on her side, perched on her elbow, her hair full of stars. And there was the Terranaut, standing in an exosuit, clutching at their helmet. Over there, the Alien, long and slithery, stars for eyes, watching the Terranaut, monstrous mouth agape. There was the Colonist, uncomprehending, small, meek-yet-greedy, eager to homestead an unfamiliar place, surrounded by nebular luggage. The eyes played tricks, and the mind happily obliged, pinning meaning to meaninglessness, placing shapes up in the unfamiliar sky, like trying to make the place home.

That Ford knew this world was out here would forever haunt his steps. Paragon would send in teams, the ISA would crawl the data and there would be a full-scale invasion of this world. This was no mere link in the Colonial chain—this world was going to be something else entirely. They would want to know every millimeter of it, find anything they could extract and learn about the aliens. This would change the dynamic of the Program.

"Everybody try to get some sleep before morning," Ford said.

But the last thing Ford wanted to do was sleep, after that bad dream. He gazed up at the three moons that orbited the planet—one bright white, one dusty grey, farther away, and one just a point of bright light.

Their proximity scanners went off three more times during the night, picking up that same large, amorphous shape. Each time they jolted up, assessed the situation, then tried to get back to sleep. Each time, it got a little harder to do so.

While they woke and slept, the radiance from the obelisks continued, a kind of green-white light—faint, but growing stronger.

DAY TWO

1

MORNING CAME. THE ALIEN SUN ROSE, a yellow sun so much like Earth's, and the world awoke, the same cold and desolate place, the obelisks looking even more dreadful in the light of the day, the green-black of the stone sharply contrasted against the white of the snow and the grey-blue of the sky. All around them was the featureless white of the snow.

On a good night, sleeping in an exosuit was like being in a sensory deprivation chamber of a sort—to the credit of the ergonomic engineers, the suits were actually fairly comfortable. In sleep mode, they served to kind of suspend the Terranaut within the suit. It was never as good as real sleep, in a real bed, of course, but they had done what they could to make it as pleasant as possible.

It was why the proximity alarms had been such an unwelcome intrusion. The protocol for sleeping on an alien world was to keep those active, to maintain situational awareness. But when the alarms kept going off every few hours, it sorely tested the patience of the Terranauts. To deactivate the alarms, however, would have been a serious breach of form, and would have been recorded and duly noted by the Psych folks back home, and it would have percolated upward to Administration, and the Terranaut would have had a mandatory sitdown to discuss why they had done this.

Ford slurped some the Nutrifill, the liquid diet formula the Terranauts consumed on their missions, which had a sweet and tangy taste, was nutritionally complete. Nobody liked Nutrifill very much, but it did the job admirably well, like so much of what they had in their arsenals.

The others were already up. Guessica was studying the obelisks, while Travers was looking skyward, monitoring some of his weather gauges. He'd launched another of his balloons. The great white-silver balloon inflating, looking kind of disgusting to Ford, like a giant mushroom. He shook off that image, got to his feet, did a stretch or two as he watched Travers release the balloon, carrying its atmospheric analytical equipment.

"They should be paying us more," Travers said. "Way, way more."

"We're well-paid as it is," Guessica said. "You're always complaining about this."

"We should get a percentage on the commerce of every planet we explore," Travers said. "Give us like nine-tenths of a percentage of all the trade conducted on worlds we surveyed."

"A commission?" Guessica asked with a laugh. "I highly doubt Paragon would approve of that."

"Yeah, it would cut into their own percentages," Travers said. "That's where the *real* money is. I mean, we're prospecting these planets, as much as we're exploring or surveying them. It's only fair we should get a finder's fee."

"Fair's got nothing to do with it," Guessica said. "It's about allocation of capital. We're only here because of Paragon's investment in us. And ALLIE is the finder; not us."

"Yes, but they're safe at home, and we're here on this ball of ice, having staring contests with alien obelisks, dealing with sleep-depriving slithery shit in the water," Travers said. "We're assuming the risk, while they reap the reward. You think the shareholders even have a clue about anything we do? Think they're losing sleep? They're fucking living it up on Eden, or Xenophon, or maybe some private pleasure planet we aren't even aware of because they've kept it exclusive and secret from the rest of us."

"Arcadia," Guessica said. "You're talking about Arcadia."

Arcadia was a bit of a Terranaut legend. Everybody knew about it, talked about it, guessed about it. Nobody had seen it, and nobody in the Program would acknowledge its existence. It was a perfect planet, one that put even Eden and Xenophon to shame, and it was a private world, one that did not welcome homesteaders like the other planets. Somebody had paid a pile of Yuan to the Naming Commission and the ISA and had gotten their own private paradise planet that put all of the others to shame. An absolute fucking paradise, with a gate that nobody could access—that was Arcadia.

But when you asked around, everybody knew about it, but nobody had seen it. That's because it was Orange Team who had found it, and Orange Team was gone. Travers could talk for hours about it, claimed that Orange Team were either bumped off by Paragon, or else they were living it up on Arcadia, their reward for the discovery of paradise.

The thing was, if you asked ALLIE about it, she would reply in a standard manner that was not altogether convincing: "There is no such planet named Arcadia in my records."

It was as close as she got to lying. No record of it existing didn't mean that it didn't, in fact, exist. Orange Team had found it, and Orange Team was gone. It was as simple as that.

"Damned right I am," Travers said. "Fucking Arcadia. I'm just saying we should get a tiny little percentage of the action we're creating for everybody else, here."

"Try running that by Payne," Guessica said. "Just try it and see how he reacts."

Travers laughed bitterly. "He'll just start swearing at me, like he always does. Man, they should let us retire to Arcadia, goddammit. We earned it."

"There is no Arcadia," Ford said.

"There is," Travers said. "Even Guessica believes it."

"I never said that," Guessica said. Travers laughed.

"Right, right," Travers said. "You believe in it, too, Ford."

"Arcadia is where all good Terranauts get to go when they retire," Ford said. Of course he believed in it—it fit too much of what he knew about Paragon for it not to be out there, and it offered a nice bit of closure for the fate of Orange Team, the big mystery of the Program, the Lost Team. He imagined those guys living it up on the Paradise Planet, away from absolutely everything unpleasant, without a fucking care in the world. It was a happier ending than them floating lifeless in space, freeze-dried debris, tumbling end over end.

"Nobody even knows where it is," Guessica said.

"Somebody knows," Travers said. "I bet they have non-disclosure agreements for anybody and everybody involved with it."

"Enough daydreaming, Trav," Ford said.

"I'm a meteorologist," Travers said. "My head's *always* in the clouds."

Ford had already made a mental note that they'd have to bring a xenobiologist on the next mission, which was standard procedure when something living was found. And an anthropologist, apparently, or an archeologist—that would be new for the Program, and he assumed that ALLIE had already prepared for that contingency.

Somebody had to be brought on to interpret and study the obelisks. He would try to put together an airtight action plan to keep Chao from being able to wade in and commandeer Blue Team. Being able to successfully map out a proper procedure for this world would mean everything to ISA, and would give Ford a golden opportunity to stand out, if he leveraged everything the way he needed to.

He consulted the topographic map the drone had given them, determining their location. ALLIE had dropped them closer the north pole of this ancient world than to the equator. That was part of the problem.

"God, the next drop, I want us at the damned equator," Ford said. "Enough of this polar prospecting."

"I hear that," Travers said. "Prospecting, Guessica. See?"

"I'm going to send up the survey drone, have it do a few more passes of this place, try to get some more readings," Ford said. "I'll patch you in on it, Trav, so you can get more climate readings, that kind of thing."

"Alright," Travers said. "How about that thing last night?"

"Don't remind me," Guessica said, from her position in the shadow of the obelisks. "I altered my proximity alarm's radius so I could sleep through it, not that it helped much."

"Bad girl," Travers said.

Ford fired up the drone, watched it arc up into the sky. By day, they usually went to straight optics, instead of the pixelated representation of the data they were receiving. It helped stave off "suit psychosis"—a kind of sensory dysfunction that sometimes hit Terranauts if they weren't getting proper stimulus. The light shining in on his three-paned visor helped counter the digital trickery of the HUD.

The desire to get his helmet off was stronger in him than before. Ford really wanted to just take it off and breathe freely.

"So, this atmosphere is breathable, right, Trav?" Ford asked.

"Yep," Travers said. "Lucky us."

"I'm tempted to fly south," Ford said. "Get us the hell out of this polar zone. How far would we have to go?"

"Technically, we're in a subarctic region," Travers said. "I know it doesn't look it, but there it is, and here we are."

Travers toggled their position on the globe, flashing red on a yellow sphere.

"I would guardedly say that it's winter," Travers said. "And we're at the border of the subarctic climate zone. Which means we could probably head down about 500 kilometers and find ourselves in a more temperate area."

"500 kilometers," Ford said. He knew that the suits could get them there and back, but was wary of getting too far from the dropsite.

It was a question of how much he wanted to get done on this first mission. Part of him wanted to be as thoroughly ambitious as he could be, just to preemptively scoop Chao. If he huddled simply on this island, there were, no doubt, a wealth of things to discover, but there might be questions as to why he didn't range farther on the world, and whether ISA would see this as a failure of nerve or imagination on his part, and it might be reflected on his report.

Yes, they had made an amazing discovery, but part of being a Terranaut was expecting the unexpected, and dealing with it.

What if there were an intelligent alien species on this planet and Ford failed to make first contact with them, just because he was too busy counting pebbles on Obelisk Island? No, he had to risk a longer jaunt. But he would not risk the entire team. Guessica likely had enough to deal with at the island, and Travers could do his work there, too. And with the drone circling the globe, and Travers patched in to that, he could gain planetwide atmospheric data. The only one who was expendable enough to risk it was Ford, himself. He fully understood this.

"I'm going down there," Ford said.

Guessica and Travers paused in their work, turned their visors to face him.

"Alone?" Guessica asked.

"Yes," Ford said. "You keep doing what you're doing. I'm going to check it out."

Both of them piped up immediately. They had any number of tests they wanted to perform in other regions. Ford quieted them down with upraised gauntlets.

"Look, I'm not risking the entire team," he said. "The dropsite is, what, sixty kilometers northeast of here? I want to keep most of us close to that, just in case anything goes wrong. I'm going to go over the topographical data we have so far and plot a straight-line course from the dropsite, see what's down there."

"Ford, we already know that there's no major landmasses within 2,000 kilometers of this island," Guessica said. "You're going to find yourself flying over open water."

"There may be smaller islands," Ford said. "Something. I have to see. I have to know."

"Deathwish McGee," Travers said.

"Chao's not here, Ford," Guessica said. She understood his unspoken competition with his peer. She had her own competitors within the Program, had that drive to do and be the absolute best she could be.

"But she will be," Ford said. "I've got to bring back a mother lode of data."

Travers laughed. "Oh, so this is political, then?"

"Everything's political," Guessica said. "Ford knows that when ISA gets wind of these...."

She tapped an obelisk for emphasis.

"...they're going to want to have as much information they can get on the rest of this world," she said.

"And we're going to give them as much as we can," Ford said. "Those change everything for us, Team."

"Blue Team! Boo-yah!" Travers said, punching the sky triumphantly.

"Something like that," Ford said.

"I mean it," Travers said. "We're going to be legendary in the Program. God, Chao is going to be sick, you know that? The woman is going to be sick with envy. They'll have to move her to Green Team, that's how envious she's going to be."

The others laughed.

"That's my point, though," Ford said. "We have to do this absolutely right. I want to give them so much data that it makes ALLIE stammer. I want to blow the roof off of the Oasis."

"I'm retiring after this one," Travers said. "Fuckin' a, yeah. I'm going to get a golden ticket to Arcadia out of this. You'll see. Or, more like, you won't see, because I'm just going, taking like a dozen of my favorite Proxies with me, and disappearing."

"It's not the worst idea you've had, Trav. Although Proxies are expensive. You'd be broke in no time," Guessica said. She would even consider negotiating a package deal for herself and her family.

Guessica walked from the obelisks to fish out a core sampler from her supply case, which she handed to Ford. "If you actually see land, give me a core sample. Hell, if you splashdown and have to walk along the bottom of the sea, get me a sample, while you're at it, assuming you're not dead. Don't you dare bring it back to me empty, Ford."

He took the sampler, which was a portable silver cylinder, stowed it on his suit.

Travers didn't have anything for him. "And they think *I'm* the crazy one. Just patch me in on your sensor feeds, so I can record them."

"I'm figuring one day out, and one day back," Ford said. "Maybe less if there's no land."

"If you don't come back, we're just going to assume you're dead, you know," Guessica said.

"I'm counting on that," Ford said.

"Crazy," Travers said.

"Not that crazy," Ford said with a grin. "Guessica's in charge while I'm away."

2

FORD LEFT THEM IN A WHOOSH OF EXHAUST, flying away from Obelisk Island, over an unbroken field of white. At least it would be easy to see if and when he entered the temperate zone.

The first drop was always the most difficult, and so far, this one had been comparatively easy, relative to other drops in his past. Until mathematical markers were placed to guide ALLIE, it was sometimes hit or miss with the dropsite, at least until something permanent could be established. He didn't sweat it; the exosuits were designed to help the Terranauts through any rough points.

Ford felt some sense of relief—their own mission had not had any real complications, and they had made historic discoveries. That alone would guarantee him a promotion at ISA. If he were able to gather additional information on his field trip, so much the better for him, for them.

He had rigged the drone to fly in a spiral pattern around the world, so he could get additional information en route, in snapshot glimpses.

And Ford felt better, the more distance he put between himself and Obelisk Island. While he wasn't one to be superstitious, there was something unsettling about that place. He couldn't really articulate it. Could it simply be a result of Guessica's "wrongful geometry?" He didn't know.

As a Terranaut, he'd seen any number of unsettling things. The profligacy of life in the universe was, in itself, unsettling. There were more living things out there than anybody on Earth was comfortable admitting. And the rules of life that they followed were not always rules that people could properly accept.

There were trees that weren't trees, and symbiotic organisms that pursued an alien mutuality that could turn the stomach of the most seasoned explorer.

The absence of life was its own set of philosophical problems; the presence of alien life was something else entirely. Ford had walked on worlds where profane, symbiotic monstrosities had gazed at him and his peers with uncomprehending, alien eyes, with appendages and mouths and limbs that only ardent xenobiologists and xenozoologists could properly identify.

There was a ghastly fecundity to life in space—it was a source of wonder and of terror. For all of the diversity of life on Earth, all the varied lifeforms that lived there, they were all part of one great family—everything on Earth was related, when you traced it back through time. As a result, everything on Earth "made sense" in a way, because of this intimacy of origin.

But alien species were not part of Earth's family by their very nature, and were the results of different sets of rules, were parts of different families, and had nothing to do with Earth. Some of the xenobiologists theorized that life on Earth, in fact, came from someplace else—that microorganisms landed here when a comet or asteroid smashed into the Earth. In which case, even the native life on Earth was of alien origin. Whether that was so was beyond Ford's knowledge—all he did know is that the full sense of the word "alien" was experienced by every Terranaut, as they encountered life in all of its enigmatic diversity on faraway worlds.

The message most Terranauts received on a new world was simply this: *you are not welcome here.* The palpable sense of intrusion in a new xenocology always loomed large in the eyes, hearts, and minds of Terranauts. They had seen numbers of worlds where entire ecosystems had evolved for millennia without even the remotest awareness or consideration of human existence. Life forms that had been tested and measured without the slightest human involvement, and had survived and thrived.

And then, thanks to ALLIE and the conduits, in came humanity.

There was a usurpation in this, an unnatural invasion that the technology allowed—humanity became the invasive species, not unlike zebra mussels or kudzu or any number of other species that were introduced into previously pristine biospheres. For all of the ISA's care about not allowing new organisms to pollute Earth's biosphere—and, to their credit, they had been very, very careful—any human presence, even on habitable worlds, was the rampant pollution of a formerly untouched biosphere, one that had gotten along fabulously in the absence of humanity, but which was irrevocably changed because of the presence of Man, as surely as the New World was changed by the invasion of the Old World, in ancient times.

Ford couldn't pretend to be bothered by it too much; it was his job, and he had seen wonders and horrors that most Earthlings couldn't even comprehend. He thought he might create some memoirs someday, get everything down, let people understand just what he'd seen. He figured that Paragon's nondisclosure agreement couldn't be in place for all time, and that he'd be able to talk about what he'd seen one day.

Down below, some of the ice was showing fissures. First, some lengthy breaches in the field of white, which then increased in number and complexity in a fashion that was kind of pleasing to Ford in their fractal multitude.

It struck him, as he watched the cracks spread and widen and multiply, that he was one of only about sixty people in the universe—he supposed he should say "humans"—who had ever seen these kinds of things. On one level, ice was ice, no matter where one went, but this breaking ice was on a world 2.3 million light-years from Earth, in another galaxy. The distance made it matter. No single human being had seen this before. Not on this world. Someday, maybe, it would be as commonplace as anything else, when the settlers came, the homesteaders claimed it and domesticated it, the conglomerates profited from it, but in that moment, he was the first. And knowing this filled him with joy he seldom ever found back at the Oasis.

Miranda wouldn't be able to understand or comprehend this place. Her world was his life, at least for the duration of her employment as his Proxy. It was kind of weird—she was an explorer, too, but of Planet Ford, versus the wider universe. He wondered if he was as alien to her as this place was to him.

It wasn't that ISA trusted them particularly, or that Paragon thought that the Terranauts were that exceptional; they were simply the handful of individuals who had successfully passed the batteries of tests that gave them the opportunity to do these amazing things, and to perform reliably in the field.

Yes, it was just ice. Yes, it was just another massive body of water (even if it was a freshwater one). But nobody from Earth had ever seen it before. Nobody from Colonies had been here before.

About midway through his trek, he saw the ice give way to free-floating bergs and ice flows, and then to open, churning sea.

"Travers, you'll be pleased to know that the ice is breaking up here," Ford said. "I'm beaming back the coordinates. I'm staring down at open water."

"Be careful, Ford," Travers said, over the intercom.

"Yes, Ford," Guessica said. "Be careful."

And he saw another island.

Or, more specifically, he saw another obelisk even before he saw the island. It showed up on his scanners, at extreme distance, and he had the image pixelated and magnified, and there it was, another oddly-shaped spire, and eight smaller spires around the central one, on a small knot of land that looked to be about half the size of Obelisk Island.

Ford dropped his altitude and took himself down carefully, landing on this rocky island, grateful for the peace and quiet, to give his thrusters a bit of a break. The exosuit could fly marvelously, but extended flight still took a toll on the suit's systems. Where he walked, the ground crackled at the points of contact with his boots. He liked the feel of it.

The island was a rocky lump, dominated by the spires.

"Are you seeing this, Trav?" Ford asked.

There was a delay.

"Copy that, Ford. I see it. Told you the whole place wasn't ice," he said. "How's the weather there?"

Ford eyed the temperature monitor.

"Looks to be around 15 degrees Celsius," Ford said.

"Balmy," Travers said. "At least compared to what Guess and I have up here. Any plant life?"

Ford looked around. The island was devoid of it. He scanned carefully, thoroughly, but the island was barren.

"No. Nothing," Ford said.

It was more than a little disappointing. Even some moss or grass would have been nice to see. But there was only sun-bleached rocky soil, some sand.

"Guess, should I take a core sample?" Ford asked.

"Naturally," Guessica said. Ford pried the sampler loose from his suit's storage pack and activated the thing, tamped it to the ground the way he'd seen Guessica do it before, watched the sampler drive itself into the soil like a kind of silver syringe, drawing forth a core. He pulled the sampler out of the ground and turned it, which sealed the thing, digitally marking the time and place of acquisition. Then he restored it to its place on his suit, a magnetic-secured clamp on his pack.

On a whim, he removed another of his markers, and drove it into the ground at the highest point. At least this way ALLIE could find this location if she wanted to, once a permanent link was established. The markers were solar-powered, would keep pulsing as long as the sun shined.

Having done that, he approached the obelisks. These weren't snow-choked like the ones on Obelisk Island, so he looked forward to being able to investigate them more directly.

The swollen stone of the spires was the same green-black hue as the others, and in the more temperate climate, seemed to glisten. Behind him, waves churned against the rock.

"Guess, with three moons, this place has to have some pretty good tides, right?" Ford asked.

"Yes," Travers said, sounding a little piqued that Ford had asked her and not him.

"How can these islands still be standing in the face of billions of years of wave action upon them?" Ford asked.

"I think the stone here is incredibly dense," Guessica said. "I don't know where the obelisk stone came from, but if the island rock is even half as dense and hard as the obelisks, I suppose it would be very resistant to erosion."

Ford ran his hand along the studded surface of the spires, the arcane, almost profanely intricate glyphs along them. Every inch of the things was covered in the elaborate writing. Whoever had built these, they had the means of manipulating this incredibly hard stone, and almost in mockery of its hardness, had carved these glyphs upon their surface. And not just a little, but along their entire length. They seemed to radiate light, or else it was a trick of the sunlight on them.

Overhead, the drone shot by, far above, trailing a white contrail.

He walked in among the spires, and, again, saw no doors. There were no tell-tale passageways, and no clear purpose to the things. Ford walked among them, between them, looked up at the sky through them. From that position, there was a sense of enclosure, he felt—the central spire was surrounded by the other spires. Everything closed in on him from that vantage point.

"Trav, could these things be some kind of alien observatories?" Ford asked.

"Damned if I know," Travers said.

Ford shoved at the central spire, just to see if it would move. He could feel the suit's servos strain as he brought several tons of pressure against the stone, but it didn't move. The stone looked wet enough that he checked his suit's gauntlets, but there was no moisture on them. He kept looking over his shoulder, only to see the smaller spires hunched over him. Ford felt himself lose his balance and recovered himself again.

"There's something off about these things," Ford said. "Are you experiencing, I don't know, vertigo around them?"

"Yes," Guessica said. "We have. Don't look at them too long."

"Are they emitting any radiation?"

"None that I can detect," Guessica said. "I checked that already."

Ford wanted to take a scroll of Smartpaper™ and run it along the glyphs, copying them. Somehow, gazing at them wasn't enough. He wanted to take off his gauntlet and touch them, to feel their texture. The urge was very strong, actually had him standing there, holding his hands out in front of him, considering it.

He stepped back and steadied himself, caught his breath.

Around him, only the sound of breaking waves, of a breeze. The hard light of the alien sun overhead, the grey-blue sky, the spreading contrail, the only cloud he could see.

The compulsion to take off his gauntlet actually made him sweat and take another step back, prompting him to bump into one of the smaller spires, which startled him, making him turn around, facing the thing. From within the circle, it felt more confining. There was definitely a sense of being surrounded, and, to his eyes, it almost seemed like there was less space between the spires than there had been before.

Ford strode out of the circle of spires, feeling like he had to squeeze between the stones, back out into the open air, and take in the broad vista of the endless sea and the sky to regain his bearings. It was absurd for a Terranaut to feel claustrophobia—they had that conditioned out of them in initial training. There was no room for it in the Program.

He toggled his rear monitors, rather than turning around, and the spires were there, looming large and lifeless, shining in the sunlight. A trick of perception, he thought. They had not moved. Nothing had changed. It was his imagination. He checked his oxygen levels, wanted to be sure that nothing was awry. But it was fine; he was fine. He just needed fresh air. He needed to take off his helmet and breathe freely.

> "Personal log: I don't know what's gotten into me. I've experienced dizziness and vertigo in the presence of the spires. A cumulative effect. I keep seeing things at the corner of my eyes, like hints of movement that disappear when I look at them directly. And I can't be sure but it looks like the spires are emitting light."

Ford's hand hovered near the release switch on his helmet. It was actually a triple-switch, a safety feature.

"Ford, you alright?" Travers asked. "I saw you stumble a bit, there."

"I'm fine," Ford said, bringing his hands back down. "Just got dizzy."

"Listen to Guess," Travers said. "Stop looking at them."

But it was ridiculous to stop. He was a Terranaut. A fucking professional. He could look at anything he wanted to and didn't have to worry about it. Almost out of spite, he gazed at the obelisks again, turned around and faced them, looked them up and down, drank down the dizziness they inflicted on him. He wasn't going to let them get the better of him.

"You see that?" Ford said, to the obelisks. It was a challenge. To them.

"See what?" Travers asked.

"Nothing," Ford said, forgetting that Travers could overhear him on the comlink.

"What did you see?"

"Nothing," Ford said.

3

GUESSICA HAD GATHERED EVERY ROCK and pebble she thought could be of interest, had tagged and bagged them, and Travers had actually crafted a snowman army gathered around the base of Obelisk Island, arranging them in cascading waves, all of them facing the obelisks, mouths gaping, eyes big.

"Can't you do something useful, Trav?" she asked. ALLIE would be happy with her work, if she were able to feel happiness, that is. Guessica's mind was already crafting tests for the Gold Team project, wondering what that world would be like. At such distances, such things they would see. The prospect of bringing back 13-billion-year-old core samples thrilled her. They would be the oldest rock ever discovered by humanity. She would write research pieces on them, would be the envy of every geologist on Earth and Xenophon and Midas. While she was dreaming about this, Travers was playing with snowmen. She highly doubted that Paragon would put him on Gold Team, but she wondered, anyway.

Then again, maybe Gold Team would come here. Or maybe they'd craft a new team once the bombshell of their discovery was revealed. Paragon would still have its sights on the farthest launch, but Blue Team's discovery was a game changer.

"I *am* doing something useful," he said. "Hey, I did my part. I've got some balloons up, and they're beaming information to my computer. I've taken spectrographic readings, barometric readings. I even did some of Ford's work for him. I'm covering all the bases. It's not my fault that I got all of my work done."

There had to be a score of snowmen piled up around the perimeter of their encampment, all of them gazing up at the obelisks. From where she stood, up by the structures, it was unnerving, these gape-mouthed snowmen gazing at her.

"I should blow those things to bits," Guessica said. The arm-mounted lasers, one per gauntlet. Guessica only had cause to use them once, on QED-311, when some native creatures, these nameless grey, shambling six-legged hulks with lengthy mandibles and slavering maws, had charged their team. They'd fired their weapons at them, scalding the creatures, which had driven them off in a panic. That world hadn't been claimed, yet—the Naming Commission was behind in its allocation agreements, but Blue Team had named it "Dangerworld," just because it had so much going on there, so many deadly things. Purplish skies added a weird light that left all of them with a month's worth of retinal readjustment—and there was a higher-than-acceptable acid content on that world. Travers had suspected that maybe they'd been dropped there to test some suit upgrades.

Anyway, the temptation to fry Travers's snowman army was overwhelming.

"I'm bored," Travers said. "Ford cut off the datafeed once the drone came back here."

"You're on company time, Trav," Guessica said. "I don't think Payne would like you just making snowmen."

"No Payne, no gain," Travers said. It was something they'd said to themselves in Blue Team often. "I'm studying cohesion of water molecules in an alien subarctic climate zone."

"Yeah," Guessica said. "Right. Hey, did you hear anything about Gold Team?"

"Gold Team?" Travers asked. "There is no Gold Team."

"Yeah," Guessica said. "I know. So, have you heard about it?"

"Not yet, anyway," Travers said.

Guessica paused in her work, put Travers on her HUD 3. He gazed at her with a smirk. "You're not on it, are you?"

"Hell, yeah," Travers said. "I mean, pending successful completion of *this* mission."

That filled Guessica with a bit of angst. Travers? Travers the clown was going to be on Gold Team? His meteorological work was, of course, beyond dispute, but he had been contacted by ALLIE for the Gold Team project, too?

"What, did you think you were the only one ALLIE talked to?" Travers asked.

"No," Guessica said. That made her wonder, though—two people from each team were being taken for the Gold Team, and she and Travers had been contacted, did that really mean that Ford wasn't going along? Assuming ALLIE was right about that—but then, assuming that ALLIE was right was the simplest, safest thing any person could assume.

"Yes, she told me that they're putting together some kind of super-team," Travers said.

"Do you think Ford was contacted?" Guessica asked.

"He'd have to be," Travers said. "I mean, for sure, right?"

"Maybe we should ask him," Guessica said, although if Ford didn't know about it, that would be hugely embarrassing, and would likely distract him from the mission, which might reflect poorly on her, which, in turn, might jeopardize her own prospects.

"Maybe *you* should ask him," Travers said.

"I'm not asking him," Guessica said. She and Ford she could see on Gold Team. But Guessica and Travers? That perplexed her. She really wanted to ask Travers how a goofball like him could possibly rate Gold Team. That's what was really gnawing at her.

"I'll ask him," Travers said.

"No," Guessica said. "Don't. What if he got passed over?"

"No way," Travers said. "Chao and Ford—they'd both be on Gold Team. They'd have to do that."

"But what if they didn't?" Guessica asked.

"Maybe there's a Silver Team," Travers asked. "A backup team? Maybe he's on that."

It was just speculation on Travers's part. He was prone to flights of fancy, but Guessica was sure that even if an alternate team was created, Ford would take it as a huge snub.

"It's funny, right? We're farther away than anybody has been, so far," Travers said. "And it'll be like nothing compared with that Gold Team mission."

"You who were just whining about hopscotching across the cosmos," Guessica said.

"Why do you think I was whining about that?" Travers asked. "I had a lot on my mind. I don't even want to think about being 13 billion light-years from Earth. I don't think I can. They'll probably toss us into the heart of a fucking quasar. I could see ALLIE doing that."

Guessica really wanted to talk to Ford about it, but couldn't think of a way of bringing it up without it being immediately awkward.

"Did you hear about Trashworld?" Travers asked.

"What?"

"The Naming Commission has a new planet, named Detritus," Travers said.

"Ha-ha," Guessica said.

"I'm serious," Travers said. "It's going to be the landfill for the Colonies. Trashworld. That's what I'm calling it. Natives of Trashworld, Trashies. You like?"

"Funny," Guessica said. "I don't believe a word of it."

"ALLIE confirmed it," Travers said. "I asked her."

How did Travers know all of this stuff? Travers, the most well-informed clown in the cosmos. She supposed she shouldn't be surprised—Travers was always talking, always trying to find things out. His nosiness paid dividends for him, despite his unserious nature.

"So, it's for real?"

"Yep," Travers said. "It wasn't one of our worlds, btw."

Trashworld. That made her sad. Maybe sanitation departments would figure out ways of dealing with all of the accumulated waste of the Colonies. But she wondered what kind of people would settle on such a place, and what that poor world would look like in time.

"It's a super-Earth," Travers said. "Big, so there's lots of room for all the garbage."

"How do you know all of this stuff, Trav?"

"I make it my business to know," Travers said. "If knowledge is power, I'm nearly omnipotent."

"Hah," Guessica said. "All of your courtesans. A spy network for you, I imagine."

"Battle not with whores, lest you become one," Travers said, putting another head on yet another snowman. "The Proxies know more than anybody about what's going on at the Oasis. You're missing out."

"I don't know how you do it, Trav," Guessica said. "You should've been fired from the Program years ago."

"I am unstoppable," Travers said. "Leave it to a weatherman to know which way the solar wind is blowing."

The wind blew between the spires, puffing snow about and making howling sounds. Guessica had walked in among the obelisks after Ford's comments earlier, and there did appear to be a kind of sense of something in their arrangement, like the central spire and surrounding, smaller spires. It was clearer without the snow piled up so heavily around them.

But there was a profligacy in their presentation, too, that called to mind bacteria growing in petri dishes, versus actual created structures—a kind of latticework intricacy to them that made her think that these obelisks had been grown, and not built at all.

It was an unscientific observation, perhaps, but one she was prepared to make with any xenomorphologist or whomever ISA would conjure up to accompany them on the next mission.

Maybe it was likelier that several of the other teams would be reassigned to QED-376, and they'd just survey the hell out it, rather than drawing things out for poor Blue Team. She figured that was why Ford was sweating it. The pressure would be intense.

"Ford?" Travers said. "Come in, Ford."

There was the crackle of static for a moment.

"Yeah?" Ford said. "What is it?"

"I heard some rumors about a Gold Team," Travers said. "Have you heard anything about that?"

"A Gold Team?" Ford asked. "Is this more of your gossip, Trav?"

Guessica bit her lip. Ford hadn't heard. Wow. That knowledge alone floored her. What was Paragon thinking? Why wouldn't they put Ford on the Gold Team?

"I've heard rumors, yes," Travers said, wincing at Guessica at his fib. "They're putting together some kind of super deep-space team for a one-of-a-kind mission to the edge of the universe, itself."

"Yeah, well, if that's so, I haven't heard about it," Ford said. "How'd you hear about it?"

Travers didn't want to get Salacia in any more trouble than she'd already been with her other gossip, so he owned up to it.

"ALLIE told me that I'd been tapped to be on this team," Travers said.

There was silence on the line a moment.

"Maybe it's some Psych Division test," Ford said. "Some kind of motivational protocol or something, seeing how you take it."

"I dunno," Travers said. "It felt pretty real."

"What about you, Guessica?" Ford asked.

"Um," Guessica said, glaring at Travers for just impulsively spilling the beans that way. "Yes, ALLIE contacted me about it, too."

Again there was another crackle of static on the line.

"I can't believe you just blurted that out, Trav," Guessica said, on a private line to Travers.

"Congratulations," Ford said. "When did you find out?"

"Right before the drop," Travers said. "ALLIE said to keep it under our hats, but we got to talking."

"They probably didn't want to tell me about it before the mission," Ford said. "Didn't want me to be distracted or anything. Operations guys are usually the last to know about these kinds of things, honestly."

That made some sense to Travers.

"See?" he said to Guessica. "He's fine. Ford's tough. He can take it."

"I don't know," Guessica said. "Maybe he's right. I mean, they'd want him to be focused on this mission, not thinking about any other mission. But why would ALLIE tell us about it?"

"Good question," Travers said. "Maybe it *is* some kind of Psych Division test—maybe they wanted to see if we'd talk."

"Did we pass or fail?" Guessica asked.

"I guess we'll find out," Travers said.

Guessica fretted over that. What if it was some kind of bizarre test ALLIE had been charged with delivering? What if they were supposed to not divulge any secrets about it? Maybe there was no Gold Team at all.

"I wouldn't worry about it too much," Ford said. "Paragon's always playing their boardroom games with us."

"Did you hear about Planet Detritus?" Travers asked.

"Yeah," Ford said. "How the hell did YOU hear about it?"

"Salacia," Travers said. No point in hiding that.

"Of course," Ford said. "She's a nosy one. Are you two through gossiping over there?"

Guessica gave Travers a tart look on her HUD display. He stuck his tongue out at her.

"When are you coming back, Ford?" Guessica asked.

"Not yet," Ford said.

"Call us when you're leaving," Guessica said.

"Will do," Ford said, severing the connection.

"See? Nothing to worry about," Travers said.

Nothing.

4

FORD SAT DOWN ON THE ROCKS, watched the sunset. The vertigo had only grown in him, and the message from his teammates had even compounded it.

Gold Team? Was that even possible? He wanted to head back to the Oasis and storm Payne's office, find out what the hell that was even about.

How the hell had Travers and Guessica been informed of this, while he was kept in the dark about it? It had to be some kind of mindfuck from Psych Division. That was the only rational explanation.

Or else ALLIE was told to turn some kind of screw in their heads and with Chao emergency-deployed to Franzen's sector, they likely didn't want to inform Ford before they informed Chao.

He watched the sun cut in half by the horizon, the first sunset witnessed by a human being on this faraway world. Nobody tracked little things like that—it wasn't like they were accomplishments, really, but they were experiences nobody could take away from him. Not ISA, not Paragon, not ALLIE. Nobody. These things, these countless little things he'd done in the course of his long career with the ISA, they were his.

Ford scooped up some of the alien sand, let it flow through the fingers of his gauntlets, watched the grains fall on the rocks below.

Or maybe he'd been passed over.

Maybe Chao would head this supposed Gold Team, and Ford wasn't even considered for it. It seemed incredible to him, but no doubt Prig didn't want the ISA's number two guy stepping on his star's toes.

The sun vanished beneath the horizon in a flash of light, and there was nothing but the waves and the darkness of the skies above. Two of the moons had risen already, the third was nowhere to be seen.

Three Terranauts, three moons.

Ford could see the radiance in the spires clearly, now, through his rear-mounted cameras. The sun was gone, but the radiance remained. They were glowing, most definitely.

He got up, turned around, and walked up to them.

"Guessica, are you seeing radiance in the spires?" Ford asked.

"Affirmative," Guessica said. "A green-white light."

"I'm getting that down here, too," Ford said. "They weren't doing that when we first approached them."

"Negative," Guessica said.

"It's probably safe to say that they're reacting to our presence?"

"Unknown at this time."

Ford smiled to himself, Guessica's ass-coverage.

"But they're emitting no apparent radiation?"

"Nothing I can detect," Guessica said. "If they are, it's some radiation we can't yet identify."

Ford reached out, touched one of the spires, one of the smaller ones, which was only about twice his height. He felt himself sweating, felt that strong sense of vertigo again.

"The vertigo increases, the closer you get to them," Ford said. "Maybe they're some kind of transportation devices."

"We can't know," Guessica said. "We should try to get one of these back to ALLIE, for analysis."

They'd love that at the Oasis, the three of them lugging an alien obelisk through the Conduit, marching down the Causeway with spoils of exploration, the Find of the Millennium.

"Yes," Ford said. "We should."

The glyphs shone with the most amazing light. It was like phosphorescence, although it wasn't a cold radiance like bioluminescence. He had his cameras set to thermograph, and could see that the spires were warm.

As he gazed at the light, at the alien writing, the impenetrable hieroglyphs, Ford found himself transported, felt himself grow remote from his own body, felt something almost like enlightenment encroach upon him. These glyphs and sigils told a story, they spoke to him. It was like with words, the way a word came to have a life of its own, above and beyond its component parts.

Like "Ford." His own name: F-O-R-D. Four letters. Three consonants, one vowel.

Syntactical atoms, bound together in a molecule of meaning that spelled "Ford."

That was him. He was more than his name, was more than the word that named him, more than the letters that made up his name. His parents loved the car company of antiquity, the electric car company. That was his namesake.

These symbols were that way—he was seeing them, really seeing them, and he was understanding what he was seeing, could comprehend the twists and turns of the glowing glyphs, the turn of the stone, the arcane forms that wound around the spire in a kind of dance.

That's what it was. It was a dance. Like dancing around a fire, or the mad dervishes of the dead religions, spinning like tops, or gyroscopes and gimbals. He could see the precession, could feel the nutation. The very ground beneath him shifted, and he found himself clutching at the stone of the spire to maintain his footing.

The lights grew brighter, but Ford did not squint. He felt sweat trickle down his forehead, despite the headband he wore. He laughed out loud, the dizziness, the disorientation. He was hanging on for dear life, feeling something unlike anything he'd ever felt in his entire life. He was unbalanced.

And yet, it was exhilarating, this incredible, surging sense of vertigo. There was no nausea, now; there was only this breathtaking sensation of transportation, of communion, of bathing in the radiance of the spires.

There was no fear.

There was no fear.

There was no fear.

5

GUESSICA EYED HER CHRONOMETER, watching the last moon rise.

"Trav, when's the last time you heard from Ford?"

Travers paused, giant snowball in his hands. "About three hours ago, Guess. Why?"

"Do you think he's upset?"

"I don't know," Travers said. "Why don't you find out?"

"Ford?" Guessica asked.

Silence.

"Ford, come in, please," Guessica said.

"Ford?" Travers said. "Yo, Ford?"

Silence.

"Fuck," Travers said.

"Can you program the survey drone to fly over there?" Guessica asked. Travers nodded, walking over to Ford's equipment case, where the drone was stored.

"A night flight is going to be a little trickier," Travers said.

Guessica did the math in her head. Ford had found that island around 250 kilometers southeast from their current position.

"We can try to find him in the morning," she said. "Let's hope it's just a communication glitch. Rig the drone to fly over there tonight, and we'll fly out there in the morning, if we have to."

"Ford," Guessica said into the comlink, while Travers programmed the drone. "Come in, Ford. Where are you? Come in, over?"

She tongued a message to his suit, in case his audio was out:

FORD. RUOK? PLS CNFRM.

But there was nothing.

"Do you think he got hurt?" Travers asked, looking up from the console.

"It's either an equipment malfunction or something happened to him," Guessica said. "Ford is a stickler, you know that. He'd not go quiet on us without reason."

Travers got the drone ready, launched it south, as the light left the sky, and day gave way to night.

"I've got it set for infrared," Travers said. "ETA in ten minutes."

"Fast little critter," Guessica said.

"Nothing but the best for Blue Team," Travers said. "I've got it set to zigzag over his last known location, and to circle over the island. If he's there, we'll see him."

"Ford," Guessica said. "Come in, Ford."

Guessica refused to get upset or worried. She was confident that Ford could handle anything that he might encounter. There was no team member or commander she had worked with who was steadier than Ford. Ford was more metronome than man.

"Maybe he's dead," Travers said. "Maybe you jinxed us when you said that bit about the one being left alone dying."

"Not funny, Trav," Guessica said. "Besides, we didn't leave him alone; he left us alone. It's not the same thing at all."

"Yeah, right," Travers said. "I'm patched into the drone feed. Feel free to do it, yourself."

Guessica did so, once Travers prepped it for her. With the sun having set, everything was incredibly dark around them. She'd toggled her infrared scanners, but it did nothing to limit the matchless emptiness surrounding them. She didn't want to turn on the lights on her suit; it made her feel exposed.

Travers saved her the trouble by turning on his lights, although it did nothing to alleviate her trepidation. The light threw odd shadows around them, made the snowmen look bizarre and unfamiliar. Alien, for lack of a better word.

It was strange—when they went back to the Oasis, those snowmen would be one of the few indications that anybody from Earth had even been here, at least until the weather eroded them into oblivion.

"What?" Travers asked, glancing at her.

"Nothing," Guessica said.

"ETA, five minutes," Travers said.

The HUD screen that showed the drone's view. Guessica toggled to the pixelated display in hopes of getting a clearer view of the island, which was showing up bright blue on the horizon, fast approaching as the drone flew. There was a yellow light on the island, which would be Ford.

"Ford, please acknowledge," Guessica said.

The island grew bigger, the details rendered in geometric pixel form, the island, the obelisks, the yellow shape of a man in his exosuit, lying on the ground.

"Um," Travers said. "Ford?"

As they got closer, another yellow shape emerged, from within the circle of obelisks.

"Are you seeing this, Travers?" Guessica asked.

"It's Ford," Travers said. "He's out of his suit."

"What?"

Guessica went from the pixelated display to infrared, and there it was, Ford's suit, laying there on the ground, the helmet open. And there was Ford, walking about, pawing at the obelisks with bare hands.

"Shit," Travers said.

It was beyond Guessica's comprehension. It was a violation of every protocol they had ever been given. No Terranaut in their right mind would ever breach their suit on a first-round survey mission. It was tantamount to suicide—either literally, or in terms of one's career. Ford had, in that reckless moment, thrown his lifetime of service to the Program right out the window. No more Team Leader, no more Team, no more Program. Ford would be taken by Psych Division and that would be the last that Guessica or Travers ever saw of him. He would become a footnote within the organization, a cautionary tale. She could actually see herself telling her peers about it, being on this faraway world when Ford Collins breached his suit and walked around all but naked, wearing only his silvery Paragon skinsuit.

"What in the hell was he thinking?" Guessica asked.

The drone circled the island, and Ford seemed oblivious to the drone, just kept clawing at the spires of the obelisk.

"What do we do, Guess?" Travers asked.

It was as uncharted as anything else they faced in this place, as unfamiliar and alien. There was no standard operating procedure for this kind of situation, because it had never happened before in the Program. There were, however, protocols in place in the event of a teammate losing their minds. That was something more common and comprehensible, at least.

Guessica bit her lip, considered her options.

"We have to get out there," she said. "Ford seems alright. I mean, aside from breaching his suit. I'm not willing to risk going out there until morning. First light."

"He just killed his career," Travers said. "I mean, for real."

"I know," Guessica said. "We shouldn't have told him about Gold Team."

Travers looked at her through their mutual monitors. "Oh, no, don't you try to pin this on me. Ford knows the game, how it's played. He would not have taken that so much to heart that he'd do something as crazy as breaching his fucking suit."

"Then what is it?"

"Maybe it's the spires," Travers said, switching the scan to thermographic again. "Maybe they did something to him."

Guessica hadn't considered that. She'd been so shocked to see Ford out of his suit that it had been difficult to think clearly.

The drone kept circling, capturing footage of Ford resting his forehead against one of the spires, tracing the glyphs with his bare hands, leaving streaks of fading heat with every touch. Then it headed back the way it had come.

6

GUESSICA HAD TRAVERS PLAY THE FOOTAGE back repeatedly, to try to make sense of what they had just seen. Ford ambling around the site, pawing at the spires.

"What is he doing?" Guessica asked.

"No idea," Travers said. "But you realize we're *all* fucked, now? At the very least, quarantined. Even if there's nothing definitively wrong with Ford, they're going to keep us under observation for weeks. And that's just assuming Ford had some rational reason for breaking the seal on his suit. Best case scenario for us is quarantine."

Guessica had Travers kill his lights after the drone came back, and she wondered whether they should risk a night flight out there to contact Ford. She just didn't feel comfortable doing that at night. Even with the instrumentation they had, it was no certain thing. She wasn't about to risk her life and Travers's until she was able to take proper stock of the situation.

"It must've been equipment malfunction," Guessica said. "Something went wrong with his suit, and he had to get out of it. That's the only way there's a permissible breach protocol."

"Why wasn't he waving us down?" Travers asked. "The drone makes noise; I guarantee he heard it."

"The atmosphere is breathable, right?"

"Yes."

Guessica didn't know what to do; Ford was the Operations guy, not her.

"So, he won't die if he's out in it?" she asked.

"No," Travers said. "He might get cold, but he should be okay."

"Try to get some sleep," Guessica said. "We'll leave first thing in the morning."

"We've still got days on the mission," Travers said. "What'll we do?"

"We'll worry about it tomorrow," Guessica said.

"Day Three," Travers said.

The implication didn't even need to be said, because she understood it. The exosuits recorded everything the Terranauts did, and would be reviewed by ISA and Paragon personnel. Ford would be in huge trouble when they got back, although all of them would be under observation. Their conduct had to be exemplary to meet this challenge—it wasn't just Ford's career that was on the line, here.

She squirmed in her own suit. How could Ford have done this? One of the sacred caveats of all Terranauts was to not open their suits. Once a new world had been safely studied, surveyed, analyzed, named, claimed, and settled, that was one thing—once ALLIE had determined that there weren't deadly pathogens or organisms on the world, once a permanent conduit was in place, then people could come and go with near-impunity. It would become a world like any other.

But on that vital first visit, the initial survey, when the variables were piled mountain-high, when there were so many unknowns to reckon with, the exosuits represented a kind of celestial insurance, a protection from The Great Unknown that a new planet presented. To flagrantly cast that aside was unprecedented.

Certainly, a couple of Terranauts had done versions of it in the past. There was Mace Cleaver of White Team, who had fallen ill on their mission to FED-86, and had to open his helmet because he was vomiting. It had been 24-hour bug that had evaded detection by the Medtechs on the drop day. Everybody had been aghast when they had found out what had happened, but Cleaver had come through fine, since FED-86 was a desert planet, and their location had been fairly remote, it was thought that this helped protect him from any untoward events resulting from the suit breach.

In the wake of that incident, ISA had a mandatory 72-hour sequestration of Terranauts before launch, requiring them to work carefully with the Medtechs to ensure that nobody went out there sick like that. It wasn't foolproof, but it diminished the odds of a repeat of what had happened.

There was the equipment failure of Johan Galt of Grey Team, who found that the climate control on his suit was malfunctioning, leading to a sustained internal atmosphere temperature spike that rendered his suit uninhabitable, forcing an emergency ditch on YAN-515 on Day Two of a four-day mission, once it was determined that the suit couldn't be fixed. As YAN-515 was an ultimately sterile and lifeless world, Galt had been fortunate in his misfortune, as he had not fallen ill.

It was later determined by the ISA that faulty wiring by a low-bid contractor on the project had led to the glitch to begin with, although Galt found himself railroaded by Paragon on his quick jettisoning of the suit in the field, and he was dropped from the Program as being psychologically unfit to serve. He later became a vocal critic of ISA and Paragon on the Newsfeed circuit, before experiencing eventual obscurity as the worlds moved on without him.

But to do what Ford had done certainly put his future in the Program at great risk, and that was putting it as politely as she was able. Guessica dearly hoped he had a good reason for doing it.

She gazed at the obelisks overhead, visible in her pixelated HUD display, and glanced at Travers, who appeared to have anesthetized himself so he could get some sleep. In the light of the aurora, they glowed.

"Ford, please answer," she said, one last time, waiting for a response. Nothing.

She sedated herself, as well, gave herself to the void.

DAY THREE

1

GUESSICA AWOKE WITH A START. It was morning. The upside of the sedative was that it made you sleep; the downside of it was that there was almost no sense of the passage of time, and one usually had to take some stimulant to shake off the effects of the sedative.

"Travers, get up," she said, giving him a little kick, which was suitably amplified by her suit that he felt it.

Travers groaned and got up.

Both of them took a few moments to take their Nutrifill and their Aquifier.

"Breakfast of champions," Travers said, getting to his feet. "I swear to you: I'm quitting after this one. No more of this shit. I don't care how much they improve the suits, don't care about Gold Team; I'm still sleeping on the ground, drinking my breakfast and pissing myself. This is no way for a human being to live."

Like so much that people faced, all of the hard work that went into the Terranaut Program on the front end went completely unappreciated. It was like when a person sat down to a meal someone else had cooked for them—not a thought went to where the food came from, who harvested it, shipped it, processed it, purchased it, prepared it— what mattered was only whether it was something they liked, or not.

The stimulants zapped the cobwebs from her head, and Guessica was readying her suit for flight. She directed Travers to do the same. Although, strictly speaking, Travers was senior to Guessica, she was pushier than he was, so she picked up the acting Team Leader mantle without comment and didn't think he'd object.

They flew after Ford, Guessica worrying that she should have risked the night flight to find him, but feeling better that she had waited, because in the day, things seemed more possible and seemed far safer. With all of the equipment aboard the exosuits, it seemed silly to worry, but she still felt reassurance in the rising of the sun, even if it was an alien sun, even if three moons hung in the sky, instead of only one.

"He's going to wish he was dead," Travers said, as they flew. "We're going to wish it, too. Paragon is going to walk all over us."

"We didn't do anything wrong," Guessica said. "Something went wrong, and Ford is the one with the answers, and will be the one who has to answer the tough questions from Paragon."

"Right," Travers said, like he didn't believe her. In truth, Guessica didn't necessarily believe it, either, but she had to tell herself something. What other choice was there?

They reached Spire Island in about a half an hour, as she decided to call the landing site, just to distinguish it from Obelisk Island, their original landfall.

She had insisted that Travers bring the solar-powered recharge unit, and they detached their flight wings when they landed, with Travers charged with setting that up, while Guessica looked for Ford. The recharge unit would repower the antigravity projectors, make them light as feathers, and easy to fly.

Guessica toggled her external speaker with a flick of her tongue.

"Ford? Where are you, Ford?"

His suit was where it had been the night before, laying empty on the ground, arms at its side, legs splayed—the thing looked like a kind of mockery of a jumping jack, or a snow angel.

She walked up to it, scanned it. There was a bloody handprint on the visor. That made her step back with a gasp.

"Ford?"

Turning, she looked at the spires, where Ford had been the night before.

There was blood smeared on the stone.

"Travers!"

Blood was all over the stones, including handprints.

Travers walked over, whistled.

"Fuck," he said. "What the hell happened here?"

"Ford!" Guessica said. "Goddammit, Ford. Where are you?"

"Here," came a voice from within the circle of spires.

It was Ford's voice.

The two of them looked into the shadows of the place, and there was Ford, still in his nanojumper, leaning back on the central spire, his hands raw and bloody. He had blood up his arms all the way to his elbows, and had blood on his face. A bloody handprint, like he'd pressed his bloody hand to his own face.

"Suit breach *and* broken skin," Travers said, groaning. They'd be in quarantine for the rest of their lives.

"Ford, what the hell happened?" Guessica asked.

"They're weapons," he said. "These things. They're weapons."

Guessica walked into the circle of spires, with Travers following.

In their suits, they loomed over Ford, who looked very small by comparison. She wasn't used to seeing him like this. There wasn't any standard operating procedure for seeing your Team Leader this way.

"Commander, why did you vacate your suit?" Guessica asked.

"I wanted to touch those things," Ford said. "With my own hands. We don't need the suits. Look at me. I'm fine. I drank the water. It's the freshest, purest water you'll ever know."

"Shit," Travers said. "You drank the water? We're going to have Psych Division rectal probing us at the rate you're going, Ford."

"You were right, Trav," Ford said. "You said it first, about wanting to touch the stones. I was going to shoot you, remember?"

He smiled at Travers, which, with that bloody handprint marring his face, made Travers squirm.

"Yeah, haha," Travers said. "That's great, Ford."

"We get all this information," Ford said. "And neither of you can tell me what the air smells like, what this place tastes like."

"What does it taste like, Ford?" Travers asked.

Their Team Leader closed his eyes, leaned back on the central spire, rested his head on it. The sight of this was incredible. He'd probably spent the night like this.

"The air is impossibly fresh," he said. "It smells like almost-winter— burning wood and the cinnamon scent of rotting leaves, but crisp. The chill is beautiful."

"What did you do to your hands, Ford?" Guessica asked.

"I was talking to the stones," Ford said, holding up his bloody hands. "Sign language."

"What were the stones telling you, Ford?"

He looked at her with a lopsided grin.

"Don't analyze me, Guess."

Ford got up, walked right past them. Barefoot, his feet making prints in the sand that filled the nooks and crannies of the black island rock.

"I'm not leaving here," he said. "It's beautiful."

Travers spoke to Guessica via the comlink.

"What are we going to do?"

Ford walked down to the water, and stepped in, kneeling in it, bathing in it. He walked right into the water and then stood up, arms up, facing the rising sun.

"Damned if I know," she said. "I don't think we're going to be able to talk him back into his suit."

"I understand completely," Ford yelled. "You can't see it, but it's right here. Step out of the suits, you'll see. They're Von Neumann machines. Far beyond anything we could imagine. I figured it out. I figured *them* out."

Guessica walked over to the shore.

"Ford, Paragon is going to have your hide for this. They're going to vivisect you. Then they'll dissect what's left."

"Let them come here and take me," Ford said. "I'm not going anywhere. It's safe."

He held up a double handful of water, let it run through his fingers, then poured it over his head, washed the blood from his face.

His eyes were wide, his smile, wider. Ford knelt down and drew more water up, and drank it. Travers and Guessica both gasped as they saw him drink from it, long gulps.

"Pure," he said. "Pure and clean."

"Fuck," Travers said. "That's fresh water, Ford. God knows what you've just ingested."

Ford sank into the water. "It's cold. It's so cold and pure. The Von Neumann spires made it so. They sterilized it all. The whole planet."

"You're going to die of hypothermia," Guessica said, eyeing the temperature gauge. "Ford, you need to get into your suit immediately."

"Never again," Ford said. "Don't you see? You're both prisoners. We all are."

Guessica looked at Travers, who was looking back at her.

Ford had lost his mind. Either some toxic interaction with the obelisk, or some kind of pathogen or parasite.

Something had affected him.

"What could have happened?" Guessica asked. "Can you hook into his suit, see if you can find any playback on what happened from the point when he severed the datafeed with you?"

"Sure," Travers said.

"Ford," Guessica said. "We're on Day Three. Do you remember the action items for Day Three?"

"You know I do," Ford said. "I don't care. You do it. You're the scientists. You do it."

"And do what? Leave you here?"

Ford paused in his ablutions to consider this.

"Yes. Leave me behind."

"They'll come for you," Guessica said. "This is all being recorded, Ford. You know this as well as I do. They'll come for you."

"Let them come," Ford said. "They'll never find me."

Guessica actually sat down on the rocks, while Travers was busy patching a line into Ford's suit.

"Ford," Guessica said. "Paragon will find you. How can you expect to live here? We don't even know what we can eat. You'll starve and die."

"Go back home," Ford said. "When the drop comes, go through. Tell them I'm staying."

Guessica knew as well as Travers did what would happen.

ISA would quarantine QED-376 until they found out exactly what had gone wrong, here. The discovery of the obelisks would be huge, but Ford's meltdown would lead to an intensive analysis of what had happened. It would be months before they risked another drop here, assuming Recovery didn't jump here and bring Ford back, kicking and screaming, or else tranquilized and drooling, cocooned in a transit harness.

They would want Ford, they absolutely would want him to get a sense of what had happened to him. They would want blood samples and specimens. They would want Ford, without exception.

She regretted that they didn't have a xenobiologist with them on this mission because it would at least have given them a proper biological specimen-gathering kit. As it was, she intended to gather some of

Ford's spilled blood and sequester it in a container, in hopes of finding whatever it was that had afflicted him.

"I've got the upload routed into memory," Travers said. "It's been on for the last eighteen hours, Guess. I can't pore through this willy-nilly."

"Alright," Guessica said. "We can leave him here."

"We're leaving him here?" Travers asked.

She didn't know what else to do. They could try to chase Ford down, apprehend and disable him, then put him back in his suit. As it was, he was less of a danger to them in his current situation. A madman in an exosuit was something far more dangerous than a madman playing on an alien beach.

"We've got a couple of days," Guessica said. "Maybe he's gone space-happy or something. Maybe he'll come around."

"Maybe he won't," Travers said. "Maybe he'll get worse. Maybe what happened to him will happen to us."

Guessica swabbed up some of his blood, sealed it in a canister that was intended for geological samples, but should keep the sample safe, regardless. She pried loose the geological sample Ford had taken, put that on her own pack.

"Ford," Travers said. "Look, you have got to come back with us, man."

Ford shivered in the water, shook his head. "This is my home. All those years, wandering, all those places. This is it. This place."

"We could tranquilize him," Travers said, on the comlink. "I could hold him, you could administer a sedative from his suit. We could keep him under, just truck him in that way."

"Disable his flightpack," Guessica said. "We'll maroon him here with his suit. He'll have a week's worth of Nutrifill. And he can go longer, since he's apparently drinking the water. That's plenty of time for ALLIE to figure out what to do."

Travers was clearly upset by the prospect of leaving Ford behind.

"Let me try to talk him down."

"Go ahead and try," Guessica said. "I'll disable the flightpack."

She understood what he was trying to do, she really did, and she sympathized. She loved Ford as much as Travers did. But whatever had happened to him had changed the dynamic of the mission, and they would have to get back to Earth immediately and give a full report.

They weren't equipped to incarcerate or apprehend Ford. They could manhandle him, could muscle him down and perhaps succeed in disabling him without harming him. But ISA would want him alive, so they could question him. And the brutal truth of it was that the exosuits were powerful machines, and they could easily damage Ford en route. It was terrible for her to contemplate, but she'd already thought of Ford as a specimen to be delivered to the Oasis.

"Ford," Travers said. "Where are you going to go, buddy? This island's pretty small. The tides on this planet are likely pretty special. You'll be washed away if you're not careful."

Ford stopped splashing in the water, just looked at him. It looked ridiculous, Travers and Guessica in their exosuits, and Ford almost naked, wearing only his silver-grey nanotunic, soaking wet.

"You're going to die here if you don't come back with us," Travers said.

"We're all dead, Trav," Ford said. "We just don't know it, yet. Everything is a cellular echo—we're walking ghosts, splashes of stardust."

"We have two days, Ford," Travers said. "Come back with us."

"Not a chance," Ford said. "If you're smart, you'll join me. Just dump the suit and face this place. You'll get it."

"Get what?" Travers asked.

"You'll understand," Ford said. His face was the same as ever. It was Ford's soldierly bearing, but his face was creased with a manic merriment.

"There's an old-school fix for this," Travers said on the comlink, making Guessica pause in her work.

"What is it?"

"Duct tape."

"What the hell are you talking about, Trav?"

Travers watched Ford climb out of the water, shivering, shaking himself off, walking over to some of the black rocks, finding some sand, and laying on his back on them, facing the sun in silence.

"We've got a few spools of it back at the camp," Travers said. "We come back here and we tape him up. Hands, feet, his whole damned body. Then we just cart him back like he was cargo, a madman mummy."

"Are you serious?"

"Yes," Travers said. "At least then we won't have to worry about him hurting himself, or messing with us. At least until Psych Ops can look him over, until they can see what exactly happened, here."

Guessica had to admit that it wasn't the worst idea she'd heard. The prospect of taping up Ford and bringing him back like that made her sad. Nobody deserved to come back to the Oasis that way. It would be the end of his career, but, in truth, his career was ended, anyway. He would never see another alien sun, would never be entrusted to another exosuit, let alone command of another team. Ford's life as he knew it ended the moment that glasstic visor came up. The first breath he took of alien air was the last gasp of his career in the Program.

"I'll take that under consideration," Guessica said. "I want to review the footage you uploaded, if there's anything there, and see what, if anything, went on here in that downtime when we lost communication with him."

"Alright," Travers said.

Ford just contentedly sunbathed, while Guessica had successfully disabled his flight unit on his suit by detaching its power pack, which she stowed on her own suit.

"Last chance, Ford," Guessica said. "We're going back to the encampment."

Ford raised a hand and dismissively waved at them, his eyes closed, basking in the sunlight.

"Go back," Ford said. "Tell Payne that I quit."

"Yeah," Travers said. "We'll be sure to tell him that."

Guessica watched Ford sunbathe, wondered whether Travers's idea of duct-taping him was the best option. At least if Ford was simply sunbathing on Spire Island, there was little harm that could come to him, and little harm that he, himself, could do.

"We can't leave him here," Guessica said. "I mean, right now, for now, yes. But we can't go back to the Oasis with him still here. We have to bring him back in."

"Yeah," Travers said. "That's pretty much what I thought, too."

"Let's go back to the encampment, play back the stuff, and see what we can learn," Guessica said. The business about Von Neumann machines was madness. Although nobody had ever encountered them in the Program, Guessica thought the spires were too inert to be any kind of self-replicating machines. Ford was mad.

"What if I stayed back here with him, to try to talk him off the ledge?" Travers asked. "I can do some more climate testing here, while I'm waiting for you."

"Okay," Guessica said. "But if you go loopy, too, I'm going to force-feed you guys sedatives until you're both drooling. Let me upload the datafeed you took from his suit. We can both look at it."

Travers pulled out a dataline and Guessica slotted it into a port on her suit, repeating the upload he'd done on Ford's.

Ford sat up and turned to watch them in silence.

"You know, we are so silent," he said. "We talk to each other through radios and on computer screens, with camera eyes in place of our own. Seeing nothing, saying nothing. When you're in the suit, there's light and noise, but out here, it's silence. The silence of this place is breathtaking. No birds aloft, no rustle of trees. Just silent spires and endless seas, fickle wind and fateful breeze. The Von Neumann void."

"That's great, Ford," Travers said. "Poetic."

"You'd not think that noise was nothing," Ford said. "I know. We know. But it is. Noise is pollution, like anything else. We're pollution. We're noise."

Guessica wondered about the tensile strength of the duct tape they had at the encampment. It was heavy-grade stuff, intended for robust performance in the field. It would hold him.

"This world doesn't need us," Ford said. "It's fine without us. Just fine. How many worlds do we need? We're a disease. Do you realize that? We're infecting the universe."

"You think so, Ford?" Travers asked.

"Yes," Ford said. "The conduits are letting us infect the entire cosmos. It's like the ancient times, when explorers brought diseases. It's like Rave. Only *we're* the disease. Every bit of us. Every cell."

"I'll bring the tape back," Guessica said. "I think that's the right idea. We'll do it right before we go."

"Okay," Travers said.

"Try to talk to him," Guessica said. "Try to make some sense of what happened, here, if you can. I'll go back to the camp and replay the tapes, you can do it here, too. Let's stay in constant communication. No blackouts. We can link our datafeed the way you did with Ford."

"Alright," Travers said. Guessica removed the dataline, as the upload was complete.

"If he does anything crazier than he's already done, don't hesitate to restrain him," Guessica said.

"There's something I'm worried about, Guess," Travers said.

"Which is—?"

"How this happened. Was he always nuts, or did something drive him nuts?" Travers asked. They both knew the answer to that question—Ford had a perfect service record. It was one of the reasons he was one of the most successful of the Terranauts. Somebody like him didn't just lose his mind. Something had happened to him.

"What's your point?"

"How'd it happen?" Travers asked.

"We don't know," Guessica said. "Maybe a breach in his suit?"

"No breach," Travers said. "I already ran a diagnostic on his suit. It's intact, except for him not being in it. He blew the hatch."

"Okay."

"So, whatever it was that got to him, it did so without breaching the integrity of his suit," Travers said. "Which means we're as vulnerable to it as he was, if it's the case."

Guessica looked over at Ford, who was still talking, pacing around, gesturing, drawing glyphs in the sand with his fingertips. She zoomed in on those, noting that they looked like some of the glyphs that were on the spires.

"He was experiencing vertigo," Travers said. "I'm saying he was feeling that before this happened."

"We've all experienced it," Guessica said.

"Right," Travers said. "It's the obelisks. It has to be tied to them. I don't know how, but it has to be. And we've all felt it. So, maybe we're all in danger, here. He said they were weapons."

Guessica had made a point of avoiding looking at the obelisks too much, despite being busy trying to run single-crystal X-ray diffraction tests on them, as well as electron microprobe analysis, if only to find what exactly they were made of. Her field kit had a portable scanning electron microscope, which she'd used to try to gain a qualitative chemical analysis of the type of stone. But while she had looked closely at the spires, the minute observation she had undertaken was perhaps a case of losing the forest for the trees.

Certainly Travers had been busier examining the atmosphere. Ford had perhaps been "exposed" to the spires more than the other two, although Guessica thought that she and Travers had been at Obelisk Island longer than Ford.

There was just insufficient information. They needed more time and better equipment. They needed ALLIE to look at it. But she was days from receiving them, bringing them home. Until then, ALLIE was a universe away.

"Minimize your exposure to the obelisks," Guessica said. "Just in case. Maybe there is something unseen at work with them, a way that they are able to affect us without our realizing it, or being able to defend against it."

"Okay," Travers said. "He did say something about them being weapons, as I mentioned. I mean, if they are Von Neumann devices, I don't want them turning me inside out."

"Find out what the hell he was talking about, if you can," Guessica said. "As I said, we'll stay in constant contact."

"Alright," Travers said. "When are you coming back?"

"Tomorrow," Guessica said. I'll fly back, and we can watch the playback, try to get a sense of what happened to him, assuming there's even any good information to be gained. Then I'll come back with the tape and we'll restrain Ford."

"We can't bring him back to Obelisk Island until it's droptime," Travers said. "Not unless we put him in his suit as dead weight or something. He'll freeze."

Guessica was aware of that. "We'll figure out what to do when we reach that point."

"Be careful, Guess," Travers said.

"You, too, Trav," Guessica said. "Seriously. Don't you dare cut off contact with me."

"I won't," Travers said.

"Look at the pollution," Ford said, watching Guessica launch. "Noise, smoke, sound, presence. Heavy metals. Souls. A toxic Von Neumann stew."

She shot skyward, leaving two-thirds of Blue Team behind.

"Our suits are bombs," Ford said. "Tiny walking bombs. Has anybody ever remote-detonated them? Don't they know? Maybe that's what happened to Franzen's team, yes? Maybe they detonated."

Even as she flew, his words were in her ears, thanks to the real-time link with Travers.

"A reactor breach in one of our suits would be like a tactical nuclear bomb," Ford said.

"Nobody's ever detonated a suit, Ford," Travers said.

"Not yet," Ford said, with a grin.

2

==[BEGIN TRANSMISSION]==

Pacing back and forth, falling over, stumbling.

"Fuck. You."

Hands and knees. Biostats are normal. Elevated heart rate.

HUD display 1 shows spires close by.

Back on feet.

Walking up to one of the spires, gazing closely at one of the glyphs. The shape is a circle that is wound with something cordlike, almost a spiral, but there are other shapes in it.

Outstretched hand touches it, brushes the stone.

"I see you."

Radar picks up a signal in the water. HUD display panel 3 shows it.

Spins around, gazes at the sea.

The signal fades, the mass moves away.

Then back to the spires.

Shoves at them, grunting. Servos straining.

"Open, you fuckers."

Throws a shoulder. No effect.

Steps back.

Gazes skyward.

"What were you looking at?"

Reenters the circle of spires, gazes up.

Arms up, touching the stone, the shadows, the relief. The scraping of gauntlet on stone. Walking around the central spire.

"Who was up there?"

"Who was it?"

Elevated heart rate. Drinking Aquifier.

"You fucking things."

Spins around, looking from side to side.

Runs out of the enclosure, squeezing past the smaller spires.

"Shouldn't be here."

Drops to knees and digs gauntlets in the sand, lets it run through fingers.

"After seven billion years, this shouldn't be here. This should be gone."

Toggles topographic map of QED-376, studies broad, featureless world. Flat landmasses. Structures built on land, but no mountains, no hills. No variable terrain. Only the spires and obelisks dotting the landscape. Jungle.

"Circles."

Gazing at the topographic map on HUD 1. All of the structures are circular from aerial view.

"Splinters."

Turns and looks up at the moons. Two of them are in evidence.

"Impact craters?"

Turns and looks back at the spires, walks around to the point where the obelisks meet the ground. Starts to dig.

Draws up some black stone, pulls it forth with some effort. Holds up stone, examines it. There is a clear shear line. Smooth, with grooves cut in it.

Static.

Turns stone this way and that. The cut side is shiny.

"Guessica? I think I found something of interest."

No response.

"Guessica?"

Comlink failure.

"Oh, come on."

"Computer, reestablish link with Blue Team."

Unable to comply.

"Computer, reestablish link with Blue Team."

Unable to comply. Signal lost.

"What the fuck?"

Gazes at the spires, falls over.

"I see you. You see this? I see you."

Drops the rock sample.

Static.

Suit system failure.

Warning light.

"Bullshit."

Warning light.

"Computer, what's going on?"

Suit system failure.

"Localize and identify."

Unable to comply.

Biostats spiking.

Spires are glowing. Glyphs on spires are glowing.

Hands come up, release helmet safeties. Helmet springs up.

Slips outside of suit, leaves it on the ground. The spires are glowing. The color is a phosphorescent green. The ground is wet where he touches it.

"I'm sorry."

Moves out of sight of the suit's cameras.

"I'm so sorry."

Static.

Static.

Static.

Ford's face looms in the camera.

"I saw it. Everything."

Grinning.

He puts a bloody handprint on the visor, walks out of the frame.

Static.

==[END TRANSMISSION]==

3

GUESSICA PLAYED THE FOOTAGE BACK THREE TIMES. She even ran the remaining hours of the static, in hopes of finding something else, but there was nothing.

"Travers, what do you think?"

"I don't know," Travers said. "It looked like the spires were glowing, but they're inert right now."

"What's Ford doing?"

"He's pacing around," Travers said, turning his camera to show Ford walking around, gesturing, debating himself in grunts and mumbles.

"Try to talk to him, would you?"

"I'll try," Travers said.

He walked into the circle of spires. Ford stopped pacing, watched him.

"Don't go in there," Ford said. "It's deadly."

"Ford?" Travers asked. "What did you see?"

"It's a weapon," Ford said. "We're thinking it was something built here, but it wasn't. It was launched here from someplace else."

"The spires?"

"Yes," Ford said, annoyed. "Blessed weapons. Splinters raining down from Heaven or Hell. It hardly matters now. It happened so long ago. Splinters from the sky."

Ford gazed skyward, and Travers followed his gaze.

"We walked into a mystic minefield," Ford said. "A tomb."

"How do you know this?" Travers asked.

"Plain as day," Ford said. "Invasion. Extermination."

Travers looked around, uncertainly.

Guessica walked to the spires on Obelisk Island, studied them anew. Warily, but intently. She dug at the base, the points of contact with the ground, and could see that there had been melted rock at the point of impact. It was difficult to see here, with so much snow interfering with observation. She pried loose a sample of the rock and examined it.

It did appear that the obelisks had struck the ground.

"Unexploded ordnance," Ford said to Travis with a laugh. "Paragon is going to love this. You and Guess should dig one out and bring it back like a trophy. Stab Payne in the butt with it."

She took the sample and stowed it, then went to one of the smaller spires and strained at it, tried to pry it loose. Her suit's endoskeletal servos were strong, but despite straining against it, she wasn't able to pull it free. After seven billion years, the thing was probably molecularly bound to the surrounding ground.

Guessica cued up the topographical map, studied the patterns of the spires. If Ford was correct, then what they were seeing wasn't the remains of a civilization, the structures of it, but rather the ghost of its demise, the evidence of its destruction, long ago.

It was a sad realization, although it would be up to ALLIE to determine whether it was the correct interpretation of the data or not. It didn't change a thing where Ford was concerned, nor did it explain why he'd violated protocol and slipped free of his suit.

"Ask him why he'd removed his suit," Guessica said.

"Why'd you slip off your suit, Ford?"

"Had to," Ford said. "You saw the footage. System failure. It'll happen to you, too. It's what *they* do."

Ford patted one of the spires for emphasis.

"It's a shame 'Thanatos' is already taken," Ford said. "As a name, I mean."

"Alright, so if you're right about this place," Travers said. "Why stay here?"

"It's as good a place as any," Ford said. "Ground zero. At least here I know nobody'll bother me. It's like sleeping in a graveyard. Nobody bothers you there."

"I've never slept in a graveyard," Travers said.

"Everlasting peace," Ford said. "The cessation of strife. Isn't that what everybody wants? A battlefield is the safest place to be, once the battle's over, the war's been won. This one's been over for billions of years. The land fought over, contended, claimed, lost. It hardly matters."

Ford rested his forehead against the largest spire for a moment, before recoiling and backing away from it.

"They're here, you know," Ford said.

Travers triggered the comlink to Guessica.

"Yeah, okay, not so much progress, here," he said. "You found the duct tape, right?"

"Yes," Guessica said. "I have it."

"Good," Travers said. "We can wrap him up right before ALLIE reestablishes a link with this place, and we can just walk him through."

"What if he's right?"

"What if he is? It doesn't change anything, as far as we're concerned," Travers said. "Our job is to survey this fucking planet. Let Paragon and the Polygon send people in to determine whether these things are actually weapons or not—that's their job. Let the archeologists in here. Let them do their jobs."

"Hey," Ford said, rapping on Travers's visor, startling him. "You're not taking me back."

"Computer, secure my visor," Travers said. The thing securitylocked. All visors were sealed, but a security lock would ensure that only Travers could open it externally. "Only open on my command."

Ford just watched him a moment, shaking his head, smiling at him, but his eyes were like empty caverns.

"You just don't get it, Trav," he said. "You don't see. You should just go. I just told you everything and you weren't listening. You were too busy scheming with Guessica."

Ford laughed and went back to one of the spires, which he caressed with an outstretched, scabby hand.

"They're beautiful," he said. "Beautiful monstrosities. Elegantly conceived and deadly in design."

"You're sick, Ford," Travers said. "What do they do?"

Ford looked at his hands like he'd seen them for the very first time. He flexed the fingers a bit. They were raw.

"What, these? Brute instruments from a bygone age," he said. "It's over. *We're* over."

"Why do you say that?"

Ford leaned forward, arms upraised, against the obelisk, pressing his forehead against it, then backing away again, a strange push-pull dance between himself and the thing.

"Their war may be over, but these weapons are live. No, it's bigger than that. They're living."

"They're stone," Travers said. "Guessica said they were."

"She doesn't know," Ford said. "She just sees what's there. She sees obelisks and spires, they become obelisks and spires. They're weapons, and they're alive. We woke them up. They're watching us."

Travers looked at the things. Their distended shapes continued to bother him; they were irritants. He looked away.

"They're made of some ultra-hard stone," Guessica said, over the comlink. "Don't tell me my job, Ford."

"You want me to tell him that?" Travers said.

"Go ahead," Guessica said.

"Guessica says you don't know what you're talking about," Travers said.

Ford scoffed.

"I'm out here, you're in there," he said, tapping his forehead. "Who knows better, hmm?"

"What are you going to do here, Ford? Let's talk about that, okay? Say we leave you here. Then what? You're still hell and gone from any-place. You can't possibly swim to the next major landmass. You're stuck on this tiny little island until you die. Probably until you starve."

"It'll be okay. I'll be okay," Ford said.

Travers didn't want to stay on the island with Ford. He wanted to go back to Obelisk Island.

"How do you know the weapons are, um, living?"

"They live," Ford said. "They're watching us now, trying to under-stand us. I saw them. They're going to get you next, Travers. They haven't mastered our language, yet, but they're learning quickly. Then they'll figure out what to do with us, and to us."

Travers glared at Ford, who was just holding onto the spires, run-ning his hands along the glyphs.

"Is that what they do? They just drive you batshit-crazy?"

"No," Ford said, laughing. "No, no, no, no. No. No. No-no-no. It's like when we get stung, you see? Like when something stings you, your body reacts to the invasion. But all too often, the response is an allergic reaction. These weapons weren't designed for us, not with us in mind. You see? They weren't calibrated for humanity. But they're learning. Isn't that brilliant? A weapon that learns like that?"

Travers did think he understood what Ford was talking about. Whatever war they had been used in, whatever age-old apocalypse the things had invoked on this world, wherever they had come from, it was for a species, or a race, or a culture that was as alien to people as could be.

"We're a side effect," Ford said. "Collateral damage."

"Okay, so you admit that you've been damaged, but you want to stay here?"

"Yes," Ford said. "I'm contaminated. And that's exactly it. I can't go back. We shouldn't bring any of it back. Not truly. ALLIE is going to open the portal and bring you back, you'll make your report, and Chao will come stomping in here with a huge team, and everybody will become contaminated, and they'll bring some of the spires back, and then it'll spread. It's like finding an old land mine or clusterbomb—undetonated ordnance. Just because it hasn't exploded yet doesn't make it safe to handle."

Travers watched him talk, listened to him, and shades of his friend and coworker were there. Ford the Reasonable, Ford the Wise, Ford the Capable Commander.

"So, you doffing your suit was to save the Earth?"

Ford nodded. "I think so."

"I can't believe anything you're saying, Ford," Travers said. "We need to have doctors look at you."

"Can you imagine when ALLIE deciphers the language?" Ford said. "And she will. Chao will slice off a pillar or two and they'll bring it back, to universal fanfare, and ALLIE will crunch the data and she'll decipher the language, the full activation codes, the arcana woven in these things, and then all bets are off."

"What do you suggest we do?" Travers asked. Might as well see where his head was at.

Ford considered it a moment.

"Set the suits to detonate, and destroy the Conduit," Ford said. "Wait till it opens and detonate when you're in the Causeway. Nuke the Oasis."

Guessica coughed, and Travers shook his head.

"That's pretty nuts, Ford," Travers said.

"Seal the breach," Ford said. "It's kind of funny, isn't it?"

"It doesn't matter," Travers said. "They'd bring people back. ALLIE would find the way back. You know she's not based at the Oasis. You know there are plenty more conduits and gates. The Oasis is only *our* part."

Nobody really knew where ALLIE was. Travers didn't, anyway. ALLIE was kept in an undisclosed, secure location. She had ready access to the Oasis, and to the Lunar Observatory, and a number of other places, but she was not housed in any of those places.

Travers thought maybe the Polygon had her locked up somewhere deep within its structure, but he couldn't know for sure. He assumed if she was, she would be too busy processing information for the Polygon's wars to bother with the search for habitable worlds, although her processing power was so incredible that maybe she could do all of that with ease.

"It's not just a matter of physical contamination," Ford said. "It's cultural. It's spiritual. We're so used to it being one-way—us polluting other places. But this place is polluted. It's toxic. And Paragon will bring it home."

"This is going to get him incarcerated," Guessica said. "Forget therapy; he's going to be interrogated and locked away."

"Yeah," Travers said.

"He advocates blowing up the Oasis," Guessica said. "Kiss Ford goodbye. We're going to take him back and we're never going to see him again."

"Yeah," Travers said.

Ford watched Travers, pausing in his talking.

"Guessica," Ford said. "Just leave me here. Easier for you, easier for them. Easier for everybody. Nobody'll ever find me."

"You know we just can't do that, Ford," Guessica said. Travers relayed that to Ford, who laughed.

"What if I tell you that the death of our world is here, in this place? The end of all that we know?" Ford asked.

"I would ask you how you could possibly know this," Guessica said.

"I'm closer to these things than you are," Ford said. "I took the leap. I looked into the abyss, and it looked right into me. It took a good, hard look, saw right through me."

Travers sighed. "You look fine. I mean, aside from whatever happened to your head, you look alright."

Ford held up his hands, showed Travers the injury done to them.

"That's just it," Ford said. "I'm toxic. I'm infected. Just because I can talk to you like this doesn't mean I'm not aware of the nature of my sickness."

Guessica wished they had a Medtech with them, but while the Terranauts had medical training, they never sent Medtechs on the first mission. Medtechs came later, when there were more people to worry about on a mission.

"Okay," Travers said. "So, how does it progress?"

"I don't know," Ford said. "I only know that I'm not well. And I only know that because I'm trained to pay attention to that kind of thing."

Travers triggered the comlink between him and Guessica.

"What are we supposed to do, here?"

"We just have to make it for a couple more days," Guessica said.

"Do you think he broke the seal on his suit on purpose?"

"I don't know. He might only appear to be lucid, here."

"What if I am hit next? What if I go nuts, too?" Travers asked.

"If you're hit, then I'm getting the hell to the dropsite and am waiting for the portal and I'm going to report all of this and we'll see what ISA decides to do," Guessica said.

"What if you're hit next?" Travers asked. "What do I do then?"

"Nobody's going to get hit next," Guessica said.

Ford mimed talking with his hand, smirking at Travers. He held up both hands, had them talking to each other, back and forth, and looked from hand to hand in bemusement. Then he walked into the shadows of the obelisks.

"What if we can't tell?" Travers asked. "Maybe we're already infected."

"How? If Ford is infected, if there's even an infection, it's because he broke the seal of his suit," Guessica said. "He's out of his mind."

Guessica felt herself get dizzy, glared at the spires in her vicinity. Obelisk Island was in the middle of a snowstorm, but she could see them, towering like titans.

"The Medtechs will check us out," Guessica said. "Once ALLIE reviews these tapes, once we give our report, once we're in quarantine, they'll look and determine whether we're okay."

"What if he's right about it infecting everybody?" Travers said.

"Look, we're the ones in the suits," Guessica said. "Ford's the one walking around half-naked out there and drinking the water, cutting up his hands, bleeding all over the place. Don't listen to him. If he's infected, maybe the aliens are manipulating him. The point is that we can't take anything he says to heart, because at the very least, he's out of his mind—whatever the cause of it, there it is."

"Yeah, okay," Travers said. "That said, do I really have to stay here and nursemaid him tonight?"

Guessica looked at Travers on her HUD 3. He gazed up at her with those bright puppydog eyes of his.

"Are you scared, Trav?"

"Umm, yeah."

"Did you secure your suit?" Guessica asked.

"Already did that," Travers said.

"So, there's nothing to worry about."

Guessica wasn't entirely sure of that. She felt the wave of vertigo hit her, dropped to one knee. There had to be some kind of ambient radiation, something their scanners couldn't detect. Something that had baked Ford's brain, and might be affecting her own.

"Are you okay, Guess?" Travers asked. "It's happening to you, isn't it?"

"No," Guessica said. "I'm fine."

Travers didn't believe her. He could see it on her face, the sweat, the rolling of her eyes. He could see the jolting of the camera as she moved and lurched. It was happening to her. Whether she admitted it or not, it was.

"What if we camped out on the lake?" Travers said. "Away from these things? Let Ford skinny-dip on Spire Island, and you and I just camp out at the dropsite? Just in case there *is* something toxic about the spires. Maybe with some distance, we'll be alright."

Guessica steadied herself. She was fine. It was just fatigue setting in. It was this bullshit with Ford sapping her strength a bit. She took a hit of Aquifier and Nutrifill, gave herself a stimulant, which was probably a bad move, given the time of day, because it would mean she would be up half the night.

"We have to get as much information on these things as we can," Guessica said.

"What else can we do? You've managed to scrape off some shavings, you've done your battery of tests on them. We've filmed them," Travers said. "Let's camp at the dropsite."

The days went faster, here, Guessica noticed. Smaller world, quicker days, less distance for its sun to travel, less real estate in the sky. She saw Travers's snowman army watching her, the deep shadows forming around them.

Fucking things. He'd made so many while she was busy working.

She charged one of her arm lasers.

"What is it, Guess?" Travers asked. Her expression said it all, as she glared, took aim.

She fired her laser, arcing it in a half-circle, slicing the snowmen with it. When they didn't fall over, she arced back, cut them again, watched them tumble and fall.

"What are you doing?"

Only stumps and severed torsos remained. The snow was fairly solid, so the body parts of the snowmen gaped up at her from the shadows, mouths wide, eyes wider.

"Nothing," Guessica said. "Just modifying the terrain a little. Keep contact with Ford. Tomorrow we'll camp at the dropsite."

"Tomorrow," Travers said. "That's forever."

"It's eighteen hours," Guessica said. "Deal with it. Stop looking at me."

"Huh?" Travers asked. "Me?"

She walked over to the snowmen corpses and stamped their faces into oblivion with her boots, each one, stomping them until they weren't looking at her anymore. This, as the sun got low over the sky, as everything went into shadow.

Behind her, the obelisks caught the light of the sun and seemed to glow a green-white hue, brighter than before.

"No," Guessica said. "It's nothing."

4

TRAVERS WATCHED FORD WATCH HIM AS THE SUN SET. It was disturbing as hell. It was like he was a synthcat or something. He just stood there with his arms folded, watching him.

"Are you feeling it?" he asked.

"Feeling what?"

"That vertiginous sensation?" Ford asked, tapping his ear. "It's in here, you know. I understand that much. You know what causes motion sickness? It's when you're getting competing sensory information—when your eyes and your ears are getting different information, can't reconcile what they're experiencing. All balance comes from those tiny little otoliths in our ears, in our vestibular system."

"Spare me the biology lesson, Ford," Travers said. "I know it."

Ford smiled, like he was indulging him.

"The structure of these things fucks with our sense of balance," Ford said. "They unbalance us."

He laughed at his own wordplay.

"That's funny, Ford," Travers said. "Good one."

"I'm unbalanced, now," he said. "Or I was. I reoriented, once I accepted the new information. There's a period of readjustment."

"Ah," Travers said. "New information."

Ford nodded. "Isn't it funny—those tiny, microscopic pebbles of calcium keep us standing straight? Fuck with those, and our entire world turns upside down. Have you ever read the old NASA files? Like how even seeing somebody standing in the wrong spatial orientation could make another astronaut puke? Isn't that funny? Our brains and bodies recoil against something like that. We're not supposed to be in different planes of existence. We're all supposed to keep our feet on the ground. The same ground. The same dimension."

Ford just spoke calmly, languidly, even, while Travers studied him. He seemed sane and nuts at the same time, and that was causing its own disorientation in Travers.

"Anyway," Ford said. "Absolutely everything we understand about up and down, left and right, right and wrong—it's tied to those tiny pebbles in our ears. Calcium builds strong bones and a sense of where we are in the universe. Funny that calcium's something we lose the moment we set foot in space."

"That's just a result of zero gravity," Travers said. Then it occurred to him: the gravity was lower here, too. Maybe the vertigo was simply a result of the lower gravity? The otoliths in their ears adjusting to the lower demands placed upon them?

"I think those sensitive little pellets are the early warning system for whatever it is these babies are dishing out to us," Ford said, patting one of the spires.

"Tell me this: why aren't you freezing right now? It's reading ten degrees Celsius right now."

"They're warm," Ford said, patting the spire he was leaning against. "Nice and warm. They know we're here, and they're warming up. I bet when Chao shows up with her army, they'll get hot."

Travers turned on his suit's thermal imaging, and, sure enough, the obelisks were radiating warmth. That was undeniable.

"Guess," Travers said. "The spires are emitting heat. I'm getting nearly fifty degrees Celsius from them."

"Not over here," Guessica said, a trifle too quickly. "These appear to be inert."

Travers studied her expression on the HUD 3. She looked back at him, those big brown eyes on his.

"You okay, Guess?"

"I took too much speed," Guessica said. "I'm going to be up all night, I'm afraid."

"Uh oh," Travers said.

"I'm fine," Guessica said.

"You sure?"

"Yes."

"Did you hear that bit from Ford? About the otoliths?"

"Yes."

"And?"

"And nothing," Guessica said. "He could be right. I don't know. Maybe the spires adversely impact them, maybe it's a symptom of the toxicity, the affliction, the infection—whatever it is."

"That's why we should camp at the dropsite tomorrow," Travers said. "See if proximity to the obelisks worsens the condition or lessens it."

Guessica smiled at him. "Not a bad test, Trav. Okay, you persuaded me. We'll try that out. But it'll mean we're farther from Ford, will have a long jaunt to bring him to the dropsite for Day Five."

"So be it," Travers said. "I'll make the trip myself to pick him up, if it means not having to camp in the shadows with these things."

"You really are spooked, aren't you?" Guessica asked.

"Hell, yes," Travers said. "Aren't you?"

"No," Guessica said.

Guessica wanted to ask Travers if he had felt any further increase in vertigo, himself, but doing so might open the field of inquiry as to whether she was experiencing any, and while he had commented on it earlier, when they had first run into the things, he hadn't mentioned it since. Guessica worried that maybe he wasn't being affected by it as strongly as she was, and would be reluctant to admit to that in front of him.

"You should be, too," Travers said.

"They're just things," Guessica said. "ALLIE will figure them out, she'll figure it all out."

"Yeah," Travers said.

"You don't sound convinced."

Travers didn't know what to think. Maybe ALLIE would sort it all out. Or maybe Ford's apocalyptic visions would come to pass. They simply did not have enough information to properly proceed. An empiricist, Travers believed that "wait and see" was the only rational response. Gather data, and then come to a conclusion.

The sun sank below the horizon, putting an official end to Day Three. Ford and Travers both watched it in silence.

"Could be Earth, if you just squinted a little," Travers said.

"It is Earth," Ford said. "Soon enough, it will be."

Ford condescended to grab some Nutrifill from his suit, slurped that up.

"Hungry, are we?" Travers asked. Ford held up a hand, like he didn't want to be interrupted while eating.

When he was done, he wiped his mouth.

"What's that?"

"I am surprised you'd bother eating," Travers said. "Surprised you haven't made a spear yet to snag some native fish."

Ford just smiled at him, walked back to the spires, to the center of the circle.

"It's balmy in here," Ford said. "They want me here. Inside the circle. The funny thing is, when I first saw these spires, I thought they looked weird. We all did. But now that I'm acclimated, get this: everything else looks weird to me, now. You look wrong. The shore looks wrong. The horizon. Everything looks wrong."

He touched the large spire behind him.

"This looks right," Ford said. "It makes sense. But that's just a measure of the derangement of my mind, because I know that they're not right, and I think they're trying to trap me. They're definitely trying to kill me."

Travers hovered outside the ring of spires. The air temperature *was* higher in the circle than outside it. This was very clear to him, as he took his readings.

"You claim these are weapons," Travers said.

"They are," Ford said. "Von Neumann obelisks. Highly advanced. Far beyond anything we could have created."

"Alright," Travers said. "So who launched them? And from where?"

"ALLIE will tell you that," Ford said. "Unless you stop her. She'll be able to calculate the position of this world seven billion years ago, will be able to map the trajectories based on the astronomy. She'll find the launch points. And then there'll be trouble. But I don't think these were launched from another planet."

It was dark, but the obelisks seemed to be glowing a little. It was hard to tell, as Travers was using infrared, since Ford had objected to him shining his spotlights on him.

"ALLIE will find them," Ford said. "The Source."

"Is that what they're called?"

Ford nodded.

"And you think they're still around?"

"Oh, they are still around," Ford said. "Most definitely."

"How can you know this?"

Ford stroked his chin, which was stubbly, now. He'd have a beard in another day.

"I know," Ford said. "I can see them."

"What do they look like?"

"Shadows, mostly," Ford said. "Grand shadows. Bulbous shapes. Eyes. It's hard to fully articulate, because I'm seeing them with my new eyes, and new geometry demands different perceptions. Words can't describe them. Not *our* words, anyway."

In the dark, the green-white of the infrared light, Travers thought Ford's eyes were black, and found he couldn't remember what color they normally were. The silence of the place hung like a blanket over them both.

"I'm going to try to sleep, Ford," Travers said. "If you try anything remotely weird, I'm going to pound you."

Ford laughed, and Travers walked as far as he could from the spires and Ford as he could get. He set his proximity alarms and sat down on the ground. If Ford got within five meters of him, the alarms would sound.

"Good Night, Guessica," Travers said.

"Good Night, Trav," she said. "I'm going to keep an eye on you."

"I've got my proximity alarms up," Travers said.

"I know, but since I'm speeding over here, I might as well make myself useful," she said.

"Alright, then. You do that," Travers said. "But you should definitely try to get some rest, yourself."

"Don't worry about me," Guessica said. "I'm fine. We've only got a couple more days to go; it's going to be alright."

"I hope so."

"Nothing to be afraid of," Guessica said.

5

TRAVERS'S CAMERAS WERE ACTIVE, and so Guessica could, through them, keep something of an eye on Ford. He got up at one point in the night, stood near Travers, but not near enough to set off his proximity alarms. He just stood there and watched Travers awhile, before walking off into the shadows again.

Guessica had positioned herself at the far end of Obelisk Island, thinking it wasn't a bad idea that Travers had, putting some distance between themselves and those things. She played back some of what Ford had said, and mulled over it in her amphetamine-amped condition, sipping on her Aquifier, eyeing the Conduit clock.

Less than 48 hours until the rendezvous.

Guessica had never wanted to get back to the Oasis more than on this mission. She had encountered a lot of adversity and travail in past assignments, but this mission was just off. She had never felt more adrift and alone. Losing the portion of the team that was Ford had certainly affected her. It wasn't supposed to happen. If Travers had been the one going nuts, she'd have accepted that, because, well, Travers was Travers. But not Ford. And not her.

That was what was really getting to her. She was feeling it. Three times since she'd obliterated the snowmen, she'd felt this odd disconnect between her hands and her head—there was this odd sensation of her head being miles away from her arms, like it was a weather balloon, floating freely, and her arms were light-years away.

It had been odd and exhilarating, in a way, as she fought to maintain control and composure, kept her biostat readings under control—she was not about to announce it so that the Medtechs could question her fitness to serve, for Paragon to sequester her in a holding tank. She kept it to herself, knowing that this was a violation of protocol, but to cede mission command to Travers would be a move she couldn't recover from. Payne would already have Ford's hide; she didn't want to add herself to the list of casualties.

But she was feeling it, most definitely. Maybe that was part of the reason she had jacked herself with so much stimulant; the hyper-alertness that accompanied the drug was perhaps just the thing she need to find her way back.

It wasn't fair. Why was she getting affected, when Travers seemed alright? She was stronger than he was, she was sure of it. Not that she wished any harm to befall him, of course, but it wasn't fair.

Guessica huddled at the very edge of Obelisk Island, ignoring the pings of her radar as it tracked the great unseen thing in the water that swam indolently beneath the thick ice. In the morning, she would fire radar into the heart of this world, see what was waiting below. She wished she could get to a larger landmass, but under the circumstances, in her situation, a beggar could not be a chooser. She would have to make do with Obelisk Island, and see what secrets it revealed to the radar.

It would be her Day Four project, something to occupy her.

There'd be enough time on Day Five to restrain Ford and fly back to the dropsite in time to reach the Conduit. She'd checked and re-checked the numbers—the fuel in their fliers, the ranges, the rest of it. They'd get home, and they could be safe again.

Never had a quieter place filled her with more unease. It was Ford's fault. The things he'd said had rattled around in their heads. She knew it was getting to Travers, too. Right or wrong, sane or insane, he had affected them—even infected them, in a way, with his words.

Wasn't a meme as contagious as anything else? Someone walking down the street shouting "We're Doomed!" could easily be brushed off as insane, but if you heard it every day, saw it every day, if the person was a shaggy stranger, that was one thing. But when it was Commander Ford Collins, with a long and distinguished service record, suddenly it had more weight behind it, it was more difficult to disregard.

That's what really angered her. If it had only been Travers, she could have compartmentalized it more readily.

Ford walked back in sight of Travers.

"I know what you're doing," he said. "I understand. I do. They see. They see you, Guessica."

To hear him speak her name, to see him gaze at her from the shadows, black-eyed and green-lit, it made her shiver.

Then she just told herself that he understood her as well as she thought she understood him. Of course he knew she'd be up worrying about this, keeping an eye on Travers. He knew. There was nothing supernatural in it. It was just their understanding of one another, borne of their years on Blue Team.

"You can stop this," Ford said. "Detonate your suit. This is our home, now."

She couldn't communicate with him, since she was only seeing this through Travers's own datafeed, and Travers was sleeping soundly. She could have awakened him, perhaps, but wanted at least one of them to get something close to a decent night's sleep.

"Detonate it, be done with it," Ford said. "But wait until ALLIE opens the Causeway. Just stroll in and do it. It'll buy the Earth a few months. Maybe they'll come back here. Maybe they won't. They'll be sifting through the wreckage for months to try to find out what happened, and years trying to figure it out. Nuke the Oasis."

Guessica squirmed in her suit, which felt terribly confining, Ford's ghostly face lurking on her HUD 3.

"If you don't, you'll let It in," Ford said. "You'll be taking It home with you. They won't be able to quarantine It. ALLIE won't even be able to see It."

She wanted to tell Ford to shut up, but she also wanted to listen, too.

"Everything that It touches, It will corrupt," Ford said. "You, me, Travers. The Oasis. ALLIE. Everything. It will spread. The conduits will spread it. Like spiritual plague, it will spread. We can inoculate the Earth. We can stop the spread, Guess. Right here, right now. It's 2.3 million light-years away. We destroy the Oasis, and maybe it'll be years until they return."

He just stood there, hovering, a shadow. A shade. A specter and a wraith, her commander, the ghost of the man she knew.

"We find worlds for garment manufacturers, create planetary landfills," Ford said. "Maybe we *should* be destroyed. Have you ever seen the worlds we've found for them? Once they're tamed? An entire planet devoted to nothing but shoes. This is progress? The educators on Nikedidas don't even pretend to teach their kids anything that isn't shoe- or garment-related. Do you ever think about that? Or on Midas? You think they're going to tell people that there's other things they could be doing instead of mining? No. We're finding new purgatories and hells for them to claim as their own. Do you realize the Naming Commission's naming a planet 'Fairway?' An entire world devoted to the ancient sport of golf? I'd seen the files on it last month. Golf? The reasoning is that by having a world dedicated to it, it frees up space on other planets for development, and creates a proper atmosphere of exclusivity to the sport. Another boutique world, served on a planetary platter by Paragon."

Guessica wanted to wake up Travers, just to be able to get a word in edgewise. The Terranauts had saved the Earth—by finding places for people to go, they had saved the planet and the human race from extinction. People went to the Colonies for new opportunities, a chance at new lives. Nobody on Terranova went there to be anything but a farmer; nobody on Nikedidas went there without an understanding of what it entailed. The same went for the sex workers of Eden, or the scholar-philosophers of Xenophon—each world had its requirements for its people.

If Ford was serious about Planet Fairway, so be it—a world of endless putting greens. People would probably flock there, or at least fans of the arcane sport would. There would be course designers, and groundskeepers, and caddies, and surely a hospitality industry to accommodate the visitors. It would be a huge success.

"And all strung together like pearls on a strand, thanks to the efforts of the Oasis," Ford said. "Sever that link, and the pearls fly free. Each colony forced to fend for itself, like *real* planets, instead of bound and subjected to the will of the ISA and Paragon and the Interstellar Commerce Commission. Each new pearl we put on the strand is just another slave world. That's the problem with colonies. A colony is never free; it is a wealth-generating organelle for the body politic that spawned it. The conduits keep the whole thing in place."

Everybody had their own opinions about the Colonies. For the shareholders of the companies that had colonized the worlds, it was a massive windfall on an order above and beyond the wildest dreams of the most avaricious of souls, spawned the first multitrillionaires.

It had certainly created an impetus for "personal planets"—moves by the hyper-wealthy to get a place in line with the ISA to find planets of their own on a level that made even the fabled, quasi-mythical Arcadia seem crowded by comparison.

Paragon had been more than happy to indulge this impulse, to devote some of the ISA's time to locating private worlds for their clients. Of course, the complicated nature of world-settling still required a government body to take care of much of the front-end work, much the way one depended on contractors to build one's dream home, and planetary infrastructural scale was so vast that private agencies were less than willing to reach into their pockets for this, depended on the Colonial Administration to sort this dirty work out.

Even small worlds required a lot of work to settle, but it had been a boom time for construction and engineering, which, in turn, drove the need for resource acquisition, which spurred ISA and Paragon to find ever more worlds to meet the demand for raw materials.

"This world is more than they bargained for," Ford said. "This place is virulent, and it is simply waiting for something new to infect. I was looking at the map of it, and the spires, the profligate destruction rained down from the Great Beyond, it made the planet look like a giant cell. Did you notice that? And these spires are its instruments of infection."

Guessica could not be sure that Ford was in favor of infecting the Earth, or of saving it. Maybe he was at war with whatever had afflicted him, although she couldn't be sure which side was which, or which side was winning.

She toggled Ford's comlink, on his empty suit.

"We're going to get you help, Ford," she said, pleased when his head turned at the sound coming from the comlink. He glanced back at Travers, smiled at her through Travers's camera's eyes.

"Nicely played, Guessica," Ford said. "Do you want to dance with me?"

He disappeared from view, then appeared on her HUD 2, wearing his bloody helmet.

"I knew you were awake," Ford said. "Thinking. Worrying."

"You're wrong about everything," Guessica said. "You're confused."

"No," Ford said. "I see everything, now. I see *them.*"

His face was shiny, sweaty. His eyes were dark, as he had not turned on all of his exosuit's functions, was just using the comlink.

"See how confining this is? How narrow one's vision is in these shells?" he asked. "No wonder you can't see. No wonder it took me so long to see."

"What do you want, Ford? To save the Earth or destroy it?"

"A little of both, I suppose," Ford said. "I'm not of the 'leave well enough alone' school of thinking. You ever hear the ancient myth of Icarus? The boy with the waxy wings, flying too close to the Sun, only to have his wings melt, and he falls into the sea? I hated that story. Because what did it say? It warned not to reach too high, to strive for too great a thing, or else you'll be burned."

Guessica didn't know about the myth; it hadn't been part of her education. Her family had worked hard to assimilate her into the larger Colonial cultural conglomerate, but their main goal was getting her into the Terranaut Program. As an extra daughter, it was as good a place for her as any.

"Point being?"

"I'm all for reaching and striving," Ford said. "I wouldn't have been a good Terranaut if I didn't have that urge to explore. But to what end? For what purpose? The first worlds, those first finds—those were our high points. Already, though, what's to be done? What is ISA doing? It's pimping planets to the highest bidder. That's what it's doing. We find them worlds to dish out. A thousand Planet Fairways, Arcadias, Edens—that's our future. Paragon would have that be our destiny and our legacy."

"It's commerce," Guessica said. "It's the nature of the whole enterprise. It funds it."

Ford looked at her like she was insane. The look in his eyes was unmistakable, some cocktail of contempt and sorrow.

"The conduits are instruments of control," Ford said. "They bind the worlds together in an unnatural symmetry. So what if Midas is ten light-years away? Or if Terranova is a hundred? Or Eden is 2,000? They're all one big happy family, all earning, all exporting, all trading. A half-dozen families run the entire enterprise. Do you realize that? Maybe two hundred people command the lives of over ten billion?"

The Earth was better because of the conduits; it simply was. The Earth was peaceful in the first time in its history; it was prosperous and actually clean again, thanks to the easing of the pressures it had faced. With only one billion people living on it, now, it was positively roomy. The country club atmosphere of it was reflective of its status. Why shouldn't the Earth have benefited from its savvy investments?

"This world will poison the well," Ford said. "This toxic place will bring a new variable to the equation. It will change things."

"For the better," Guessica said.

"It's hard to see how it could get much worse," Ford said. "But it can. This place where ghosts dance at dusk and dawn? I can see them. Ghosts everywhere. A battlefield. Long gone, a dead place, without even a memorial. They're all here, and they're looking for someplace to go. We're about to give them that. They'll come flooding right through the conduit, now that they know what we are, where we came from."

"Right," Guessica said.

"Don't believe me," Ford said, more a challenge than a question. Ford understood Guessica more than she could ever know him.

"I don't," Guessica said. "You're just sick, Ford."

"You'll do the right thing, Guess," Ford said, removing his helmet. "I know you will."

The view of the helmet rocked back and forth, as Ford had dropped the helmet and walked away.

Ford was kind of squaring the circle, mentally—he held that the Colonial Administration was corrupt, that the order created by the conduits was corrupt and undeserving of their support, and that the Colonies deserved to be free worlds, not dependent on Earth or conduit technology to exist.

Further, he believed that what was on QED-376 was so dangerous and toxic that, were it to reach Earth, it would infect the planet and ultimately destroy the world.

To remedy this, he advocated destroying the Oasis (and themselves), as a way of protecting the Earth from what this planet contained. And, in so doing, disrupt the means by which Paragon found new worlds for its clients to settle/conquer/colonize.

This from a man who had served with distinction for a decade in the Polygon, and another decade as Terranaut, hand-picked by Paragon's headhunters. A man who had never balked on any assignment, had successfully surveyed over a hundred worlds, who had always shown himself to be resolute and even serene in the face of alien adversity and outright danger.

To say Ford was a rock was an understatement; he was a mountain.

And to see him in this state hurt Guessica more than she could fully express. She was witnessing the fall of a great man, one of her heroes. She had joined the Terranaut Program to placate her parents, to be sure, but it was also because of Ford Collins and Wen Chao and Sandahl Foote, the Big Three. The three of them had been an inspiration to her. When she had been assigned to Blue Team, she had been beside herself with glee, had told her parents about it, and what it meant. They had been thrilled for her, and she'd been thrilled, herself.

So, to see Ford crumbling like this distressed her. I was simply outside of her realm of experience, and, she admitted, beyond her comprehension. She wanted to crawl into Ford's mind and understand what had broken him. She wanted to avenge him.

She wished she could rub her forehead, because it was a lot to think about, and she wasn't sure if she was thinking clearly or not. Guessica felt herself stifling a yawn, grateful that the stimulant edge was beginning to blunt.

If he already thought the Earth was corrupt, why would he worry about it becoming further corrupted by the intrusion of whatever it was that QED-376 possessed?

Was he fearful of ALLIE discovering how to operate the strange and alien weapons? Was there a fear of the use of these weapons as instruments of control on the Colonies?

Or was it something else?

She was dizzy.

> "Personal log entry: I fear that I'm becoming infected by whatever got Ford. I can't trace the pathology of it, can't guess the nature of it, but I worry that it's affecting me, too. I'm making this entry in the hope that any ISA personnel who may or may not come across this find it, in the event that I'm no longer coherent or even living. The spires have some ability to affect the perception of human minds. I cannot be sure precisely how, whether it's some kind of electromagnetic phenomenon, or whether it's something new and unfamiliar to us—but it appears to not require physical

contact—or it's a physical contact occurring in wavelengths our scanners are unable to measure at the moment. All I know is that I am definitely affected by it. Symptoms include loss of balance and bouts of vertigo, loss of spatial reasoning, mania, even hallucinations. I'm still collating right now, despite my infection. I can't speak to the condition of Travers. I may talk with him in the morning, get a sense of his situation. All I know is that I am infected as surely as Ford is. I recommend quarantine not only of Blue Team personnel, but of QED-376 until such time as we can determine the cause and nature of this deep-space psychosis, or whatever it is. Ford has not, as yet, become violent, although he has manifested grand paranoid visions, conspiratorial thinking, and at least latent threats of extreme violence. I don't know if this is a personal manifestation of his affliction, or whether it's a larger symptom of the malady. I fear that by the time I know for certain, I may be too far gone to be able to do anything about it, or offer any kind of objective analysis."

She paused, taking a sip of Aquifier.

"I recommend a full Medtech team investigate each of us, and the samples of the spires that I gathered. Look for anything and everything you can—brain swelling, unusual radiations, anything. Something is happening to us out here, and I cannot account for it. Guessica Rao, Geologist First Class, Blue Team."

She turned off the recording device with a flick of her tongue, and gazed at the mission clocks, watching them tick off time, marking tiny pieces of space-time in minute phosphorescence.

It was an old trick she'd learned long ago: when you couldn't sleep, just watch the clocks.

DAY FOUR

1

TRAVERS DREAMED THAT HE WAS WALKING at the bottom of a sunless sea. His suit was somehow holding up, though the warning gauges were sounding. In the shadows, just out of reach, he saw It watching him, this great, monstrous thing, with unblinking eyes.

He bolted up to find his proximity alarms going off, and Ford standing there, standing on him, on the shell of his suit.

"Wake up, Trav," Ford said. "You're missing the sunrise."

Travers got to his feet, knocking Ford off of him with a whine of servos. Ford stepped deftly away, grinning at him.

The sun was up, but they were surrounded by fog. A thick blanket of it that turned everything to threatening shadow.

"Day Four," Ford said. His beard was in full swing, now. It was largely black with flecks of white in it. For that matter, Travers's own beard was in evidence, although ISA had screened applicants, didn't want anybody too hirsute in the exosuits, as it was found that it could interfere with an applicant's ability to work the helmet controls.

"Guessica," Travers said. "Are you up?"

"Yes," she said. "I think I discovered something."

"What?"

"The spires are older than the planet," she said. "They're around 7 billion years old, but the world itself is only about 5.7 billion years old."

Travers didn't know what to make of it, exactly.

"That's weird," he said.

"Yes, it is," Guessica said. She looked uneasy on the HUD 3. "Very weird. It means whoever launched those things had them for nearly 2 billion years before they decided to throw them at this world."

Travers tried to understand how or why someone would do something like that, and came up blank. He didn't know, and couldn't know. It was altogether alien and unfamiliar.

The Source, whatever that was, had not evolved beyond their warlike and/or colonial natures in billions of years. Or maybe they had refined them. Maybe they had reached some kind of evolutionary perfection, in their eyes. It would be something he'd ask Ford.

"You okay?" Travers asked.

"Fine," she said.

"So, the Source for them is someplace older, still," Travers said.

"Much older," Guessica said.

"Do you think they were weapons?" Travers asked. "Like what Ford said?"

"I don't know," Guessica said. "All I do know is that they aren't native to this world, and appear to have impaled themselves here from space in a planetwide bombardment."

The implication of it made Travers reel a bit. There was profanity in the act—it wasn't so much the invasion of this world, as the desecration of it.

He tried to imagine the Source, this alien entity, crossing paths with this world, and, for some reason, finding it wanting. Deserving of destruction, raining down these strange spires, puncturing the land, decimating whatever had been here, using unfathomable energies.

What had QED-376 done to deserve this? And who was responsible? In a weird way, he saw the Source as the race, themselves—it seemed right, this shadowy evil that had attacked this world for reasons unknown. The assignment of evil to the Source was purely subjective on Travers's part; he couldn't possibly know. Maybe the denizens of this world had deserved it; but something about the nature of the spires themselves made him doubt this.

It was the chronology of the weaponry that bothered Travers the most. Was it a neighboring planet? That didn't make sense—the age of the spires pointed to something beyond this system, because the worlds would all be roughly the same age, if they were formed by the same solar cycle.

So, was it a roving spacecraft, or a fleet of them? Something traveling from world to world, bearing an ancient arsenal they were intent on using? Two billion years was a long time to carry a grudge, to bear a payload to a target. But the Source had done just that, when they had finally crossed paths with QED-376.

Travers triggered the topographical map of QED-376 and gazed at the forest of spires that the surveyor had seen. Such profligacy. What had they seen on this placid planet that had so outraged them that they would do this?

Or were the spires themselves a kind of colonist for the world? In the thick fog, they hulked above him in titanic mystery.

"It's bizarre," Travers said.

"To say the least," Guessica said.

Ford went to the water and did his water-sun ritual with it—cupping it in his hands and pouring it on himself, drinking the water. He was an apparition in the fog, going through his morning motions, like the way Chao did Tai Chi in the garden at the Oasis, leading a team of personnel, all of them moving to one grand, cosmic rhythm, a celestial dance.

"Are you bringing the tape?" Travers asked.

"Tomorrow, first thing," Guessica said.

"I'm not going to have to stay here another day with him, am I?" Travers asked.

"No," Guessica said. "You can come back here, if you want."

"Good," Travers said. "Because he's weirding me out."

"How's your balance been?" Guessica asked.

"Alright, overall," Travers said. He'd had some dizzy spells, but nothing incapacitating. He wondered for a moment whether it might impact his ability to fly. That was something that hadn't occurred to him. He'd hate to crash into the water. That'd be a nightmare.

"Overall?"

"A little dizzy," Travers said. "We're not going to make it, are we?"

"Don't think like that," Guessica said. "Of course we should."

Her choice of "should" was a slip, and Travers caught it.

"That doesn't fill me with confidence, Guess," he said.

"Will," Guessica said. "Of course we *will*."

"It's foggy over here," Travers said. "Thick stuff."

Ford emerged from the water and walked over to Travers. Again, despite Ford being outside of his suit, his presence disquieted Travers.

Never mind that Travers could squash him if he wanted to; the asymmetry between the two of them was unnerving. Ford gazed into Travers's eyes, while swirls and eddies of fog passed between them.

"Won't be long, now," Ford said. "You'll see it, soon enough. The whole miserable enterprise, clear as a foggy day."

Travers decided he would abandon Ford as soon as the fog lifted. He didn't want to go flying up right now without a clear view. Instrumentation could get him to Obelisk Island, but Travers had an aversion to flying by instrumentation only. It might have seemed overcautious, but the duty rosters were replete with Terranaut fatalities and injuries from less cautious souls.

"Were you able to get radar soundings of the core?"

"Yes," Guessica said. "The core is active, despite the apparent absence of plate tectonics on the surface. Of course, we're only getting a small sample, here. There may be active volcanic regions elsewhere. We need a full survey team to assess it; I can do a lot, but it's still only very preliminary."

"I want to go home," Travers said. "Ford be damned. Everything be damned. I'm going to drop out of the Program as soon as I get back. I'm cashing out."

"Cashing in, more like," Guessica said. "We're going to be famous… and infamous. Right up there with Orange Team."

Travers hoped that would be so. He was comfortable with that, could relate to it. Let him go anywhere but here. He never wanted to see this place again. But the prospect of reaching home gave him some hope.

"Are you staying in the Program?"

"Yes," Guessica said. "I don't think I could go back to normal life, Trav. My family needs me to excel here and everywhere. And I cannot possibly pass on that Gold Team initiative, assuming it's legitimate."

It was weird to think of that, like Ford could be incarcerated, at the very least. Guessica would stay with the Program. Travers would work the media circuit, likely with a stack of nondisclosure agreements in hand, settle comfortably in retirement somewhere, his life and sanity intact, if all went as he'd planned.

Talking of the future cheered them both up. It was like a parting of the clouds, a momentary respite. Meantime, Ford stalked through the fog, talking all the while.

"You're running out of time, Trav," Ford said. "We all are. Everything is. We should blow this place to bits. It's a tombstone. A crypt. Can't you see, yet? The ghosts? They're absolutely everywhere. They hate us. They hate you."

Travers scanned around them, full-spectrum, hoping for something, an indication of what it was that Ford thought he was seeing. But he was a climate scientist, not a paranormal researcher. And there was nothing to see.

"You're imagining it, Ford," Travers said. "Your bruised brain is playing tricks on you."

"Like hell," Ford said. "Absolutely everywhere. They're watching us. I want to tell them that we didn't send the spires. It wasn't us. It might as well have been, though. We'll come and plow the ground under, sow it with salt. Nothing will grow here."

"Poor Ford," Guessica said, although from the look on her face, she was as worried about herself. "What a way to end a career. From Program poster boy to bureaucratic basket case. They're going to have to cover for this, you know? Especially once word gets out about what we found here. Newsfeed will want it, they'll all be wanting to interview Ford. Not you and me—it'll be Ford, it's always Ford. And ISA is not going to be able to serve him up."

"They'll have ALLIE simulate him," Travers said. "There are enough samples of him that they'll just craft a hologram for him and have that do the talking, instead. Ford's face, ALLIE's words, Paragon's script."

"Maybe they'll let you or me talk," Guessica said. "Although I doubt it. I'm just The Scientist Chick and you're the Whey-Faced Worrier."

"Oh, thank you very much," Travers said.

"Nothing personal," Guessica said. "It's just how they'll play it, or how they'll want to. They'll want Commander Ford Collins front and center on this."

Ford had disappeared in the fog. Using the pixelated scan, Travers saw that he had retired to within the circle of spires.

"Again, let Mediation worry about it," Travers said. "Not our problem, out of our pay scale."

"Yeah," Guessica said. "You're right."

Guessica wished she were truly as confident as she sounded. But, in truth, she was holding on by her fingernails. The vertigo was only getting worse, the contamination growing. She found herself using her yoga to control her breathing, to provide her with a framework to maintain her hold on reality. The problem was that inside the suit, it was just too difficult to move around. The exosuits were as comfortable and advanced as ISA made them, but they were still prisons.

She could do more than just yoga breathing outside of it, in the open air. Cold air, yes, but the obelisks were now radiating heat, here, just like the ones on Spire Island; they would keep her warm. Even now, the snow around them had melted away. It was a dazzling change from the inert spikes of lifeless stone they had been when they had first come here.

Now the things were glowing greenly, a beautiful shade of green that called to mind grassy knolls. It made her think of home. Even as the snow fell, the spires were warm and radiant. She knew if she just went within the circle of them, she would find comfort and peace. She could take off her suit and laugh at the alien elements, could shrug them off.

Breathe, she told herself.

Breathe.

Breathe.

Breathe.

2

TRAVERS WALKED CAREFULLY THROUGH THE FOG, not wanting to run into any-thing, not wanting to stumble. He was getting dizzy, too. He could tell that Guessica, for all of her breezy bravado, was seriously affected, perhaps worse than he was.

"Ford?" he asked. "Ford?"

"What is it, Trav?" Ford asked. He had emerged from the fog behind him. He had taken a strip of cloth from his tunic and turned it into a shiny bandana that he had secured to his head with the Paragon head-band they were provided. He had pried loose a tube from his suit and held it like a swagger stick.

"What the fuck are you doing?"

"Waiting," Ford said. "We're all waiting, aren't we? You, me, them, everybody. It won't be long, now. I don't know how long it was, how long they waited, but now that we're here, they have something to fo-cus on. You think maybe Franzen's team found something like this? I was thinking about that."

"We can't know," Travers said. "Nobody knew."

"Can you imagine that? Yellow Team goes belly up. Now us. Chao is going to be ecstatic," Ford said. "But this place is going to gobble her right up. Can you imagine her here? All of these ghosts will devour her."

"Ghosts don't eat," Travers said. "Ghosts don't exist."

"Ghosts might not eat, but they *will* take a bite out of you," Ford said. "They're here. Quantum universes, Travers. An infinite number of planes slicing through each point—infinite perspectives and possibilities. Say we're A, and the ghosts are G—we're both there, but we've got B, C, D, E and F between us. Universes. Who's real? Who's the phantasm? The supernatural isn't super if you can account for it. They're all around us. They're not happy. It's funny, really. The spires are watching, and the ghosts are watching. Two sides in a confrontation, waiting for us to choose sides."

"You already chose your side, didn't you, Ford? I mean, you're with the spires, right?"

Ford considered this. In the fog, he weighed it, looking this way and that, seeing nothing. "That's a good question, Trav. The spires let me see, but in so doing, they let me understand their purpose. And the one constant that is apparent to me is that they are evil. And yet, out here, what is evil? We're so far away from everything. The most grandiose of laws of the Colonial Administration are less than meaningless at this many million light-years, Trav. It has no jurisdiction here, in Andromeda Galaxy. Only the conduits make them matter. They are the enforcement mechanism, the delivery system for our own kind of corruption."

It bothered Travers to even factor the spires into his thinking, as if they were sentient, had a part to play. Maybe it was a sign of his wavering sanity, what was plaguing all of them. Just as soon as the fog lifted, he would leave Ford behind on Spire Island, he would reconnoiter with Guessica, and they would incapacitate Ford, and then bring him back home, along with all of the data they had accumulated. Mission fucking accomplished.

"In Conduits We Trust," Ford said. "Wormholed worlds, like a basket of riddled, rotten apples from the Garden of Eden, itself."

At the mention of Eden, he snickered. "You never saw that place. A gorgeous world. Lush, forgiving, fertile. Prettier than Terranova, just brimming with life. Verdant. Marvelous. Sandahl was Team Leader for that one, I was just there as support on Missions 2 through 6, because she'd done the initial survey work. Never seen anything more beautiful than Eden. You just knew that the Naming Commission was going to be all over that one. We all knew where it was going. They turned it into a brothel."

Travers had never been to Eden, but he knew its reputation, had seen the advertisements for it, the leering women, perfectly assembled, pneumatic breasts and legs that went on for light-years.

"Enter a World of Sin" and "Paradise: Found"—those were the marketing terms for Eden.

"I'm not a moralist," Ford said. "But how the developers saw Eden and thought they could put casinos and brothels there is beyond me. It was so beautiful. Alien, to be sure, but so gorgeous. A resort planet. A pleasure planet. And when the xenobotanists found out what a pharmacological goldmine that place was, lordy, it went through the roof. Pharmacom was on that immediately. They have drugs that take you places you didn't even know you wanted to go."

"I've never been to Eden," Travers said.

"They always talk about how tastefully they've planetscaped it," Ford said. "Like a perfectly sculpted body under a surgeon's hypersonic knife. The transition from virgin to whore—oh, what a pretty whore, but a whore, just the same. Do you understand that? Can you? That is Eden. It took just a few years to do it. The Rape of Eden."

Travers had nothing to add to it. He'd never thought about it, nor assumed that Ford worried much about the fate of the worlds they surveyed. But then, this trip had revealed a lot about Ford that Travers hadn't known, or even suspected.

Ford and Travers faced each other in the fog—madman and cyborg—that's really what it was, what he was, Travers admitted only to himself.

"Tell me why they smote this world," Travers said. "Tell me about the Source."

"Why do you want to know? Why do you even care?"

"I want to know what you know," Travers said. "I want to know what you see. I want to know who *they* were."

All around them, the tendrils swirled and grasped for them.

"A fleet," Ford said. "Old beyond reckoning."

"That's the Source?" Travers asked. Ford shrugged.

"Colonizers," Ford said. "Like us. And conquerors. Like us."

"Where are they?"

"Still here," Ford said. "Ghosts, I told you. Spires and spirits, victors and vanquished, braided together."

Travers didn't want to wait for the fog to lift; he wanted to leave Ford right now. He could risk an instrumentation-only flight.

Behind Ford, the spires appeared to glow. No, they *were* glowing, Travers was sure by now. The fucking things were glowing.

"Do you ever think about how limiting 'life as we know it' really is, Trav?" Ford asked. "In all the multiverse, the vastness of space, which we know more than anyone, we few who've walked it—can we really hope for life as we know it? Can we accept life as we *don't* know it? As we don't understand it? It is like taking a one million kilometer field and marking off one millimeter of it, and saying that that millimeter is life as we know it. Sample size, my friend. Sample fucking size. You're the scientist—sample size affects outcomes. Selection bias."

"I understand that, Ford, but what are you talking about?"

"The ghosts," Ford said. "They're all here. This entire planet is stuffed with them, lousy with them. You're almost seeing them, I can tell. You're being bent as sure as I was. You know how it is—something gets bent, you can't ever get the shape right again. You ever try to make something right, once it's bent out of shape?"

Ford walked over to his abandoned exosuit, reached a panel on its back, at the side of the great backpack, which contained the power pack, among other things. He pressed a switch, one of the patented Paragon three-finger security switches, and a little door came out.

"Ford, don't do anything stupid," Travers said.

Ford glanced at Travers, looking him up and down a moment, as if assessing a challenge. He dug out the survival pack, a small box that every exosuit was equipped with, in case all other systems had failed.

He sat down and opened his with a sigh.

"These always made me laugh," Ford said. "These little kits. Like these'll save us."

Ford pulled out a survival knife, a diamond-shaped blade with a saw-edged length on either side of it, as well as a knobby handle.

"Knife, saw, and hammer," Ford said. "All of civilization, in the palm of my scabby hands."

Ford ripped some more fabric from his tunic and used it to lash the knife to the tube he had been carrying, crosswise, perpendicular to the tube. Ford tied it and bound it tightly to the tube. He tested it, once secured, with a few test cuts, this way and that. Then he tore some more of his tunic off and wrapped it around the handle of the thing.

"What are you doing, Ford? Going spear-fishing?" Travers asked.

"This is a warhammer, Travers," Ford said. "Not a spear."

"Are you going to war, Ford?" Travers asked.

"We've been at war with this place the moment we landed—or this place has been at war with us, anyway," Ford said. "We just didn't see it."

Ford dug out a tightly-packed metallic foil poncho, unpacked and carefully unfolded it, put it on.

"Fog leaches the life from you," Ford said. "You ever notice that? Eats sound and heat. Of course you'd know that, right, Weatherman?"

Travers watched Ford warily, unsure what he had in mind with his makeshift weapon. He thought about grabbing it and hurling it into the water.

"Leverage," Ford said, gesturing to the length of metal tubing, which was a high-tensile strength alloy custom-made by Paragon. In fact, the name was laser-etched on the side of it. "What was it that dead guy said? 'Give me a large enough lever, and I can move the world?'"

"What are you planning to move?" Travers asked.

"You," Ford said.

3

GUESSICA WAS ON HER HANDS AND KNEES. She's propped herself onto her knees, and pitched forward, holding herself up by one hand. The mission clock showed that they had about 23.7 hours left until ALLIE opened the conduit.

They were getting down to the final hours of the mission. She had done all of her fieldwork, gathered every scrap of data she could about the planet's geology, as well as about the spires. The subsequent mission teams would have an easier time of it, thanks to her efforts, and the work of Travers. Maybe even when they figured out what had happened to Ford, and to Guessica, herself, that would help them, too. She didn't want to let anybody down, least of all, ISA.

She had cut off the feed with Travers for a special project she was undertaking. She didn't want him to see her in this condition.

The vertigo had settled into her skull, nestled itself right in there, and was showing no signs of abating. She knew she was lying flat on her back on Obelisk Island, but felt like she was falling almost constantly. It had taken an act of willpower not to gasp and cry out, but she did not want there to be recorded information about her losing herself in the suit. She had made her personal log, but she wasn't about to scream and wail and make a spectacle of herself.

But she kept tumbling and falling, and it was getting harder to stand. With the augmentation of the exosuits, she could easily catapult herself across the island and into the water. Any number of adjustments could be made.

She had one last test to perform. She had cut off auxiliary systems to make it possible, to charge up her lasers after her snowman massacre. She intended to take a sample back to spite Ford, to spite the spires, to spite everyone. She would bring it in and let ALLIE digest it and discover its secrets, if any.

The green light indicated that the 75-kilowatt laser was fully charged. What she had in mind required precise work, and while it might have given xenothropologists fits, she was going to do it, anyway. A sample was a sample, and she wanted to deliver more than simple molecular scrapings. She wanted to give them something to cheer about.

She couldn't rely on her arm being steady enough to run the auto-targeting, so she just propped up her arm while the ground spun, and she took aim. If what she intended came about, it wouldn't require much finesse.

Guessica pointed the laser at the nearest spire and fired it, the red beam lancing through the spire in a diagonal slash. It went right through the stone, and the thing fell like a tree in a virgin forest, only the thing fell toward Guessica.

She lurched out of the way, the thing smashing to the ground, narrowly missing her leg as she fell. They faced one another, the fallen obelisk and the Terranaut.

Guessica crawled over the thing, pleased that her laser had managed to cut the material. She went to the stump and examined it. The contact point with the laser was boiled and bubbly, looking like melted wax. She fished out some tongs and grabbed a quick-cooling blob of it, putting it in a sample container, along with the tongs. She was finding it increasingly hard to see clearly; everything was distorted to her eyes.

Gazing at the severed spire, it was clear that they were solid, not hollow, and made of the same green-black stone.

She managed to find her footing and heft the spire, the servos of the exosuit straining to bear the load, but ultimately succeeding.

> "Personal log: The spire appears to weigh about 3.75 metric tons, if the gauges on my suit are accurate. It's solid stone, if this material is, in fact, even stone. The laser cut right through it, to no ill effects that I can determine. We'll see what ISA can uncover. I'm going to walk to the dropsite with this, starting now. I can't fly out there carrying this load."

She toggled the comlink with a sloppy slap of her tongue. "Travers, I'm going to need you to bring back the camp equipment. I'm leaving it. I'm heading to the dropsite."

Travers appeared on her HUD 3.

"I thought we were supposed to stay in touch," he said.

"You were supposed to stay in touch with me," Guessica said. "I'm Team Leader; I reserve the right to tune out as needed."

"Why are you leaving me the gear to haul?"

"I am bringing a spire back to the dropsite," Guessica said. Might as well be forthright, see how he takes it.

"Is that a good idea?"

"It's an idea," Guessica said.

"I think Ford is going to try to stab me," Travers said. "I don't know why, exactly, but I'm definitely getting that kind of stabby feeling, watching him work, here."

And then talking to Ford: "What are you planning to move?"

"Get out of there, Trav," Guessica said. "Come back to this site."

"Yeah," Travers said. "I just might. Oh, shit—"

The comlink cut off, and Guessica couldn't reestablish a link.

"Shit," she said.

Then she tried to take a step forward, but staggered to one side. The horizon was at about a twenty-degree angle to her eyes.

"Computer," she said. "Plot course for dropsite marker. Set suit to autopilot for dropsite marker."

The on-board computer acknowledged this, and Guessica began running for the horizon, across the frozen plain, carrying the spire, which looked more radiant than before.

> "Personal log: I thought perhaps physical integrity was vital for the preservation of power of these objects, but this one is still radiating heat and emitting light, despite having severed it from its base. I can't account for this, but it is definitely apparent."

Now that the suit was doing the navigating for her, it freed her mind up to contemplate what she was carrying, and to ponder what had happened to Travers.

"Trav, are you there? Trav, come in?"

There was no answer.

Maybe Ford had killed him.

"Trav, if you can hear me, answer me," Guessica said.

She held tight to the obelisk as her suit ran, commanded the suit to hold that armature posture, because, in her vertiginous state, she could not be certain that she could continue to carry it.

> "Personal log: Team Leader Ford Collins may have killed Team Member Travers. I've lost contact with Travers and can't reestablish contact. If I'm able to get this obelisk dropped off at the dropsite without incident, I'm going to head directly to Spire Island to assess the situation."

At the edges of her vision were shapes and colors, hovering above the ground. Alien apparitions, only somewhat visible to her eyes, but radiant in the way that the radiance of the obelisk was, an almost greenish-white hue. The shapes were first at the corners of her eyes, then were perhaps somewhat more apparent to her, although Guessica found it hard to focus, let alone concentrate on the things.

"Who are you?" she called out, using the loudspeakers, although she was certain her own words would be incomprehensible to the phantasms.

All the same, she did it.

> "Personal log: I think I'm hallucinating. I am seeing apparitions all around me, watching me. They are wholly alien, and difficulties with my vision are preventing a clear view of them, but there are black eyes, three black eyes, rendered in a triangular position on a bulbous head, and they seem to be shrouded in some kind of webbing that flows from them like a net wrapped in glistening beads that hang from their bodies. I know it seems bizarre, but I'm merely reporting what I'm seeing."

She gazed at her scopes, and, of course, there was no sign of the things.

"Computer, give me a full EM scan," she said, and the computer obliged. Guessica didn't trust her tongue to be able to find the switch.

The HUD 2 flashed with color and light as the suit combed the air around them for unseen energies.

> "Personal log: I'm doing a full-range scan, and I'm not seeing anything with it. But when I look out of my glasstic visor, I'm seeing them. I hope the cameras are picking these up."

Guessica checked her camera feed on HUD 1 and, indeed, the cameras did appear to be picking up the images.

> "It looks like the cameras are seeing them. But maybe that's just my hallucination continuing. Whatever they are, they are entirely unlike ourselves. I almost think they are aquatic by their structure, although I'm in no position to scientifically judge this."

The autopilot actually took her through several of them, and the things seemed to pass right through her, their radiance passing from without to within, imparting a sense of something as they did, glimpses of something long ago, ages past, in sudden glancing blows as the shock of the phantasms struck her again and again, like jolts of cold water run through with low-voltage electrical shocks.

In the sky, the spires fell like rain, brightly-lit, almost incendiary to her eyes, that same green-white, only far brighter. And not her own eyes at all, but the eyes of these revenants—that's how she saw them. The Revenants.

She saw them strike this world with great force, ancient explosions, felt the concussive waves as they came, and something else, another wave, something far beyond anything on Earth, another wave of an indescribable energy.

But all too quickly, the images faded as the Revenants passed through her. It was like having a seizure, Guessica thought, these fleeting flashes of insight as they passed through her.

She almost felt like she had a third eye in the center of her own forehead, actually checked herself on her internal monitor to see if she did.

The afterimages of apocalypse hung heavy on the backs of her retinas, the thundering cascade of spires piercing the ground of this world, the coruscating waves of energy laying waste to all that was beneath the Source.

Ford had named them, and the name stuck in Guessica's brain: the Source.

Invisible to the Revenants, beyond the reach of their planetary defenses, these shadows beyond the clouds that rained luminescent death down on them. She could see the sky shining with them, these spears—not spires at all, but spears—of light laying waste to it all. So many of them, until the world bristled with them like a monstrous urchin, and the things ate the Revenants, and something else, something she could not clearly see, for the images were evanescent, dreamlike, but something else on this bristling battlefield of a world.

"I see," Guessica said, gasping. "I see."

4

FORD STABBED AT TRAVERS WITH HIS MAKESHIFT WARHAMMER, catching Travers in his glasstic visor. The force of the thrust actually scored the protective material. He hit him with the butt end of the weapon, the flat hammer end. The spang of metal on the glasstic actually jolted Travers's HUD displays, cracked the visor. Ford reversed the weapon in a quick turn of his hand, climbed onto Travers's suit, even as Travers tried to grab him, and struck again, harder, the knife blade puncturing Travers's visor, the blade mere millimeters from his face. Ford grunted, prying the thing free with his other hand.

Travers repelled him with a sweep of his hand, the augmented strength sending Ford flying off into the fog.

"What the fuck, Ford?" Travers said, watching the cracks spread across his visor as the glasstic shattered, as his HUD displays fractured and flickered away. The image of Guessica on HUD 3 looked particularly haunting, as the cracks shot right up her face as she looked on nervously, and then vanished.

"Just trying to pry you out of that can you're wearing. Come out of there."

The alien air mingled with his own air supply, the wet scent of unfamiliar fog. Travers staggered and pried open his shattered helmet.

"You crazy son of a bitch," Travers said. "You fucking bastard."

He couldn't believe he'd done this. Without his helmet visor, the exosuit was blind. Travers toggled the emergency releases and blasted off the helmet.

With the helmet disengaged, the suit would go into prep mode, as Ford had no doubt intended.

Travers popped the releases and slipped out of the exosuit, setting foot on the alien soil with his own bare feet. The emotion of the moment, his rage at Ford, his terror at his situation, the alien-yet-familiar feel of the place on his feet, the vertigo—it left Travers reeling.

He fell to the ground and Ford emerged from the shadows, tousled Travers's hair.

"You're free, Brother," Ford said. "Just like me."

Then he walked back into the fog, a shadow among shadows.

Travers couldn't believe how easily Ford had sabotaged his suit. But then the man was a longstanding Terranaut veteran, a soldier, too, so he would know the ins and outs of the exosuits. Travers was actually gasping on the ground, like a fish out of water, in a kind of psychological reaction to breathing the alien air, which wasn't so unlike the air of home, except for the knowledge that it wasn't the air of home, was the air of QED-376.

"You know, I thought of a name for this place," Ford said, wiping blood from his lips from where Travers had struck him.

Travers couldn't answer, was still getting used to the relatively thin alien air, and the fact that he was breathing it, that goddamned Ford had contaminated him, doomed him to perhaps the rest of his life in Quarantine. Travers wanted to vomit.

"Tartarus," Ford said. "I'm calling this world 'Tartarus' from now on. Fuck ALLIE's assignations. Fuck QED. It's Tartarus or bust, Baby."

Travers threw up. He knew it was just a stress reaction, but he did it, just the same, the nutritionally complete Nutrifill and Aquifier colorlessly splashing the rocks.

Ford snickered from the foggy shadows.

"First man puking in the Andromeda Galaxy," Ford said. "More history in the making, Trav. Congratulations."

Travers got to his feet, swaying, wiping his mouth. The scent of the world was like wood smoke—there was an ashy sweetness to it, a desolate richness to it, despite the thinness of the air.

"You crazy motherfucker!" Travers said, stomping after Ford, who just watched him approach with growing amusement.

"I'm liberating you, Trav," Ford said. "I've just set you free."

Travers took a swing at Ford, who just dodged him with a catlike spring to his feet, which caused Travers to lose his footing and fall into the sand.

"I'm giving you a fighting chance, anyway," Ford said. "You think I want to kill you? You're my brother."

Ford tossed aside the warhammer, out of reach of either of them. As he did so, Travers lunged at him again, catching him around his thighs in a half-assed tackle that sent them both to the ground.

"You just doomed me," Travers said. "Paragon is going to lock us *both* away, now."

He swung at Ford, who just shoved him off of him. Older than Travers, he was stronger, and well-trained in combat.

"Trav," Ford said. "I'm giving you the only way out we've got, here. We bring those fucking things back, and it's the end of everything."

"But you can't know that," Travers yelled, chest heaving. The thinner air precluded much in the way of robust movement, let alone hand-to-hand combat.

"You'll see when you see," Ford said. "You'll understand."

Overhead, the sun shone, but where they were, it was thick with fog. The obelisks loomed like hulking, misshapen giants. Fomorians, waiting to lay claim to them.

"Whose side are you on, Ford?" Travers said.

"Ours," Ford said. "You have no idea."

Travers watched him warily, perched himself on his haunches, breathed the alien air, wondered if it was all in his head. Oxygen was oxygen. What did it matter that this world was millions of light-years removed from Earth? And yet, it still filled him with fear.

"You fucking maniac," Travers said. "You couldn't go nuts with Chao; no, it has to be here, with me."

The spires glowed with a sepulchral light, made more so by the fog.

"They're feeding on us," Ford said. "Tasting us."

"And you want to stay here," Travers said. "With them."

Ford nodded, picking up his warhammer again, drawing glyphs into the sand while the waves crashed beyond them.

"Yes," Ford said. "Oh, I want to leave this little island behind, you were right about that. I want to see these jungles on the mainland and see just what's down there. Do you know what a proving ground is?"

"No," Travers said.

"It's a place where the Polygon tests its ordnance," Ford said. "It's an off-limits area where they fire weapons, where they test them. Proving grounds are used for training and for testing. As a result of this, there is lots of unexploded ordnance out there in proving grounds, with the result being that these places become wildlife sanctuaries—a wolf doesn't care one bit if there are landmines or high-explosive shells wedged in a hillside. Because of this, they become wildernesses, places where people can't go, or won't go—sure, a few professionals, some soldiers will go there, but they're dangerous places."

Travers could see where he was going with this. "And you see this place like that."

"It wasn't a proving ground," Ford said. "It was a battlefield. But those things make this place unfit for colonization—so this place will always be a wilderness. Only I—we—have an advantage: we recognize the danger these things pose. We may not understand it, but we recognize it. And because of this, we can survive this place."

"We don't know if there's food here, Ford," Travers said. "We're talking about a habitat that evolved completely independent of us. Everything here could be poisonous."

Ford shook his head. "I'm willing to take that chance, rather than risking everything by going back home and killing everyone. These things are alive, and they are watching us. And I'll tell you something I suspect—they draw strength from us."

Travers gazed at the faintly-glowing stones in the fog, walked over to one of them, held out his hand, and touched it. He had wanted to do so earlier, when they'd first seen them—it had been an honest compulsion. But he felt something different in the moment, facing them like this, without anything but his own skin to protect him.

The glyphs were glowing faintly, and they were emitting warmth.

"We are being irradiated," Travers said. "I'll bet you anything that they are irradiating us."

"Tenderizing us," Ford said. "But you can touch them."

The stone felt warm, the stone itself, almost greasy to the touch. Travers felt his fingers traveling on their own against the glyphs. One of the drawbacks of the exosuits was an absence of tactile sensation, so, almost despite himself, Travers found himself probing the surface of the spire with his fingertips.

Ford looked on, watching.

"What kind of weapons are these?" Travers asked.

"Von Neumann, like I said before. Look at your fingertips," Ford said.

Travers drew back his hand, dismayed to see his fingers had smears of blood on them. Painless. He didn't even feel the rupturing of his flesh. He stepped back with a squawk, while Ford laughed.

"Isn't that something?" Ford asked.

Travers studied his fingers. There was no sign of a cut. The blood had simply leached through the flesh.

Ford held up his own scabby hands. "I discovered that pretty quickly. They liquefy us. I don't know if that's the purpose of these things, if it's simply a side effect, but they're pretty good at it."

The glyphs just glowed, his blood on the green stone.

"Are they feeding on us?" Travers asked.

"I don't know for sure," Ford said. "As I said, 'tenderizing' is a better word for it. What they are doing, in my unscientific estimation, is studying us. Taking samples."

Travers felt the disorientation, the vertigo, the sense of spatial unreason inherent in the shape of the obelisks, and swayed on his feet a bit. He backed away.

"Yeah," Ford said. "I can't account for that, but my guess is that the otoliths somehow are being impacted by them, or else there is maybe even some kind of damage occurring to our brains."

Travers kept backing away, until he reached the rocks that separated him from the water.

"I think Guessica was wrong," Ford said. "She claimed that for these islands to still stand, they'd have to be incredibly dense. And that's probably true. But I think maybe the spires ensured that there would be land here. They wanted to be found."

"Um," Travers said. "Right."

"We have a geologic impossibility, here," Ford said. "Unless Spire Island is some tiny bit of a much-larger landmass that has eroded away over billions of years—and only Guessica can tell us that for sure—then maybe the spires themselves created the island, so that living things could shelter near them, and feed them."

Travers couldn't imagine the malign intelligence that might craft such a thing.

"One part artillery barrage, one part smartbomb, one part cluster-bomb, one part landmine," Ford said. "And worse."

"How so?" Travers asked.

"They talk to you," Ford said. "Not in so many words, but I think some of what I've seen is coming from those fucking things. They want to know what they have in store for us. Crazy as it sounds, they *want* us to know."

It was too much for Travers to take. He had always hoped that when ISA finally ran across some aliens, it would be something more pleasant, like what they showed on the trideo, like a happy union between man and alien, a peaceful coexistence. Or at least a comprehensible invasion—that he could handle.

This was something else; it was like sedition of his soul. Or at least of Ford's.

And yet, Travers could feel the things looking into him, too. There was a presence to them that he could perceive. Maybe not directly, but it was the way a hypersonic frequency could sometimes create that sense of something there, even if you couldn't quite hear it.

"Fuck all of this," Travers said. "And fuck you, too, Ford, for putting me through it. Cross-contaminating, protocol-breaching motherfucker."

Travers walked over to Ford's own abandoned exosuit and pried loose his helmet.

"You crazy fucker," Travers said. He was beyond angry with Ford. He couldn't believe the man would do this to him.

"You're the second man on Tartarus," Ford said. "We just need to get Guessica down here, and we can start our own colony."

"She's going to the dropsite," Travers said. "She's getting out of here. And so am I."

Travers hooked the bloody helmet to his own suit, Ford's handprint looming large on the glasstic visor.

Ford walked over, and Travers turned around to face him, bringing up his own broken helmet, brandishing it like it was a club. Ford stayed out of reach, his own face shrouded by the fog.

"Easy, Bro," Ford said. "I didn't want to kill you. I don't want to kill you. I just wanted you to taste this place. To feel it. Tell me true—still dizzy? No? I know you're not. You're already acclimating. That's what our bodies do, you know—they acclimate and adapt. It's what we do."

The forest of protocols that Ford had violated on this mission was endless and vast, a trackless wilderness of madness. Travers was so angry at him, he wanted to kill him for what he'd done. Words eluded him.

"This is our home, now," Ford said. "Tartarus."

Ford ran a hand through his hair, shaking his head.

"Stay away from me," Travers said. "Seriously."

The sun was high above them, now, but the fog still clung stubbornly around their rock. The light of that sun shone through, but the fog was slow to burn off, diffused the light, made everything around them strange. And Ford was right, of course—the fog did draw away heat, or at least felt like it did. Travers found himself shivering.

"I cured you," Ford said. "I saved you. What are you going to do? You're still going to be on the receiving end of whatever ISA has on hand to probe you with. You might as well stay here with me and wait for Chao to come. Or Vic, maybe."

"I have a mission to complete," Travers said. "As do you. This isn't my home. I'm going back."

Ford gripped his warhammer in his hand, flexed his fingers a bit, watching Travers slip himself back into his suit.

"The snail crawling back into its shell," Ford said. "Spineless, after all."

As much as Travers hated using Ford's bloody, contaminated helmet, it at least would let him get his suit online again. He snapped it in place, and Ford just watched him, a look of disappointment on his face. He looked nearly sad.

"I could break this one, too, you know," Ford said. "I could crack your shell, Hermit Crab. I could crack it and leave you on the beach to scuttle in bewilderment. You tasted Tartarus, Travers. You have it inside you. You can't run from it."

Travers got his exosuit back online immediately, quickly as he could, and Ford just watched him powering up.

"I'm disappointed, Trav."

"Good," Travers said. He was dizzy, but wasn't incapacitated by it. Yet.

The suit was powered up again, and Travers got up, backed away from Ford. Travers couldn't believe it had even happened, that he'd been outside of his suit. He could feel alien pebbles on his feet, inside his suit with him. Intergalactic gravel between his toes. The techs would have an absolute field day with that.

"Guess," Travers said. "I'm back online."

"Trav! I thought you might be dead," Guessica said. He put her on the HUD 3.

"Ford tried to, I don't know, emancipate me," Travers said. "Violently."

"Get out of there," Guessica said. "Just get out of there. We'll let the Recovery Team get him."

Travers couldn't wait for Slaughter and his Recovery goons to turn up at this place, what they'd do to bring Ford back.

"I'm contaminated," Travers said. "He broke my suit."

Travers was keeping an eye on Ford, who had retreated back into the circle of spires.

"I'm sorry," Guessica said. "Are you okay?"

"Pretty far from okay," Travers said. "About 2.3 million light-years from okay, Guess. I'm almost afraid to go home. I mean, I want to, but this is going to be crazy. A homecoming like no other."

"Not our fault," Guessica said. "Not your fault. Ford's fault."

"It's the fault of these things," Travers said. "Ford's either out of his mind, or else he's onto something."

"Why not both?" Guessica asked.

Travers activated his suit's wings, and the antigravity projector hummed to life, making him light as a feather.

"Leaving so soon, Trav?" Ford asked.

"You're on your own, Ford," Travers said. "Good luck."

"You need it more," Ford said. "Way more than I do."

Travers fired his engine and flew from the island, fog be damned. He went by instrumentation, got up over the fogbank, which cleared as soon as he got a few hundred feet up, and got a look at it.

He hated the brown-red bloodstain on his helmet, wished he'd rinsed it in the water before he'd put it on, but didn't want to wait a moment longer, just in case Ford reconsidered and went at him with his warhammer again.

> "Personal log: I've been exposed to the alien climate,
> thanks to Ford's sabotage of my operating system. I
> know this is borne out in the recording, but I wanted
> to confirm it for the record. I am contaminated, and

will have to be put into immediate Quarantine. I do
this of my own free will."

Ford be damned, Travers had already started thinking of QED-376
as Tartarus. That was the power of naming. Names created their own
reality.

"Guessica," Travers said. "Ford's going to die out there."

"Yes," Guessica said. "Probably."

"I will try to bring him back," Travers said. "Like how I planned."

"Yes," Guessica said. "You should. I can't. I'm about halfway to the
dropsite."

"You left me the duct tape, right?" Travers asked.

"Affirmative," Guessica said.

She looked bad. She looked loopy, her big eyes were watering.

"Are you okay?"

"Fine," she said. "Just bearing a heavy load. Look, until I get to the
dropsite, let's just keep communication to a minimum. You're free to
try to recover Ford, and to bring back the equipment. Sorry I couldn't
bring more with me."

"Yeah, okay," Travers said. He wanted a bit of payback, he admitted. He wanted to wrap Ford up in his survival smock, like a fucking
mummy. He had to do something in the wake of what Ford had done
to him.

Travers grimly imagined how they would look, coming back through
the Causeway, this motley, ragged crew—Ford a duct-taped mummy,
Travers in a bloody suit, Guessica toting an alien obelisk like she was
carrying a log on her shoulder—it would be legendary.

The image of it made him giggle a little. Guessica's eyes flicked up
toward him on the HUD 3.

"What's so funny?"

"We are," Travers said. "We have to keep our suit recorders going
when we cross the Causeway, if only to see everybody's reaction when
we come back. I want to see the look on everybody's faces."

"Yeah," Guessica said, without humor. "Funny."

"I hope Payne's there," Travers said.

"He's probably on Eden right now," Guessica said.

"Fucker," Travers said.

"Exactly."

5

GUESSICA'S MARCH, AS SHE CAME TO SEE IT, took her across that alien lake—she'd already determined that the dropsite had put them at a large freshwater lake, not a sea at all—exceedingly deep, but a lake, all the same.

She understood that the ice was thick enough to bear the burden of herself and her cargo, but it still unnerved her more than a little to walk across this massive body of frozen water that way, knowing that a rupture in the ice would send her into the depths, and she'd be unable to get out.

Guessica swayed this way and that, but always keeping true to her course, which flashed as a beacon light on her HUD 1. She was exhausted. Even though the suit was bearing the load of the spire, the strain of the high-velocity movement, even with her as a passenger within her suit, was wearing on her. And the drugs she'd been taking to keep on-task were wearing off, too.

And she suspected that her proximity to the thing, having it right up against her, was compounding whatever effect it had on human beings. She assumed she was being bathed in toxic radiations. ALLIE would sort everything out. That's what she told herself, over and over again.

She was grateful that Travers wasn't dead. It was distressing seeing him blank out, and being unable to do anything about it.

To jog along a field of white, hour after hour, entirely alone, under an unfamiliar sky, was an unsettling thing, but Guessica continued, mindful of the chronometers, understanding full well that she should be able to make it with time to spare, if she kept to a steady pace.

That was exactly the challenge, however. Her vertigo was so strong that she didn't think she could man any of the controls if she tried to. In the absence of balance, in being completely unbalanced, she simply concentrated on hugging the obelisk to her, trusting the suit to be able to get her to the dropsite.

She kept it all inside, refused to talk to herself, didn't want to give them anything to pin on her. She felt bad for Travers, who had now become another test subject, thanks to Ford. She felt bad at leaving him the rest of the stuff to bring back, but in her eyes, this was more important.

Far more important.

So strong was the drive that she had a moment's doubt as to whether she should be working so hard to get this alien artifact to the dropsite. Maybe it's what the thing wanted. That was just addled Ford-thinking, though. That's how she saw it. It was just a lump of stone. It was not magical or incomprehensible. Maybe it *was* a weapon. But it was still just stone. And it was billions of years old. Maybe when they broke down the structure of it, it would yield newer, more robust construction materials.

Guessicanium, she thought, with a sudden bit of amusement, despite herself. Yes, they owed her that. Guessicanium, the new building material Paragon would unveil in the wake of the discovery of Tartarus. Vulnerable to lasers, but immune to erosion. Light- and heat-emitting. Structurally very dense. Probably a gridlike structure to its molecules, very tightly packed. She'd have a villa made of the stuff.

She would be promoted after this, she was sure. She was getting the job done. She was adapting to an enfolding mission and handling it. She would be the one ISA would trot out in the interviews. Of course, Ford's absence would be telling, but Paragon's press people would handle it, would find some suitable lie to explain it all away.

It would be Guessica's show, from start to finish. The gyrocompensators kept her on her feet when the thing was on autopilot. She could pitch forward and the thing would correct for it. Most Terranauts were reluctant to use autopilot; the variability of terrain and circumstance made it unpopular with them, but in this circumstance, with her own vestibular system thrown far out of whack, and with the flat terrain of the frozen lake to navigate, it had been a logical, even an inspired move.

In fact, the more she thought about it, the more she liked it. "Computer, ETA at best speed?"

"Four hours," the computer said.

"All ahead, best speed, on current course," Guessica said.

Her suit lurched as it began to run across the snow. It was such an odd place to be, occupying this cybernetic chassis, having the thing run for her, while she hung on inertly within it, cocooned and ill.

The nausea was building, and there was no real cure for it. She took some analgesics and narcotics to try to counter it, but with her head spinning, it was getting harder to function.

"Guessica?" Travers asked. "Your eyes are whirling."

"What?"

"They're going back and forth," Travers said.

She closed her eyes, hard. But they were still moving.

"Better?"

"Yeah," Travers said. "Look, I'm about thirty minutes from Obelisk Island. Did you leave your flightpack there?"

"Yes," Guessica said. There was euphoria in imbalance. She felt that, too, once her stomach settled. Like diving off a steep cliff, like the gravity tests they'd done, hurling them in modules off of spires. Towers. Not spires.

"Good," Travers said. "When I get to Obelisk, I'm going to recharge my flightpack, then I'm going to fly to the dropsite with as much of the gear as I can carry. I'll shuttle back and forth and get the stuff there, then I'm going to fly back to Spire on my pack and get Ford. I'm bringing that fucker back."

"Yes," Guessica said. "Good plan."

Shorter words, simpler syntax. She held it together by threads. Threads like the webbing around the Revenants.

"Your eyes are still bouncing around," Travers said. "Like you're in REM sleep, almost."

"Thanks, Trav," Guessica said. "All clear here."

"Yeah," Travers said. He didn't believe her, and she didn't want to open her eyes to see him. His tone told her everything she needed to know, and she felt the tears going down her cheeks. "Go easy, Guess.

We're all going to be in Quarantine. ISA is going to not take any chances."

"I'm fine," Guessica said. "Thanks for asking."

"I wasn't asking," Travers said. "And you're far from fine."

Guessica could see with her eyes closed. The images were more apparent, the shadows and shapes, all around her. Everywhere. They were absolutely everywhere, these apparitions, watching her. Like Travers's snowmen, only so many more. Even against the green-black canvas of her shut eyes, she could see them. Especially there.

She could not be clear on what they were, whether they were the colonizers—the Source—without any real basis for her conjecture, she thought they were, instead, the victims of the Source, the Revenants. Long buried, deep within the ground, now. So long ago. Older than the Earth, itself, these victims, this dead place.

"Tartarus," Guessica said. It was Ford's word. She had heard.

"Guess? Have you taken anything?"

"Yes," Guessica said. "A lot of drugs, Trav. I'm so glad they give us so many. Thank you, Paragon."

"Be careful," Travers said. "You know, don't operate heavy machinery while intoxicated, that kind of thing."

"Intoxicated," Guessica said, laughing. "God, you are so right."

The shadows weren't shadows at all; they were such radiant things. The light they shed was green, the same shade of luminous green that lit the glyphs of the spires. It was the same hue. She could see this as clearly as she saw the sun overhead, back when she was able to look at it. Now, with her eyes closed, traveling blind, she could see the others in their multitudes, trailing after her in ever-growing numbers. What had the Source done to them, why had they even come? In an empty universe, a place of matchless endlessness, that they would have murdered the people of this world—it was almost cosmically cruel. Had they sought them out? These poor people? Was it just chance?

To just come to this place and take it. And then what? Abandon it? No one was here. It was like a crumpled ball of debris. They had used it up and moved on, in their infernal fleet, from world to world, this way. She could see it.

She could see it as clearly as Ford saw it, and that caused her no end of anguish.

Just a little farther.

6

FORD WATCHED THE FOG BREAK, just sat there, hungry, watching it go its merry way, broken apart by the sun. It was beautiful. He'd never watched a fog lift. His life had been too busy for that, and there had been so many other things to distract him from it. But here, on Tartarus, he could just pause and watch the winds blow, could feel them.

He wanted to laugh, seeing Travers scrabble across the island, panicked, puking, fearful, gasping on air that was fit to breathe. There was no disease here, nothing that the spires themselves didn't bring.

Ford got up, stretched, walked over to his suit, drew a straw and drank his fill of Nutrifill, that nutritionally-complete slurry that kept them alive in the field. He had enough for a few more days. He hadn't planned further ahead than that.

Then he went to the water, sank his feet into the stuff, the cold of it waking him up, although he'd not slept for days. He tossed his warhammer behind him, safe on the shore. The tides were up with the moons, the waves were coming. He saw that. Surging waters.

Travers would come back for him. He was sure of this. He would be ready for Travers. There was nothing to do but be ready.

Behind him, the spires hummed, seemed to hum. It was just the wind, traveling through them, the oscillation of wind through the circle of spires, like a musical instrument.

Ford drew handfuls of the water and drank from it, the sweet broth that nourished him, a taste unlike anything he knew, could ever know. So cold and beautiful.

The dizziness was gone. He had adapted himself to the new geometry, the fearful geometry of the Source. Which was funny, really, because in that frame of mind, even his scabbed hands looked profane, and the spires looked normal and right. It was all a matter of perspective. He had gained a new perspective.

Walking out of the water, he reclaimed his warhammer, began writing with it in the sand, while the tides rose and the waves claimed the shore. He had so much to do, and didn't know if he had enough time to do it. He had to get cracking, and, climbing atop the corpse of his career, the empty exosuit, he got cracking.

The last will and testament of Ford Collins, the King of Spire Island and Lord-Governor of Tartarus.

7

TRAVERS REACHED OBELISK ISLAND BY LATE AFTERNOON, could see the carnage wrought by Guessica—the decimation of his snowmen legions, and the sundered spire. Hell hath no fury than a woman with a 75-kilowatt laser.

He walked over to the ruined section of spire, the bubbled, broken thing, and touched it with his gauntlet, on a whim. Already, the snow was claiming it. It looked like stone. However the spires operated, they looked like stone.

There were six cases to take. It would mean three trips. He couldn't take the gear and recover Ford, too. He would expend all the fuel in the fliers, making those trips.

They already had a marker at Obelisk Island. They could leave that and the gear in place and let ISA send another team in, let them recover it.

Travers looked at the surveyor case. The surveyor was largely played out—there would be enough fuel for it to reach the dropsite, and not much more. He opened the case and removed the surveyor, dumping it to one side. Travers programmed the surveyor drone to reach the dropsite, launched it and sent it on its way. That was one problem solved.

The case could hold Ford. He'd fit in there. Good enough for Travers. Then he consolidated the other cases, put the samples and the datafeeds into a second and third case, just carefully put that stuff in there.

Then he could fly with the two loaded cases, using up his own flight module. He almost wished that Guessica had removed the flight module on Ford's suit, rather than simply taking the power pack for it.

But that worked fine for him. Travers would carry Ford's pack on him, which could get him from the dropsite to Obelisk. Then he could use Guessica's to reach Spire Island and back. Then maybe whatever was left would get him to the dropsite before the portal opened.

It was a big pain in the ass, but Travers thought he could do it, if he didn't get distracted. That was the key. Guessica was looking like hell. She had turned off her HUD feed, so he couldn't see her pinwheeling, watering eyes.

"Guessica? Are you still with us?" Travers asked.

"Yesssssssss," she said. "Fine."

"High as a kite, am I right?" Travers said.

"Rhyme time?"

"Yeah," Travers said.

His own vertigo was somewhat less pronounced than it had been. He wasn't sure why this was so, why Ford and Guess seemed harder hit by the affliction.

"Tartarus," Guessica said. "The Naming Commission won't like that one bit. They'll come up with a name like 'Epiphany.'"

"Assuming they even bother to name it," Travers said. "I think this'll be one of those secret planets we hear about. Or don't hear about, anyway. The flip side of Arcadia. Acheron, perhaps."

They both knew that. Most of the worlds that the Terranauts surveyed never went public, for various reasons. Tartarus seemed ripe for that treatment. He imagined the Polygon would send weapons specialists here aplenty to study the obelisks in detail.

"Do you believe in ghosts?" Guessica asked.

"Um, no," Travers said.

"Ghost ships? Ghost towns? Ghosting?"

"Not so much, Guess," Travers said. "Why don't you pop me on the HUD? Let me have a look at you."

"Ghost planets?"

He could see where she was going with that. It was a funny thing to consider. Was this a ghost world? What did that even mean? It was a dead planet, that much was clear—sure, there was something growing in the temperate regions, but whatever intelligent life that had been here was long since dead. It was, therefore, a haunted place.

It was funny for him to understand that—how could one believe in haunted places without believing in ghosts? What could haunt a place in the absence of ghosts?

Toxins. Chemicals. Those things could haunt a place. Unexploded ordnance. Sentry guns—he remembered a battery of sentry guns that had been left in place. They had caught a group of kids playing in an old war zone. They'd just run into it, and the guns woke up and shot them all dead, blazing away. Where had that been? He'd only remembered the guns, the photographs of them on Newsfeed—death on a tripod, shiny and black, like deadly insects.

Travers thought about the basics of communication, and whether Ford's talk of the spires talking to him was just nutbabble or whether there was something to it—there had to be a sender and a receiver for there to be communication. A haunting required two pieces of the puzzle to form the circuit. There had to be something there, and a mind to connect those things, for there to be a sense of haunting. Or something evocative enough to create that haunting feeling. Forget Schroedinger's Cat; this was Schroedinger's Ghost.

"Why are you asking me about ghosts, Guess?"

"I see them," Guessica said. "They're following me to the dropsite."

"I don't think you're seeing anything," Travers said. "I think you're hallucinating. I think maybe we all are."

"I see them. And, more importantly, they see me."

"What do you see, then?"

Travers didn't think much for Blue Team's chances if he was the only sane one left. And yet, with Ford doing lord knew what and Guessica seeing ghosts, it made him more than a little worried.

"They're watching me," Guessica said. "It's not my fault. That's what I want to tell them."

"What do they look like?"

"Black eyes and radiant hearts," Guessica said. "So many. I can't see their faces. My eyes won't let me see."

Travers looked around him, but could see nothing but falling snow and the equipment.

"You're tripping," Travers said. "You've got to dial back on the drugs, Guess."

"Fine," Guessica said. "I'm fine. Everything's fine."

"I'm going to send the drone to the dropsite," Travers said. "I don't want you to be startled by it. It's got enough fuel to touch down there."

"They're so angry," Guessica said. "They hate us. They think we're the Source. They never saw the Source. Do you realize that? They never saw the faces of their executioners."

"So, you think Tartarus is a ghost planet? Is that it?"

"Yes," Guessica said. "No. Maybe."

"A quantum answer," Travers said.

"These are quantum times, my friend," Guessica said.

Travers wondered if ALLIE could even understand the idea of a ghost. Could the machine understand a ghost? He wasn't sure. ALLIE could perceive things they couldn't. Incorporating the Loonies' dark side data, ALLIE was able to find planets that nobody could ever see with their own eyes. Things that might as well have been invisible, but were mathematically inevitable. He didn't know how she'd take the information from Tartarus.

"It's not our job to figure it out," Travers said. "We're just here to gather information."

"I'm 2.5 hours from the dropsite," Guessica said.

"Alright," Travers said. He had tapped into the survey drone's feed, and got a glimpse of Guessica sprinting across the snow, bearing the burden of the obelisk. It was a curious image, seeing her running flat-out like that. "You're running your suit awfully hard, aren't you?"

"She'll make it," Guessica said. "She's fine."

"Right," Travers said. "You set it to autopilot, didn't you?"

"Yes," Guessica said. "Smart, huh?"

"Yeah," Travers said, as the drone left the image of her behind. It was a good idea. "What happens when you reach the dropsite?"

"I'll lie down," Guessica said, a trifle quickly. "And wait for you. And Ford."

He knew why. She was relying on the autopilot to keep her balance for her. He really wanted to ask her that, but knew Guessica would be reluctant to answer.

Travers finished arranging the portable gear, and readied his flight-pack. He would fly to the dropsite, drop off this stuff, and then wait for Guessica to reach him. Let her try to bullshit him face-to-face. He knew she was worse off than he was.

He turned and gazed at the obelisks, which glowed softly. One life obviously wasn't enough to impress them too much; they wanted more.

8

SOMETHING WAS HAPPENING.

To her.

Guessica knew this, but couldn't stop herself.

Too close.

Too long.

Too much.

Too something.

Was it a bad idea? Had it been a bad idea? It was her mission—good or bad did not come into it. ALLIE would be so disappointed, if she could even feel that. Guessica had not wanted to let ALLIE down. There would be no Gold Team for Guessica, no gold star, nothing. She had done her job, and this was what it had gotten her.

The sensation wasn't entirely unpleasant, so much as it was disorienting. Absolutely everything she was seeing was bending and distorting, like through a fisheye lens, like through a conduit, where space-time itself was bound to the dictates of anti-gravity.

She wanted to laugh, because it was euphoric, this sensation, this loss of self in the face of wrongful geometry, her own legacy, her epitaph.

Transformation.

Reincarnation.

That was something she fixed her closed eyes upon: reincarnation. She wasn't dying; she couldn't die. Death was just a passing through a gate—a conduit to another plane of existence. That's what she was seeing.

Metamorphism.

Yes. She understood that better than anyone on this mission. She was the protolith, changed by heat and pressure. Yes. They all were.

That made sense to her. There was logic in this. What was reincarnation but spiritual metamorphism? There was nothing to be afraid of, here. There was simply the resignation to the inevitable. It was as inevitable as breathing, as inevitable as death and oblivion.

The pressure wasn't literal, here; it was something else, a pressure on her spirit. The awareness was piecemeal, like sifting through the debris in a crater, trying to find the clues to the impact, the source of the destruction.

Guessica was trying to excavate her own spirit, to understand what had befallen her, assembling the pieces, so carefully, a dig, really, with everything laid out in a grid, mapped and marked. But grids were meaningless to her, now—she had lost her way. The old geometry didn't apply, she lacked the words for the new geometry, the reorientation to supplant the disorientation.

Matter, energy, plasma, transformation, metamorphology, reincarnation. The words weren't able to capture it. But still, she tried. A scientist, from beginning to end.

Evanescence.

Yes. Evanescence.

She was evanescing. That was it.

She wanted to cry out, felt that sense of satisfaction in her discovery, but she'd forgotten how to speak. No, that wasn't quite right. It's just that words were part of the old geometry, and she did not yet know how to speak. The tools weren't there, weren't in her hands. But she had no hands to grasp them.

I am the Evanescent Guessica Rao.

It was metamorphic poetry.

There was music and beauty in it, she could see this, even with shut eyes, she could see it, could still hear it.

There was no stopping it.

I am the Evanescent Guessica Rao.

I am the Bangalore Torpedo.

I am coming for you all.

She couldn't stop herself if she tried. And speaking of stopping, Guessica had forgotten to breathe, and had realized that she'd forgotten.

She opened her eyes, at last, only to realize that she didn't have eyes to open, anymore—or, there wasn't anything to distinguish the state of her having her eyes closed or open. Somehow, they had become one and the same, in her eyes.

In her eyes.

She could see them so clearly, now. All of them. And they could see her. They would take her from this place, and yet she would remain here, with them. Part of them, one of them.

Tartarus.

Acheron.

Home.

9

 and reached the dropsite in about a half an hour, which meant that he had about an hour until Guessica reached him. Her suit had been gamely sprinting toward the dropsite, with singular focus and drive. Travers doubted that anybody short of a test pilot had run one of the exosuits at such a high level for such a length of time. It was fitting that it would have been Guessica, ever the overachiever.

He carefully put the cases near the snowman he'd made, which was still standing, although the wind had sculpted it a little bit, taken a bite here and there out of its formerly pristine planes, turned its smile into a sneer.

Then he lay down in the snow, and made a snow angel with his suit. He felt better than he'd felt in days, being away from those things. Maybe Ford had been right about them.

Out here, on the ice, it was peaceful. There wasn't the dread that accompanied the spires. In fact, the only thing Travers was dreading was Guessica bringing that spire here. He did not want that thing nearby. She was, for now, Team Leader, so he put up with it, and certainly ISA and Paragon would love to get their hands on it, but Travers wanted nothing to do with it.

At the very least, the thing was toxic in some unknown way.

He sat down, could not wait to get out of his suit. The last couple of days were always the hardest on a mission, even a routine mission. The confinement of the suit was taxing, and nanotech aside, Travers wanted simply to get out and take a shower, get himself scrubbed clean under hot water. The Oasis had many things available for Terranauts, but the showers were some of his favorite things.

Then he realized that they'd sure as hell not let him shower when he got there. He'd have to announce that he was contaminated, and that meant that while he would be taken out of his suit, the last thing they'd do is let him shower. They'd probably run him through scanners and remove every stray pebble and bit of xenogrit that came from Tartarus, and then they'd be likelier to hose him off with bleach or something to ensure that no pathogen came riding in with him.

Only then, after a 12- to 18-hour decontamination protocol, would he maybe be permitted a shower, his favorite post-trip ritual.

Goddamned Ford.

He couldn't wait to truss him up and bring him back.

Travers knew this would be the last trip for him as a normal Terranaut. Not that "normal" and "Terranaut" ever shared the same sentence, but that would all change when they got back. He would make a huge splash when he got back home.

If they got home. At this distance, home felt infinitely far away. An entire galaxy away. Tonight, he'd gaze up at the sky and look at the Milky Way, and know that the next night, he'd be there and could gaze up at the sky and see Andromeda Galaxy.

The first human beings to set foot in Andromeda Galaxy. Nobody could take that away from him. Not Ford, not Payne, not Paragon. He had made history. They all had. And to have discovered alien life and civilization—or, more precisely, alien artifacts of some ancient war— it meant that he would matter. Whatever the outcome of this mission, however it ended up for them, he had a place in history.

"You still out there, Guess?" Travers asked.

"Skrrk," came the reply. Static.

"Guess, come in, over?"

"SKRRK."

Travers tongued an instant message to her.

GUESSCA. OK?

SHRAKRAKKAKARLLLBDLFT.

Travers got up, scanned the horizon. There was no sign of her, yet.

"Guess, come in. Come in," Travers said.

"SKRRK."

"Fuck," Travers said. Something had happened. Maybe the spire was interfering with her comlink. He hadn't noticed any kind of interference before, but something had happened.

> "Personal log: Something's happened to Guessica. I'm still getting a reading on the radar, she's still approaching, should be here in about 45 minutes, at current rate of speed. But I've lost communication with her. I am trying to reestablish contact."

"Guessica, come in," Travers said.

She had cut off the connection between them, and he could not reestablish a visual link without her help.

He wanted to head out to her position, but since she was coming to him, he figured he'd save power and wait it out.

Travers took time to gather up some snow and scrub the bloody handprint from the glasstic. A few minutes of scrubbing, and Ford's handprint was gone, and Travers felt much better.

> "Personal log: I don't believe in ghosts. I don't think there are ghosts on this world. There is something here, something that is not us, but to call it a ghost? I don't know what to make of that, or whether I can accept it. Ford calls this place 'Tartarus,' and it's as good a name as any. Something terrible happened here long ago. We may never discover exactly what. Or maybe we will. And maybe that's worse."

He paused to breathe.

> "It's hard to know which is worse, I guess, but if the choice is between knowledge and ignorance, I side with knowledge. Knowledge is power, and ignorance is weakness, not strength. We'll take our chances, and we'll learn from it. I don't know if ISA will willingly return anyone here. It's out of my hands. But if you do, please use all appropriate cautions. There is something awful here, in the fullest sense of the word."

Travers could see Guessica at the horizon, now. Just a speck. She would reach the dropsite by sunset, at the rate she was going.

"Guessica," Travers said. "I can see you. Come in."

"SKRRK."

"If you can see me, give me some sign," Travers said.

"SKRRK."

He tongued the message, sent another text.

GSSCA: RUOK?

This time, there wasn't even the garbled message she'd sent before.

GSSCA: RUOK?

Nothing.

Maybe she had passed out. Overdosed on her drugs. She always was prone to making full use of the pharmacological buffet that ISA included in their suits. Not to say she was a hypochondriac, but she fully subscribed to the "better living through chemistry" school of applied medicine.

He imagined her snoring in her suit, deep in a narcotic-induced haze, and laughed. Everything about this place had put him on edge. She'd reach the dropsite, stoned out of her mind, and they'd eventually have a laugh about it, once they were home.

"Computer, magnify image times ten."

The image of Guessica filled his HUD 1, resolutely running for the dropsite, bearing the obelisk in both arms, held across her chest. The glyphs on the obelisk were glowing brightly. Even from this distance, he could see that.

> "Personal log: Guessica's in sight. Although she severed the spire from its moorings—for lack of a better term—the spire appears to be active, just the same. The writing on the sides of it is shining brightly. I don't know what the power source could be for this thing, or if 'power' even qualifies."

He kept an eye on Guessica, watching her get closer and closer, until he no longer needed to use magnification. He kept trying to hail her, but she was unresponsive.

At last, she reached the dropsite encampment, and her suit stopped moving.

"Wake up, Guessica," Travers said. "You made it."

She stood there, motionless, holding the obelisk. The three of them stood there—the snowman, Guessica, and Travers, as the sun set. The glyphs weren't glowing as brightly as they had been glowing before.

Her visor had been set to block out the sun, was tinted black. It had been a wise move, since she'd been running into the sun the entire time.

She still held the obelisk.

"Wake up in there," Travers said, tapping her visor. "Guessica? You made it."

He tapped her shoulder, but there was no response. Although she'd be pissed, he went to the latches on her visor and triggered them, but got no response. She'd locked them, much as he had when he was with Ford.

"Fuck," he said. "Guessica. Wake up in there. You reached the dropsite."

She just held the spire, motionless, silent.

The exosuits responded to body movement. It was a very intricate system whereby the suit responded to the body movement commands of the Terranauts. They instantly responded to them.

Something was wrong, because Guessica shouldn't have been able to hold the obelisk in that static posture like that, just because the force-feedback system on the suit would respond to any range of motion, and nobody could hold that still.

Travers tried to pry the obelisk free of her arms. He was able to do so, dismayed that the close proximity of the thing brought back the vertigo quite readily. He tugged the thing free, and grunted, straining, bearing the load of it, walking to the far side of the dropsite, setting the thing down next to the snowman.

Then he walked back to Guessica, who stood there with her arms in exactly the same position as they had been before.

"Guessica?"

He was now very worried. Even if she were dead in there, for whatever reason, there should have been some kind of force-feedback on her arm units. Instead, they were in the last position she had made for them.

It could have been some kind of monumental suit malfunction. In which case, the protocol was to breach the suit and ascertain her condition. But here, in the cold zone of the dropsite, it was a worrisome proposition. He could breach her suit, but it might jeopardize her life.

Maybe she'd locked in the position of the suit's armatures, because the vertigo was so bad that she couldn't trust herself to carry it without dropping it. She must've doped herself up and intended to ride out the remaining seventeen hours asleep. This pissed Travers off, since it meant that he was the only functional Terranaut operating.

"Goddammit, Guess," Travers said.

He had to ascertain her condition. Even if she had voluntarily tranquilized herself, as a team member, he had to determine her situation. ISA would flay him if he let her overdose, or at least didn't check on her condition.

Travers went back to her helmet. There was a pair of emergency release buttons on the back, which was a security failsafe in the event that a Terranaut was experiencing an equipment failure and was unable to release their own helmet using the standard release mode. For a functional Terranaut, it could be done by bringing both hands up and pressing the buttons at the same time.

"Guessica, if you don't respond in five seconds, I'm going to blow your top," Travers said.

He watched the chronometer, gave her exactly five seconds. There was no response.

"Alright," Travers said. "You can't be pissed at me for doing this. I gave you every opportunity."

The buttons were red and round. He put his gauntlets upon them.

"Last chance," Travers said. "I'm not fooling around, here."

Nothing.

He depressed the switches, and the micro-explosive bolts deployed, and off popped Guessica's helmet, with a puff of smoke. It flipped over three times in the air, catching the waning sunlight, before landing on the snowy ground with a thump.

If she was doped up, the cold air would wake her up quickly enough. And she'd be infuriated at Travers for breaking the seal of her suit.

He walked around to face her, talking, as was his way.

"Look, Guessica, I'm sorry, but you know the proto—"

There was nothing in the suit. It was empty.

"What the hell?" Travers said.

He went to the opening of her suit and peered in, using his suit's sensors. There was no sign of her.

"Umm," Travers said. "Oh, shit."

It wasn't possible. She had to be in the suit. It wouldn't have remained operational if she'd ejected from it. That was one of the features of the suits.

He needed to patch into the datafeed. Giving the suit a shove to drop it on its back, he went to one of the datafeed ports.

But as the suit fell to the ground, a slurry of fluid splashed out of the open mouth of the suit, staining the snow pinkish-red.

"Oh my god," Travers said, jumping back with a squawk. The fluid began to freeze on the snow, a slush of ice and Guessica.

Travers gagged, staggered away from the suit. Its arms were still locked in that pose, which, Travers assumed, was the last position Guessica's arms had been in before she had liquefied.

"Oh, god," Travers said.

He wanted to cry and vomit at the same time. It had to have been her sustained close proximity to the spire that did this. He wished that he could tell somebody, but there was nobody to talk to. At least nobody right there.

> "Personal log: Guessica's dead. You can see the audiovisual file. I think extended close proximity to the spire caused her to, um, liquefy. She was a good team member. We flew several missions together, and she always did her part, always was an exemplary professional. I don't know what the hell happened. You can upload the datafeed on her suit, see what happened. I don't know if I can look at it."

He stopped, choking back tears.

He toggled off the log, watched the sun dip below the horizon, plunging everything into darkness. The obelisk glowed faintly in the snow, some distance beyond. Travers felt completely alone.

It bothered him that "SHRAKRAKKAKARLLLBDLFT" were Guessica's last known words. He wondered what that had been, whether it had been her liquefying tongue trying to contact him, whether it was a cry for help, or the delusional flailing of a dying brain, or even a greeting in an alien tongue.

He dropped to the ground and sat by the empty shell of her suit, watching what was left of Guessica freeze, the steam leaving the suit as the cold bit into it. ISA would insist on the sample being returned to the Oasis. A frozen omelet of Guessica, brought in with everything else.

Another absurdity—Ford, duct-taped captive, transported in an equipment case, Guessica as an ice floe, an empty exosuit, a broken, deadly obelisk. A wealth of data and a mystery that would have Paragon's personnel interrogating them perhaps forever.

How had the spire done this to Guessica? Trying to pull himself together, he analyzed the freezing matter that had been his teammate with his sensors, although doing so filled him with grief and disgust. She would have hated to be so scrutinized.

She had been turned to liquid. That was what the scanners indicated. There was little to distinguish between Guessica and the snow around her, except some organic matter that had been her.

"Personal log: Although I can't be entirely sure what happened, my suspicion is that the spires have some kind of ability to convert matter, through some unknown means. Guessica appears to have been reduced to her component parts—water, principally. Maybe the vertigo is a manifestation of this liquefaction process, some kind of disorientation induced by the dissolution of form. I need to talk to Ford, since he was the first one affected by the spires. I have to ascertain his situation, see if he's liquefied as well. He spoke of the vertigo abating from his exposure to the native environment, whereas Guessica was strongly affected by the vertigo and yet didn't risk exposure to the native climate. There could be a correlation, although I understand that this is a premature conjecture. I occupy a middle point between those two poles, since I tried to maintain system integrity, but was briefly exposed to the climate of Tartarus. I would also stress, however, that I spent the least amount of time in the proximity of the spires—I would guardedly hypothesize that close contact with the obelisks is definitely perilous for human beings. The weapons—if Ford was right about guessing their nature—while not specifically geared for human beings, still possess the power to do us grievous harm. I may log into her suit's datafeed tonight and see what I can see, although I do this with only great reluctance. There is enough time to do this and to recover Ford in the morning, before the Conduit reopens."

He turned off his personal log and gazed at Guessica's empty suit, then he looked at the sky above. Overhead, the northern lights shimmered and cascaded in resonant waves of charged particles.

"Where'd you go, Guess?" Travers said, feeling horribly alone.

10

FORD CROUCHED BY HIS SUIT, glanced over at the spires, which were faintly glowing. He flexed his fingers, then balled his hands into fists.

He had lost track of time, but assumed that they would be coming for him before too long. It was what he'd do, if their situations had been reversed. Against their augmented suits, there wasn't much he could hope to do.

Ford could don his own suit again, wait for them to come for him, and fight them, perhaps to the death. But he didn't want to do that.

So, what was there to do? He had marooned himself on Spire Island, and couldn't hope to swim to shore.

He had watched the sea life swim in the water, saw the eddies and swirls, but hadn't seen the creatures, themselves. Ford doubted he could eat them. It was risky enough eating sea life on Earth; on Tartarus, it could be suicide.

But then, marooning oneself on an alien world was much the same thing. Part of him wanted to wade into the water and serve himself up to whatever it was that swam in these fresh, foreign waters. Another part wanted to just huddle in the warm and glowing shadows of the spires, to see the lights of the departed victims of the things illuminate the evening grow ever-brighter, and watch himself dim, feel himself liquefy, become part of the environment. The other part of him thought to wait until Guessica and Travers returned to bring him home.

That had been one of the things that had motivated him to attack Travers to begin with; to force his hand, to keep him here. To have someone who understood. He hadn't expected Travers to cannily switch the helmets the way he had. He should have thought of it, but didn't. He had a lot on his mind, after all.

To be brought back would be to be disgraced. Payne would enjoy inflicting himself on Ford. They would subject him to countless tests and endless interrogations. He would probably, in some way, shape, or form, become property of Paragon. They would want to know What Went Wrong™, without being able to really understand that nothing went wrong at all; everything was happening as it was supposed to. Drop something, it fell. Action, reaction. Cause and effect. To expect otherwise was irrational.

That was the truth of it. As inevitable as sunset. Tomorrow would be the last day of the mission. They would come for him.

He opened the pendant Miranda had gotten him, pressed the crystal, saw her face appear in the cool glow of the hologram, as she smiled at him fetchingly.

"Come back soon, Ford," she said, her voice like a windchime. "I miss you."

She was so beautiful, and the pendant was lovely. The holographer had done marvelous work, their camera traveling slowly up and down her body, settling on her face, and Miranda just smiled at him, her eyes filled with convincingly counterfeit warmth. She barely knew him, but to someone who didn't know that, they'd have thought they were long-lost lovers.

She wouldn't be waiting for him, should they bring him back. Paragon would waive the contract, and she'd go someplace else. Just like that. There was nothing to go back to. Nothing waiting back there for him.

Nothing.

Ford snapped the pendant shut, stuffed it back inside his nanotunic.

Ford would be ready. For them. He got to work.

11

GUESSICA'S GHOST SPOKE TO TRAVERS on the datafeed. He saw her, eyes closed, comlink closed. But she could not turn off the suit's internal monitors; they were always on. It was something the Terranauts always had to deal with—constant observation. Retroactive, of course, but everything they did was scrutinized by the Psych Division and both ISA and Paragon professionals.

It was why Terranauts like Guessica so often maintained a stoic presence in the face of adversity—they knew that their performances would be evaluated. Travers never self-censored. He liked to think of that as part of his charm, although it surely cost him promotions within ISA, as he lacked the gravitas of the straight shooters like Chao, Ford, or Guessica.

She was shivering, sheened in sweat. Her eyes were clamped shut, and were going every which way underneath her eyelids.

"Please," she said. "No. I'm sorry."

Her eyes snapped open, and she was seeing, her black-brown eyes wide, bulging, watering. Seeing something.

"Yes," she said. "Not my fault."

> "P-p-personal log: The Source came and claimed them. All of them. The Revenants. I'll call them that hencef-f-forth. The Source and the Revenants. They rained down spires from the sky and claimed and tamed Tartarus for themselves. The Source. All taken. Every last one. They're here. Ghosts. Every last one of them is still here. To be taken that way, snuffed out—

an eyeblink. Bombardment. The Source from the sky, their ancient fleet and older weapons. Bred for war, conquest, colonization. Bred for it. I can see them. All around. Quantum shadows—does that make sense?"

She paused, swilled some Aquifier.

> "I'm so thirsty. Can you believe it? Drenched and sweating. The Source took them in one stroke. The Revenants are the shadow flickering after the light has been extinguished—they yet remain as ethereal embers. All this time, and they are here. They're the glow on the back of your eyelids after a flash of light forces your eyes shut, the retinal afterburn. I don't know why or how. The Source is not here; they moved on. They took what they wanted, left nothing behind except their spires, and the Revenants. I c-can't know how I know, except that I can see them all around me, can feel them. They see us. They're following me. My feet are soaked. I'm going to short out my suit."

She paused again, clearly embarrassed.

> "I am trying to get to the d-dropsite. Sorry. My tongue is numb. My whole body is numb. Not cold. Warm. But warm and numb. Enervated. I should call Travers, tell him. But I don't want him to see me l-like this."

Her face was drawn.

"I can't feel my arms. Computer?"

She slurred it, flicked out her tongue to try to communicate with the onboard computer. Her tongue was sloppy.

"Travers."

"Travers is trying to reach me," Guessica said. Water was pouring down her face. She bit her tongue. "They're absolutely everywhere."

She tried to text with her tongue, but the loss of muscular control was evident. Guessica began to scream, as rivulets flowed from her, as her hair ran like a waterfall, as her face flowed away, she screamed, a gasping scream that bucked like a dune buggy across a craggy moonscape, she screamed and screamed, what looked like tears flowed from her eyes, until Travers realized that the tears *were* her eyes, and what she was ran from her and splashed on the suit's internal monitor cameras, and ran down the empty helmet, devoid of sound except the whine of the overdriven servos and the sloshing of Guessica, the churning of her in the depths of the suit, unseen.

Travers gagged and stopped the datafeed, bringing his hands up to his head, his gauntlets against the helmeted visor in a cybernetic parody of grief. It was insufficient to the occasion. He wanted to remove his helmet and feel it properly. To climb from his suit and bury his face in the silent snow beside his fallen comrade.

But in the crackling darkness, on a sheet of ice, beneath the sky on an alien world in an alien galaxy, he could not mourn properly. It was not yet time to mourn.

"Guess," he said.

He gazed at the spire in the snow, the glowing thing, and felt hatred. It had done this to her for reasons he couldn't comprehend, but it was responsible.

Travers got up and began walking in the snow, his lights on. He wrote "Welcome To Tartarus" in giant letters, taking advantage of the big size of the exosuit's feet, the cybernetic clodhoppers. The letters must've have been ten meters long. He'd set them behind the great snowman he'd first made when they'd landed.

He cried and laughed as he did it, drew a giant arrow in the snow, pointing south. Gave the wind something to scrub away, something to show that they'd been here. Something for Chao to trample when she got here.

Travers thought of crafting a monument to Guessica, but felt like anything he could have come up with would have not done justice to her memory.

His comlink chirped, and Travers actually jumped. It was Ford.

"Travers," Ford said. "Are you reading me?"

"Ford," Travers said. "What do *you* want?"

"Where's Guessica? I've been trying to hail her for the last twenty minutes."

"She's gone."

"Dead?"

"You tell me."

Ford was visible to Travers, thanks to the internal cameras, but not the other way around, because he'd smashed the visor. Served him right.

"It wasn't my fault," Ford said. "You can't pin that one on me."

"What happened to her? Can you tell me that? And what are you doing in your suit again? I thought you'd gone past that."

Ford looked into the camera. He was on Travers's HUD 2.

"I have," Ford said. "This is for your benefit, not mine."

"What happened to her?"

"I told you the spires were weapons," Ford said. "I told you both that. I warned you about it. About them."

"How did it kill her? Do you even know?"

Ford chewed on his lip a moment before replying. "I only know what I know, and what I know is next to nothing."

"Why aren't you liquefied? Can you at least tell me that?"

"Proximity matters," Ford said. "I gathered that early on. Remember my bloody hands? Remember yours? You probably thought I was, what, handfucking those spires until my fingers bled? But I wasn't. My hands started to melt. That woke me up. Too long against them, and they do things to you. We're a side effect, Travers. We're an unhappy accident, as far as these things are concerned. We're roadkill, not their primary targets. But it doesn't mean we can't be hurt by them."

"Yeah, okay."

Travers sat down in the snow, folded his legs and rested his elbows on his knees. He felt like a child in the incredibly dark night sky, the sun setting, the moons yet to rise.

"Guessica was too close for too long," Ford said. "That's my guess—sorry. You know how stubborn she is…was. She probably thought she could outlast the effect, or overcome it. Maybe she ignored it, or didn't recognize it when it was happening. I think the spires convert living matter, or they break them down into their component parts, turn them into something else."

"Like a solvent?"

"Why not?" Ford said. "I'm not the scientist; you are. But I guess it's how the Source did away with the locals. It's just my guess. Transformed—turned them into raw materials, fertilizer, whatever they needed."

Travers swept up some of the snow with a pass of his hand, like a great paw. The flakes were like the snow he had learned about, when Earth was colder and actually had snow. He packed the flakes into a snowball, let it grow larger, pretended it was Tartarus. He set it down on the snow, gingerly.

"The Source—they did this," Ford said. "There's no way of knowing how the things were supposed to work; it's just how they work on us."

"Why did you call us?" Travers asked.

"I'm telling you to *not* come get me," Ford said. "Just don't do it. Tomorrow's when ALLIE picks you up. Leave me behind."

"You know I can't do that," Travers said. "You know I won't do that."

Ford smiled to himself, nodded.

"I know. But I'm *not* going back. I'm not going to be their lab rat. They've taken enough out of me. I'm not going to be run through their microtomes. I'm not letting them get another piece of me. Right here, right now, I'm free. I mean to stay that way."

"And you know this conversation is being recorded," Travers said. "So, you know they'll know."

Ford nodded, looked into the camera's eye, into Travers's eyes.

"Yes, of course I know that," Ford said. "You're not taking me, and they're not taking me. I set my suit to detonate. I rigged the powercell to blow. It's going to do just that. I'm warning you off Spire Island, because I don't want to take you with me when it goes."

"I don't believe you," Travers said.

"Fine," Ford said. "Don't. But you know the potential destructive power of a suit detonation as well as I do. They love telling us that. If you're close, you'll feel the burn, and the EMP will snuff out your own systems and you'll end up splashing down and having a long walk home. Look, you're, where, at the dropsite?"

"Yes," Travers said.

"Perfect," Ford said. "You barely have enough juice left in your fliers to get here and back, right? Not if you factor in transporting me, too? I'm not going quietly. Why take the risk? Why bother? Get yourself home. You'll miss the explosion, sure, but you'll have guaranteed your ticket back."

Travers looked into Ford's unseeing eyes, and wondered if he was crazy enough to actually do it. He thought he was, but it was just as easy for Ford to be bullshitting him to save his own ass—Missing and Presumed Dead. AWOL on an alien planet.

"You can't survive here," Travers said.

"Nothing can," Ford said. "It's a tombstone of a planet."

"So let me take you home," Travers said. "Where we belong."

Ford shook his head. "You're going to destroy home with those things you bring back. This place is going to destroy our home. I'd rather stay here, in the petrified shadow of the Source's evil, where it's safest. Poor Guessica—she beat me to the punch: the most distantly-dead human being yet in history. But you know how meaningless history is when you face this universe of ours, now, don't you?"

Travers did. It was impossible not to. The unimaginable vastness of the universe made everything smaller. And the sad truth of it was that everything was moving away from itself at ever-increasing velocities, and eventually, even the Loonies would no longer be able to see the most distant galaxies, which would move beyond even ALLIE's ability to see them. Maybe that's what drove the frenetic pace of ISA's stellar surveying program. Maybe they were in an interstellar land rush before, one by one, the galaxies moved out of sight.

Once out of range, they could never be seen or known, and even the conduits couldn't recover anybody. Andromeda Galaxy, for all of its distance, was easy—it was speeding toward the Milky Way at greater than 100 kilometers per second. Or maybe establishing outposts at ever-greater distances would let human beings hopscotch their way across infinity—a very long string of pearls, indeed, bound body and soul to the power of the conduits that leapfrogged distances, opened up the way indefinitely.

"You don't know what those things'll do," Travers said.

"They're telling me," Ford said. "They're in my head. They'll get in your head, too. Then you'll see."

"Why would they even do that?"

Ford looked at him, though Travers knew he couldn't see him. "The Source wanted their victims to *know* what was happening to them, and why. It wasn't geared for our brains, so the message is garbled, but some of it comes through."

"And you expect me to accept that? To be persuaded?"

"Look at Guessica," Ford said. "Doesn't that persuade you?"

Travers couldn't look at what was left of Guessica.

"The Source were smart," Ford said. "They came, they saw, they conquered. Never stopping. We're celestial pretenders compared with them. Shit-shoveling simians."

"Ford, I'm coming for you in the morning," Travers said.

"I won't be here," Ford said. "I'll be gone. Spire Island will be radio-active slag."

"I'm going to have to take that chance," Travers said. "I just can't leave you here."

Travers couldn't tell from Ford's face whether he was bluffing or not. Part of him wanted to remain at the dropsite and not bother with re-covering Ford; the other part wanted to go after him just out of spite.

"Alright, then," Ford said. "You can't say I didn't warn you."

"Nope," Travers said. "I can't say that."

"I'll call you before I go," Ford said.

"Don't," Travers said. Ford nodded and severed the communication.

Travers was convinced that Ford was bluffing. He'd find out in the morning. Looking at the mission clock, the conduit would open around midday. So, he'd have a busy morning of it, flying out to fetch Ford, and coming back. Ford was right about that—the fliers were running low on fuel. Travers would risk a straight shot from the drop-site to Spire Island, and hope that the flier held out. He'd bring Guessica's fuel cell with him, and hope it all worked out.

All he wanted to do, however, was just to stay at the dropsite, wait for the conduit to open, and to go home. But he had to at least go through the motions, so that ISA and Paragon could say that he had done everything he could do to get Ford back, that he had completed the mission successfully.

It galled Travers to have to do this, but a review board would defi-nitely investigate his conduct, and Travers had to do everything by the book, and that meant at least attempting to recover Ford. He had to, or else he'd face Payne.

The first moon rose, big and shiny-bright, a shade of grey-blue.

His radar pinged, and the whatever-it-was swam beneath him, a mere fifteen meters away. He wondered what it was that lived in this freshwater sea, whether it was a school of some alien sea life, or one great, big thing, or one of many great, big things.

The thing stayed beneath him awhile, just floating there, and it un-nerved Travers to be out on the ice like this, alone—or worse—not completely alone.

Maybe it could sense the radar pinging at it. Maybe it could see his shadow on the ice. After a few minutes, the thing swam away, moving with a slow and horrible grace. Whatever it was, it was massive. Travers took some comfort in the thickness of the ice. He doubted anything could punch through ice this thick.

Then again, he'd been wrong before.

DAY FIVE

1

MORNING CAME, AND TRAVERS WOKE to an alarm he'd set before going to sleep. He woke with the alien dawn, the sun lancing over the horizon, the colors so beautiful—shades of lavender and magenta, as the sun came up.

Its superficial resemblance to Earth made it all the more unnerving to Travers, this sense of otherness wrapped in planetary similarity. That was the issue with seeking out Earthlike planets—they were Earthlike planets. They could operate on entirely different principles than Earth, play by different ground rules, but they spoke the same language—the way that languages sometimes had the same roots.

His comlink chirped, and it was Ford, as Travers had expected. He answered.

"Beautiful sunrise, isn't it, Trav?" Ford asked.

"It sure was," Travers said.

"It's not over, yet," Ford said. "Keep looking."

There was a detonation to the south. Travers couldn't see it, but he sure as hell heard it on this quiet world.

Ford's comlink cut off the moment the thing went off.

"Shit," Travers said. "Ford? Come in, Ford?"

There was only static.

Travers got to his feet and faced south. He could see a mushroom cloud reaching skyward, far in the distance. He'd done it. He'd actually done it.

> "Personal log: It looks like Ford detonated his suit's
> power supply. I'm going to fly there to confirm this."

He didn't want to. Travers wanted to do anything but this, but he had to check, he understood that they would expect him to check. So, he warmed up his flier, plotted the course, and jetted off for Spire Island, one last time.

Travers sped over the ice, knowing full well that if the flier failed him, he'd be marooned. He hoped everything went smoothly, because he most certainly didn't want to remain here. Not that ISA wouldn't send other shore parties in, Recovery Team, all of that. But it still bothered him, the prospect of being left here.

The flight to Spire Island went quickly; he was already getting used to the lack of scenery at the landing site, when the island appeared on his scopes, and he brought his suit down upon it. The spires were melted, here—a mangled fist of molten stone, and his radtracker clicked disapprovingly of the amount of radiation, here. The blast zone was where the suit had been, and there was only a shiny crater.

"He did it," Travers said. "You crazy motherfucker."

He looked around, walked across what was left of Spire Island, taking stock of the surroundings. The water was surging today, the tides coming in with a vengeance. Overhead was a hole in the sky, where the explosion had punched upward into the clouds. And a fog was rolling in—locally, it had been burned away by the detonation, but the fog was reclaiming its terrain.

> "Personal log: It appears that Ford Collins committed suicide here, detonating his exosuit's micro-reactor. I don't know how many safety protocols he had to have overridden to get that to happen, but if anybody knows a suit inside-out, it's Ford. I can't believe I've lost two teammates on this mission. Moreover, I can't believe I'm still alive."

He walked over to the ruined spires, which were blobs of blackened stone.

> "It appears that enough heat can destroy the obelisks, as Guessica's laser determined, and Ford's reactor meltdown confirmed. They're not invulnerable to harm, for what that's worth."

Travers scanned the area around him, but there was nothing, only surging waves. The water was terribly active today.

> "The tides are up today. I've lost two friends within twenty-four hours. This is the final resting place of Commander Ford Collins. With him gone and Guessica dead, I'm Team Leader of Blue Team. I'm heading back to the dropsite to wait this out."

He saw a flash of something across the water, then another flash. Looking up, he saw it across the water.

"Computer, magnify image."

The computer did so, and on the HUD 1 was Ford, paddling in a makeshift kayak he'd crafted out of parts he'd drawn from the shell of his exosuit.

> "Personal log: Correction, Ford hasn't killed himself. He's made a kind of boat out of some of his suit and appears to be attempting to make landfall."

Ford was wearing the shiny poncho, the survival wrap, and was rowing with one of the armatures.

> "Personal log: It looks like he donned the suit and used it to tear itself apart. He's got one of the arms as a kind of oar, using one of the flight wings gripped in the hand as the paddle. It appears that he's pried off the backpack and used that shell for the hull of his boat. Not the most comely of craft, but it's wide enough to offer enough displacement to float. I don't know why he detonated the reactor. Maybe to see if it could destroy the spires."

Travers eyed the mission clock, and his own fuel consumption monitors for the flightpack. He had visions of swooping in and snatching Ford, trying to bring him back.

He toggled the loudspeaker.

"Ford. You crazy bastard! Where are you going?"

Ford looked over his shoulder, then pointed. South by Southwest.

Travers toggled the topographic map. No doubt Ford had consulted it as well. From this launch point, he was about 700 kilometers from land.

"You'll never make it," Travers said. Although he knew that if anybody would or could, it would be Ford.

> "Personal log: Ford's heading south-southwest. From this location at Spire Island, he's approximately 700 kilometers from the larger landmasses. I am unsure of the currents and eddies in this water body, but with a favorable current, maybe he'll get there. I can't imagine him rowing that entire distance. I'm plotting his course from here, so the Recovery Team can know which way to go."

The computer logged his position on the topographic map, making Travers smirk, the idea of a straight line course being ludicrous, of course, for a man in a kayak, but it at least would give a datapoint for the RT to fix upon. If all went well, they'd have a team here in the next 24 to 48 hours, and they could bring Ford back.

All Travers knew was that he couldn't risk it. His fuel supply was too low. He had enough to get back to the dropsite, and nothing more. He couldn't risk trying to reclaim Ford.

"I'm going, Ford," Travers said into the loudspeaker. "They're going to bring you right back, you know. So I'm not even saying 'Goodbye.' How about this, instead: *See you soon.*"

Ford raised a hand and waved at him. Already, the currents were taking him farther away.

Dereliction of Duty.

Breach of Contract.

Absent Without Leave.

Destruction of Property.

Homecoming would not go well for Ford, when it happened. It would be a scandal for the Program, one that Paragon would be hard-pressed to deal with, even using skilled Mediators.

Travers watched Ford until he had vanished from sight, always with an eye on the mission chronometer, which was ticking things down. Just a few hours left.

> "Personal log: This is a last glance at Commander Ford Collins, for the record. A good man, an able commander, a dedicated Terranaut. I can't explain why he is choosing this course of action, why he'd turn his back on everything he was to stay on this dead world, but I am noting his location so that he can be brought back, and we may learn more about the Source."

Then he walked around the ruins of Spire Island, studied the slag of the obelisks a moment. Ford was traveling in the direction of the wind, which was blowing any fallout away from him. He was lucky in that respect, at least. He had not managed to irradiate himself in his foolhardy and pointless destruction of his suit.

Why had he done that? Taking the micro-reactor with him would've been smart, as it would've provided him with a ready, steady power source in the field. Then again, the things were heavy. It probably would've made his little boat trip impossible.

Travers surveyed the damage once more, just let the cameras do their work.

> "Personal log: In the absence of the spires there is definitely an abatement of the vertigo. Clearly, the spires have a range limit, and while they appear able to survive some damage to their integrity and remain operational, a nuclear detonation does seem capable of destroying them. I'm getting no sign of radiance from the ruined spires, here, and am feeling no vertigo, experiencing no hallucinations. Nothing."

He replaced the power pack of his flier and set off for the dropsite again, still reeling that Ford had marooned himself rather than undergo whatever ISA and Paragon would have in store for him. But then, it also made a kind of sense—better to go out like that than face disgrace and worse back home.

Still, Travers felt terrible. The mission had not gone at all as he'd planned, and he couldn't imagine having to do the debriefing all by himself, or having to answer all the questions that would be thrown his way.

He missed Guessica, and he missed Ford.

Travers even dreaded the return, when all the teams onsite would be watching him, seeing how it went. He'd be the last one any of them would think of coming back by himself on any mission. He knew that. But there it was.

His flier sputtered out about ten kilometers from the dropsite, and Travers brought himself down as carefully as he could, left the flier there, walked to the dropsite the remaining distance. While he walked, he reviewed the tapes of Spire Island, just to replay it, to see and understand what had happened.

Looking at his mission clock, it was getting very close to intersection with the conduit clock, the yellow numbers dancing with the blue. It was always his most tense time, those last few minutes.

He gazed at Guessica's empty suit, already half-covered in snow. Walking over, he gave it a kick, knocking the snow clear. It still horrified him to think that he'd have to bring that frozen Guessica spill home.

Being at the dropsite, he could feel the presence of the spire, laying there, softly glowing in the snow. It had made a kind of bed for itself, he could see, having melted a bit into the ice. The warmth of the thing was enough to do this.

"I should leave you here," Travers said. "Just out of spite, I should do it."

He walked over to the thing and pried it loose of the ice with some effort, setting it on another patch of ice with a grunt, gazing at the melted impression the thing left in the ice.

> "Personal log: I can't know what the thing is feeding off of, where its energy is coming from. Maybe it's from me, or from what's left of Guessica. But some of the energy is spilling off in the form of heat and light. Enough to melt the ice a bit. I must admit to being more than a little wary of bringing this obelisk into the Oasis. It'll be the find of the century, maybe of the millennium, but all the same, it still makes me nervous. However, I'm not going to let some other Terranaut come strolling through the conduit with it. Blue Team found it. It's ours to claim. And since Guessica gave her life trying to bring it back here, I

owe her that, at least. Ford's dead-set against bringing it back, but Ford's out of his mind, paddling across an alien lake toward a jungle that's as likely to kill him as it is to shelter him, so what does he know? I'll complete my mission, I'll do my duty, and let greater minds than mine decipher what the spires mean, who the Source were, and what happened to Tartarus."

And then he lay on his back and looked up at the sky. It would be the last silence he would enjoy for a long, long time, and he made the most of it, just savoring it.

He could just make out the shapes and shadows, at the corner of his gaze. The Revenants, is what Guessica called them. Of course.

Then he saw that one of the Revenants was Guessica. She gazed at him forlornly, reached for him with glowing hands.

"Oh, shit," Travers said. It was her, alright. She was floating there, radiant green-white, her eyes black as the Tartarus night sky.

"Personal log: I'm hallucinating again. I'm seeing Guessica standing here with the other Revenants. A whole army of them. I've never seen so many. Obviously the radiation from the spire is affecting me again, since I'm back in range of it. I suppose I could make use of my time remaining to try to ascertain the actual range of an individual spire's capacity to mindfuck a victim."

He got up and began to back away from the dropsite, away from the spire. Guessica watched him, as did the others. There were so many.

"Ten meters out, still seeing them."

He kept walking, and the Revenants didn't follow him, but simply watched him pass.

"Maybe some kind of interaction with the Aurora Borealis and the spire, causing hallucinations," Travers said. "Fifteen meters, still seeing them."

The conduit would open in an hour. He had sixty minutes left on Tartarus.

"Twenty meters," Travers said. "Everywhere I look, I see them. These glowing Revenants, malevolent things. The hatred is palpable. I can feel it. Not Guessica; she just looks sad."

An ocean of radiance.

It was like what he'd seen on a company cruise Paragon had taken the Terranauts on—the boat stirred up phosphorescence with its propellers, and in the dark of the sea, at night, a stream of radiance flowed in its wake. This was like that, only far brighter.

"Thirty meters," Travers said. "If this is, in fact, caused by the spire, the range of an individual spire is extraordinary."

He kept going, until, about eighty meters out, he saw no more Revenants.

"I can't be sure if this is in any way accurate," Travers said. "But eighty meters away from the spire, I'm not seeing any Revenants. However, when I step back within that limit, I'm not seeing them, either. Maybe it's a cumulative effect of exposure to the obelisk, I'm unsure."

Travers programmed his suit to walk in a circle around the obelisk, and shuffled his feet as he did so, to craft a great circle in the snow. At least they'd have this information, when he brought the thing back.

When his suit tracked the 160 meter-diameter circle, Travers stopped and ran his suit's sensors.

> "Personal log: I'm going to indicate the point at which I begin to see the phantasms. At least then we'll have a benchmark for onset of psychosis, or toxicity, or whatever this is. Proceeding inward from the circle."

Steeling himself, Travers plotted a course for the obelisk again, walking resolutely toward it, keeping his senses attuned to anything out of the ordinary. Shadows, shapes, lights, anything.

> "Personal log: It must be some kind of cumulative toxicity, because on the way out of the range of the spire, I saw apparitions all over the place, and I'm seeing nothing at the moment."

Closer still, he had his suit in full sensor mode, tracking anything out of the ordinary. Travers was actually kind of proud of himself for being so methodical in the face of the uncanny action of the obelisk.

He was helping ISA attain data on the phenomenon of the spires, and this would help them immeasurably.

> "Personal log: I'm about forty meters away, still nothing."

At about thirty meters he thought he saw something in the corner of his eye, a shadowy shape. He immediately reported it, then traced another circle around the spire, talking as he did so.

> "Personal log: I saw something just now, just some shape at the edge of my perception, so I'm indicating it as the start of the hallucinogenic region of the spires, or at least the point of initial influence and/or damage."

He got closer, and as he did so, felt the vertigo reappear. Again, he reported this, as well.

> "Personal log: Vertigo sets in at twenty meters, worsening as one gets closer to the spire."

He traced another circle around the spire. He imagined Chao and the others would be wondering just what the hell he had been up to, making snowmen and snow angels and tracking concentric circles in the snow with his suit. But they'd understand, soon enough.

The vertigo did set in again. Maybe Ford had been wrong about that—or maybe Travers's re-immersion in the suit's microenvironment had prevented the natural alteration and assimilation of his senses that resulted from exposure to the spires.

> "Personal log: Definitely experiencing stronger vertigo as I get closer to the thing. And I'm seeing Guessica again. She's luminous, reaching for me. Not hateful like the Revenants, but just pleading, by the sight of her. She's saying something to me. I think she's saying my name."

And she was. Guessica—or, "Guessica," as Travers thought of her, since he refused to rule out that she wasn't a hallucination—was, indeed, saying his name over and over again. And something else. He couldn't read lips so well, and the radiant effect made it harder to make out her words.

"Are the cameras recording this? Can they see?" Travers asked. He tongued a quick playback, and, sure enough, the cameras did appear to be seeing this. "Guessica apparition is attempting to say something to me. It's harder to see, because the Revenants are crowding around her, around me. At fifteen meters the visual hallucinations are growing in number and intensity. I'm perceiving something—images—the Source. I would guardedly say that I'm seeing the Source. I'm seeing the destruction of this world. Raining splinters of light down from beyond the sky. An endless bombardment. The images are intense but fleeting. I can see them, though."

The Guessica Revenant floated toward him, reaching for him.

> "Personal log: The Guessica shape is approaching me. I don't know...."

He reached out for her, his armored hand passing through her. Guessica passed through his suit, her radiant face growing in Travers's visor, eclipsing everything around him. He broke out into a sweat, was breathing hard, felt an unspoken dread and terror claim him, even though the apparition simply gazed sorrowfully at him with shining black eyes.

She passed through his suit, was right in there with him, and the intimacy of it terrified Travers, as she was right there in front of his face, the luminous motes that comprised her right there, her hands upon his face, passing through him. A ghost.

"She's in here with me," Travers whispered, panting, triggering his internal camera on the HUD 3, to see if it could see. He could not see himself, the image was one of simple green-white radiance, a cloud obscuring the camera.

This close, right against him, her eyes mere centimeters from his face, Travers let out a howl, and the Guessica apparition passed through him, into him.

"Stop this," she said.

It was her voice in his head. He could hear it, feel it. For a moment, he could see her in this dire place, of this world, not part of it, exiled on Tartarus, claimed by the Source, another casualty to calamity, with all of the others.

The sense of her vanished, leaving Travers drenched in sweat, shaking. Then he composed himself.

> "I see them. Everywhere. What does she want me to stop? The Guessica apparition urged me to 'stop this'—her exact words, if 'words' is even right, here. A feeling, a mental aftertaste? The spire is shining. The luminescence definitely grows with proximity, although it's unclear to me whether this is a reflection of my actual presence, or whether it is a trick of the light. I will say that the spires were initially dormant when we first encountered them, and this is borne out in the record."

His thoughts drifted as he watched the counter drop to zero, saw the rift in space-time form, saw the conduit open, saw the gravity lens gazing at him. The portal would only be open for a minute or so.

ALLIE's smooth voice chirped in his ears, funneled through the gravity lens that was the conduit, like she was speaking through a megaphone, muffled and distorted.

"Blue Team report," ALLIE said. "Contact restablished."

"This is Travers," Travers said. "Reporting. Guessica's dead. Ford is missing in action."

It wasn't factually accurate, but there was time to elucidate further on it once he'd get inside, once he was in Quarantine.

He lugged the equipment in first, slid in the trunks, let them chew on that bit of information. He dragged in Guessica's empty suit, hurled it across space-time. He pried up the frozen remains of Guessica, the colorful chunk of ice, put that through.

"That's Guessica," Travers said. "Full report pending."

"What the fuck is this?" Payne said, over the Causeway intercom, as alarms went off. "Travers, what in the fucking hell happened?"

Payne had made it after all.

"We've found something," Travers said. "Something extraordinary."

He paused, for he saw the Revenants flooding toward the conduit, passing right through the maw of folded space-time, this massive flood of them, a spiritual tsunami.

"Um," Travers said. Did he report what he was seeing? Was he even seeing it?

"What?" Payne said.

"Nothing," Travers said. "You'll see."

The Revenants surged through the Conduit, and ALLIE didn't say a thing. She couldn't see it, couldn't see them.

"ALLIE, are you seeing anything unusual?" Travers asked.

"What did you find?" Payne said. "Travers, what the fuck happened?"

The only thing left to bring was the spire, itself.

"Negative, Travers," ALLIE said, her voice so smooth in his ears, so coolly competent. "I'm not detecting anything at the moment."

"Alright," Travers said. Maybe it *was* all in his head. "Proceeding."

Travers walked to the obelisk and picked it up, held it up on a shoulder, and turned to see Guessica standing there, the last apparition, gesturing. All of the others had flown through the conduit, nobody the wiser, no alarms sounding, beyond the one that signaled a problem with Blue Team, when Travers had tossed Guessica's suit and remains in.

"Sorry, Guess," Travers said. "Duty calls. ALLIE, initiate quarantine procedures. I'm bringing something in."

He stepped through the conduit, into the Causeway, and on to his destiny.

When the obelisk crossed the conduit barrier, its glyphs flared to life, blindingly bright, bathing the Causeway in green-white light. Different, unfamiliar alarms sounded all around him, the Causeway flashed red, and ALLIE was speaking quickly, authoritatively, on all loudspeakers.

"Initiating emergency quarantine procedures, initiating emergency quarantine procedures," ALLIE said, klaxons sounding. "This is no drill. This is an Omega-level alert."

The crashing vertigo brought Travers to his knees in seconds, and he felt water pouring from him. He removed his helmet, tossed it aside, and wriggled out of his suit as Medtechs and security personnel flooded the Causeway, both figuratively and literally. Up above, at the observation area, Payne and the others shrieked and liquefied, splashing against the reinforced glasstic panes, as a pulse of green-white energy claimed them.

"Initiating emergency quarantine procedures. This is no drill. This is an Omega-level alert."

Blast doors were coming down along the length of the Causeway, but they wouldn't do any good—Travers could see the water surging, could see the splashing, could see the suits collapsing, the shapes of men and women gone limp and lifeless, slapping on the ground as the spire laid claim to them, transformed them. Waiting. Waiting for the Source to lay claim to this place. Fertile land, ripe for the taking. Someday they would come for this place, the spire pulsing, marking its location in space, a steady, endless pulse. It would be waiting for them.

The thing had already taken root, incredibly enough. It stood aloft, having somehow pierced the floor of the Oasis, yielded a dozen other spires around it, branching out, growing, the green-black stone spreading.

Travers glanced back through the distorted fisheye of the conduit, could see Guessica's ghost gazing forlornly at him. He could see her for a moment, before his gaze went watery, before ALLIE closed the conduit. He held his hands up, watched them turn painlessly into fluid before his eyes, in the radiant, dizzying light, found giddy laughter amid the sea of screams.

It would now be *his* time to shine.

FINIS

ABOUT THE AUTHOR

Dean Vale lives and breathes Science Fiction at all hours in an early 20th century brownstone, where he conjures up progressively more dystopian and utopian visions for the future of humankind. *Farther* is his debut novel.

DeanVale.com

NOSETOUCH PRESS

Nosetouch Press is an independent book publisher
tandemly-based in Chicago and Pittsburgh.
We are dedicated to bringing some of today's most
energizing fiction to readers around the world.

Our commitment to classic book design in a digital
environment brings an innovative and authentic
approach to the traditions of literary excellence.

*The Nose Knows™

NOSETOUCHPRESS.COM

Science Fiction | Fantasy | Horror | Mystery | Supernatural

Available in

PAPERBACK | HARDCOVER | EBOOK

Available in
PAPERBACK | HARDCOVER | EBOOK